THE SEVEN YEARS PRINCESS

A RETELLING OF MAID MALEEN

THE CLASSICAL KINGDOMS COLLECTION
BOOK ELEVEN

BRITTANY FICHTER

WANT MORE FAIRY TALES?

Sign up for a free no-spam newsletter and free short stories, exclusive secret chapters, and sneak peeks at books before they're published . . . all for free.

Details at the end of this book.

Grieving the loss of loved ones is not a switch we can flick on and off. This book is dedicated to the beloved souls you, Dear Readers, lost in 2020 and 2021. My prayer is that you can look at your loved one's name on this list and smile. Time doesn't heal all wounds, but God can use our losses to draw us closer to Him and put us on the right path, the memories of our loved ones safe in our hearts as we go. That said, this book is dedicated to:

Lorn Starling * Glenna Lee Southerland * Alexis R. Brock *George N. Vastis * Isabel * Phillip Durham * Joan Fleener * George Barnhart * Bill Hackbarth * Annette Miller * Connie Gulling * Pat Steen-Carr * Casey Jackson Starnes * William Henry Akridge III (Mark) * Elyse * Dolores M. Martin * Anat Birman * Carissa * Baden P. Ratterman * Oscar (Rocky) McCallick * Solon Beals * William Marcus * Linda Hodges * Julia Rose * Grandma Flo * Craig * Shirley * Betty Ann * Ralph * Mary Jo * Linda * Chloe

CHAPTER 1
FRIENDS

Mistress Emille gave Maleen a wry smile. "I saw that, Your Highness. Your uncle will go into convulsions if he sees you wearing those shoes in public." She bent and studied Maleen's feet. "Where did you even get such shoes?"

Maleen shifted and looked down at her newly acquired boots. "Um, I borrowed them."

"From whom?"

"Brandon Tate."

Maleen's governess blinked at her. "You got them from the pig farmer's son?"

Maleen nodded. "Don't worry, though! I'm going to give them back! And I gave him something as payment for his troubles."

Mistress Emille rubbed her eyes. It was strange. Her brown hair had seemed perfectly in place when she'd come to Maleen's room just a few minutes before. And now it was already looking a bit "piqued," as the servants would say.

Mistress Emille sighed. "Do I *want* to know what the payment was?"

"Four loaves of bread."

Maleen's governess took a long, deep breath through her nose and held it in for a long time before letting it back out.

Maleen sighed, too. Maybe this idea hadn't been her finest after all. It had seemed so simple, though. For the first time in her life, her uncle was letting her play outside with the other royal children. Boots had seemed more practical than her pretty white leather boots.

At the time, at least.

Her discussion with her uncle the week before had not been encouraging.

"I'm still not entirely sure this is a good idea," Uncle Perseus had said with a frown. "But the other royals are beginning to gossip about it, so I might as well let you out with the other little hooligans for a few hours."

Maleen had nearly fallen over in surprise. "I'll listen and be obedient, Uncle! I promise! I won't get into mud, and I'll make sure to stay tidy, and—"

"Just stay near your guards," he'd growled, "and try not to catch cold. If you're ever going to grow up and rule, it would be best for you not to die before you're of age."

Maleen had known better than to point out that it was summer, and she was hardly likely to die of catching cold while chasing the other children on the gently sloping green hills that backed the palace. So she'd merely thanked him and darted out of the room before he could remember any other stipulations to place on her playtime.

"I did it for Uncle," Maleen explained now as her governess helped her out of the shoes.

Mistress Emille let out a laugh. "For your uncle?"

But Maleen felt on the verge of tears. "He's always so worried about me. I figured these boots are sturdier than my white shoes. If I wore them, I'd be less likely to fall and hurt myself. Then he won't forbid me from playing with the others again."

Mistress Emille's smile faded as she knelt in front of Maleen. Maleen wiped her face with the back of her hand, suddenly angry at the tears that were falling uninvited. Princesses of eight years didn't cry about shoes. But Mistress Emille only smiled softly as she pulled a handkerchief from her reticule.

"Your uncle doesn't mean to be cruel," she said softly as she wiped Maleen's face. "Losing his brother...your father was very difficult for him. Losing your mother at the same time meant he not only had to mourn his lost brother, but he was now responsible for the kingdom and for you as well." She sighed. "He's doing the best he knows how. And he's terrified of losing you, too."

Maleen frowned. "I never thought of it that way."

Mistress Emille lifted Maleen's chin gently. "No more tears, love. This is a day for fun." She held up Maleen's white leather boots. "In your *own* shoes."

An hour later, Maleen found herself dressed, primped, and shining as if the servants had scrubbed every bit of color out of her skin. *This is the day!* she thought as she followed Mistress Emille down the stairs to the palace's entrance hall. Today she would do as she'd so longed to for as long as she could remember. She would play on the lawn with the other royal children instead of watching the merriment through a window.

For some reason, though, her feet moved slower and slower as they neared the bottom of the stairs. And by the time Mistress Emille had reached the ground, Maleen's feet had stopped completely. Mistress Emille looked back and saw Maleen still standing four steps up.

"Your Highness, what's the matter?"

"I'm scared," Maleen whispered, holding tightly to the banister.

Mistress Emille blinked at her. "Of what? I thought you wanted–"

"I do." Maleen nodded rapidly. "I only..." She swallowed. "I've never been allowed to play with them. What if I don't know what to do?"

Mistress Emille climbed back up to where Maleen was still clinging to the banister and gently took her hands. "You'll be just fine. Watch the other children and learn from them. Be kind. And who knows?" She tilted her head, her brown eyes thoughtful. "Perhaps you'll find someone special."

Maleen wasn't convinced. All her life she'd dreamed of being allowed to mix and play with the other royal children at the gatherings her uncle was always dragging her to. But as she watched them now, already paired off or divided into their own little groups, she wasn't sure she even remembered how to say hello. Her mouth went dry, and her throat seemed so swollen she couldn't have talked if she'd wanted to. But Mistress Emille didn't stop until Maleen was standing in a large group of children.

Sure enough, as soon as Mistress Emille had left her side to go stand with the other nannies and governesses, all eyes were on her. Little girls her age, older girls, little boys, and even big boys were peering at her.

Was it possible to forget how to breathe?

"You're new here, aren't you?" one of the older girls asked. She looked to be at least four years older than Maleen, but her smile was kind. Maleen managed to nod.

"Well, I'm Elizabeth, and I'm from Staroz." She pointed to the other side of the room where the adult guests were taking refreshments. "That's my mother, Lady Janulis. And that," she pointed at one of the younger girls, who looked to be around Maleen's age, "is my sister, Margaret."

"Hello," Maleen whispered.

"And this," Elizabeth continued, "is Princess Monique from Ombrin."

Princess Monique sniffed and studied her nails.

"There's Lady Priscilla from Vaksam."

A girl with strawberry blond curls gave Maleen a measured smile and polite nod.

"And that's Prince Henri from Destin." Elizabeth pointed to one of the older boys. He was one of the biggest boys Maleen had ever seen. Not fat. Not fat at all. Just...big. And strong.

"This is Prince Nicholas from Ashland." She gestured to the boy next to Prince Henri. Prince Nicholas wasn't nearly as muscular as Prince Henri was, but he was a whole head taller. He had friendly blue eyes and gave Maleen a kind smile. Then Elizabeth continued down the line.

The names began to run together in Maleen's head. How in the world would she remember all these people? Why had her uncle made her wait so long to meet them all? She began to panic silently as Elizabeth reached the final edge of the circle. "And this is Prince Roburts from Metakinos."

At the mention of her uncle's least favorite kingdom, Maleen stiffened. She'd never met its prince, as her uncle certainly wasn't about to break his strict rules for the son of his hated neighbor. But she knew the name. The boy was tall and thin with dark hair and an unusual shade of green eyes. She knew from her uncle's tirades that he was two years older than her, but aside from that, she knew nothing.

Except, of course, that his father wanted nothing more than the downfall of her kingdom, something Uncle Perseus was desperate to prevent.

Prince Roburts gave her a nod, but his smile wasn't as open as Prince Henri or Prince Nicholas's had been. He, too, seemed aware of the divide that already stood between them. Maleen turned to the other children, hoping they started the games soon.

"Where are you from?" Prince Nicholas asked politely.

She turned and blinked at him. "I'm from here."

"Here?" one of the other girls asked with a frown.

Maleen nodded. "This is my home."

After another very long second, Prince Nicholas gasped with what looked like understanding and seemed like he was on the verge of saying something, but Prince Henri elbowed him in the side.

Why hadn't they started the games yet?

She didn't have to wait long, though. Just two minutes later, the children were herded outside into the late spring sun. There were refreshments for anyone who wanted them, and as Maleen had been told to expect, the older girls wandered over to sit on the chairs that had been placed in the shade of the large oak trees. The older boys and the younger children were left standing on the green. The palace steward divided them into teams, separating Prince Henri and Prince Nicholas, despite their protests, and told them that each team had a colored flag hidden somewhere on the green. The first team to find their opponents' flag and bring it back without having their own stolen would win.

Maleen was on Prince Henri's team, and Prince Roburts was on Prince Nicholas's team. This relieved Maleen, as she wasn't sure what she would do if she were forced to talk to Prince Roburts for the game. For good measure, though, she made sure he was on the opposite side of the green.

The horn sounded for the game to begin, and everyone darted off into the trees. Maleen fell quickly behind. She wasn't used to such exercise. Her uncle had strict rules about what outdoor activities were safe and proper, and running in a dress wasn't one of them. Though, Maleen found as she ran that she didn't really care. She was tired soon, but the sun was on her face, and she was going faster than she could remember ever running in her life. Speeding down and up the hills through the interspersed trees was thrilling, and the sensation of the wind against her face made her laugh.

Soon, they were so spread out that Maleen couldn't see her

teammates any longer. Not that it bothered her. She was simply overjoyed to be outside without her governess or bodyguards shadowing her every step. Soon, she forgot to look for the flag and simply began to wander.

After several more minutes, though, she began to feel thirsty. Too thirsty to run all the way back to the refreshment tables. Besides, her uncle might glance out the window and see that her hat had fallen off her head and was hanging by its ribbons from her neck. Then he would call her in for sure.

So that left the stream. It wasn't a deep stream. At least, it didn't look deep. And there were plenty of rocks on the edge that she could sit on.

Carefully, Maleen edged her way onto one of the larger rocks. She sat on it, careful to keep her pale pink dress off the mossy parts. Briefly, she mourned the loss of Brandon Tate's sturdy boots. But there was naught to be done about it, so with a slight groan, she placed her white boots at the edge of the water and leaned forward to drink.

Then she was falling.

Cold water rushed over her head. In her nose. In her ears. She tried to scream, but water choked her and pushed her down. Not only down, but it shoved her forward, hurling her downstream, allowing her to come up for breath only to pull her back down. The stream that had looked calm and tranquil from the bank was a thousand times stronger than Maleen had imagined.

The water roared in her ears, dulling the outside sounds to a gurgle until they popped before she went under again.

As the water continued to bully her downstream, carrying her past stones and boulders, she eventually became aware of another figure to her left. Somehow, she managed to look over to see a boy running alongside her. He was shouting something, but she couldn't make it out.

"Help!" she shrieked.

He cupped his hands over his mouth. "Put your feet first!"

"What?"

"Feet first!" he screamed back.

Maleen tried to put her feet first, though she didn't know why she should. But it was hard as the water continued to roll her like a pebble.

The boy put his head down and sprinted, this time faster than the current. At first, she felt utterly betrayed as she watched her only help speed away. Rather than leaving her, though, he veered right, and she looked up just in time to see a bridge coming fast.

He threw his body down on the bridge and lay on his belly, his arms outstretched toward her.

Maleen reached her arms up as well. He tried to grab her leg, which floated beneath the bridge first, but the material of her soaked stockings slipped out of his grasp. She shrieked. If he wasn't able to catch her, she doubted he'd be able to catch up again.

How far would the water take her?

But just as her stomach began to go under the bridge, he snatched her left hand. Their wet fingers immediately began to slip, but he used his other hand to grab her wrist as well. Slowly, and with much pain to Maleen's arm, he pulled her up until she could place her elbows on the bridge.

The wood was rough beneath her wet, slippery fingers, but he stuck his arms on top of hers and leaned his weight against them. Only when their faces were inches away from one another did Maleen comprehend who her savior was.

His hair was lighter than she'd first thought. The roots were dark, but they were covered by a thin layer of blond on top. And his eyes were a more brilliant green in the sunlight.

"P-p-p-prince Rob-rob-roburts!" she exclaimed through chattering teeth, though she couldn't tell if the shivering was more from the cold or her shock at her new situation. The son of her uncle's sworn enemy was the only person standing...or laying, rather, between her and getting washed away down the stream.

"I can't pull you up!" he shouted over the sound of the water. "You're too wet!"

She looked around as much as she dared turn her head. There was no one in sight. Her legs floated beneath the bridge as he continued to hold onto her arms. Her neck was already beginning to ache. "What do we do?" she cried.

"We wait. Someone will come."

She nodded, and her shivering grew more violent, her chin nearly knocking on the bridge as she did.

He scooted even closer, his hands reaching nearly up to her shoulders as he put more of his weight on her arms. "Tell me something!" he called.

"Tell you what?" She couldn't remember the last time her arms had hurt so much. They were cold and tired, and he was leaning on them as well.

"Anything. Try to think of something else."

She tried to blink droplets of water from her eyes. "Um, my uncle is never going to let me outside again?"

He gave her a look like she was crazy. "Why?"

"He's always afraid I'll get hurt." She squeezed her eyes shut then opened them again. "I think he might have been right."

He shook his head, a lock of wet hair falling over his face. "Think about something else."

"I can't," she said breathlessly. "I'm too tired." As if agreeing, her body gave a shiver so hard that Prince Roburts nearly lost his hold.

"Don't give up!" He squeezed his fingers into her arms so hard it shot sharp pains up to her shoulders. "Don't you let go!"

Maleen shook her head, her body sagging in defeat. Her dress trailed deeper into the water once more. "I can't," she said through tears.

"Hold fast!" he shouted. "Someone will find us soon! They will!"

She gave him the best pout she could manage. "I don't even know what that means!"

"My father's commander always says it. It means you don't let go! You don't let the water win!" He glared, leaning his face toward hers until they were almost touching. "Hold. Fast."

Maleen couldn't say for sure how long they stayed that way, him leaning on her arms as her body dangled off the bridge. He said a lot, most of which she couldn't remember. Something about silk and dye and the festival and a duchess's wig falling off.

But eventually, just as shivering and exhaustion were about to overcome her, she heard another sound. It was a shout. Then two more. She couldn't make out what they were saying, but she didn't care. Moments later, she had been swept up into someone's strong, warm arms, and they held her close.

"Henri!"

"Yes, Uncle Launce?"

"Go get your mother! We'll meet you on the way."

Maleen somehow managed to open her eyes just enough to see a large man wrapping Prince Roburts in a cloak just as the man who held her was wrapping her up in his. She shivered, and when she looked at her fingers, they were a strange shade of blue.

"How is she, Launce?" the other man asked.

"Too cold." The young man who held her was thin and tall. There was a grim set to his mouth as he wrapped the cloak even more tightly around her. "But that's the best I can do here. We need Isa."

"Launce!" a woman called, her voice growing closer as she did. "Henri says you found her!"

Maleen was on the verge of unconsciousness, but she saw a flash of copper hair as the thin man handed her to the woman. She heard little after that, though, because the woman wrapped her arms around Maleen and held her close, and for one brief moment, just as she fell asleep, Maleen dreamed she was in her mother's arms.

Maleen didn't remember being carried back to the palace or being placed in her bed. She did briefly, afterward, recall more glimpses of the woman with copper hair and kind, midnight blue eyes. The woman was always there when she awakened. Sometimes, she fed Maleen. Other times, she sang to her or rocked her close as if Maleen were a small child. But Maleen didn't mind. The woman's embrace was warm, and for the first time in a very long time, Maleen felt completely safe. Not even her uncle's worries could reach her when this woman held her close.

Eventually, though, Maleen no longer had to sleep all the time. She stopped shivering, and her fingers returned to their usual color.

Then one morning, she awoke to the brilliant morning sunshine streaming through her window. Sitting up, she looked around her room. The rocking chair beside her bed was empty.

"Where did she go?" she asked as Mistress Emille walked in. The sight of the food on the tray she carried made Maleen's stomach groan.

"Who?" Mistress Emille set the tray on Maleen's lap.

"The woman with copper hair."

Maleen's governess laughed. "You mean Queen Isabelle of Destin?"

"That's who that was?" Maleen had heard the name before, but she would never have expected such a soft, motherly creature to be the most powerful queen in the western realm.

"She saved your life, you know." Mistress Emille knelt by Maleen's bedside. "She's been watching you for the last six days. Only this morning did she think you out of danger enough to go back down to the gala."

"Six days..." Maleen added in her head, then she gasped. "The gala ends today!"

"It does." She tucked in Maleen's bedsheets. "But you're staying right here."

"I feel fine."

"And I'm the queen of Ashland. No, you're going to lay here and eat and sleep some more. If you do that well, your uncle might let you out of your room in ten or so years." She gave Maleen a look. "And I'm only half-joking at that."

"But I have to say goodbye to Prince Roburts! I need to thank him!"

Mistress Emille raised her blond eyebrows. "Your uncle–"

"He saved my life!" Maleen glared at her governess. She loved Mistress Emille dearly, almost like a mother. But the way everyone in the palace, including Mistress Emille, tiptoed around her uncle was sometimes downright odd.

Mistress Emille sighed as she folded a towel that had been laid on Maleen's bedside table. "I'm aware of that. But with your uncle...it's complicated."

Maleen was about to argue that her uncle was nonsensical. But that would get her nowhere. Then she had another thought. She would do something she'd never considered before, and it filled her with guilt just thinking about it.

She was going to lie.

"I'm getting tired," she said, rolling over on her side. "I think I shall go back to sleep."

"That's what I want to hear." Mistress Emille came over and kissed her on the head. "Sleep and heal. You'll be well in no time."

But Maleen didn't need to heal up. She'd been healed by the queen of Destin, for goodness sakes. So she waited until she was alone. Then she climbed out of her bed, put her shoes on, slipped into the only dress she could put on without help, and darted out the door.

As she made her way toward where she knew the children would be, she thought of all the ways that she might thank a prince for saving her life. She didn't know how Prince Roburts would like to be thanked. Would he just want the words? Or perhaps a hug? Or what about gross things? Boys liked those.

In the end, she settled for making a quick stop at the stables to visit Brandon Tate. After hesitantly accepting Brandon's suggestion of an appropriate thank you present, she made her way to the dining hall through the servants' shortcuts that ran throughout the palace. When she first arrived, her heart fell. She couldn't find him. The festival was ending that day, and many of the guests had already gone home.

But just as she was about to give up hope and go back to her room, she spotted him sitting beside the fire. Taking a deep breath, she left the doorway and sat beside him.

He gave a start when he turned and noticed her there.

"Princess! Aren't you supposed to be healing?"

"I had a powerful queen heal me." She rolled her eyes. "I'm healed enough as it is."

He blinked at her. "Um, very well. How can I help you?"

Butterflies flitted around her stomach, and she nearly got up and marched back out.

Hold fast.

The words came back to her, floating in on the collection of vague memories she had of the near drowning experience. The water didn't beat her. Her fear wouldn't either. She'd come downstairs six days ago to make friends in the first place, and that's what she was going to do.

"I, um... Do you like snakes?"

He stared at her again, then started to laugh. "Not necessarily, no." Then he cocked his head. "Why?"

"Uh, no reason."

He glanced at her reticule, which was hanging dangling from her wrist. "Then why is *that* moving?"

Maleen froze and then looked down at the little bag. Sure enough, it was writhing and wriggling against her leg. She let out a stifled shriek and let it fall to the floor. When it hit the ground, the drawstring loosened, and a little green snake wiggled its way out and slipped beneath one of the cloth-covered tables. Maleen stared at it, her mouth hanging open. "Brandon...Brandon didn't tell me it would do that!"

Then she heard laughing. Turning back to Prince Roburts, she saw that he was laughing so hard he was rocking back and forth in his seat as tears ran down his face. Tears sprang to her own eyes as she realized how incredibly silly she must look.ortification making her face and shoulders tingle, she had taken two steps toward the door when she felt a hand slip into hers and pull her back.

"I'm not laughing at you," Prince Roburts said, wiping his face with a handkerchief, his skin still flushed from the laughter. "I'm laughing because I like you."

She frowned. "That doesn't seem like a reason to laugh."

"You're not like most girls." His eyes gleamed. "You're far more interesting."

Maleen wasn't sure if she considered this a compliment or not. "I just wanted to thank you for saving me," she mumbled, looking at the ground.

"I'm glad I did." He bent and retrieved her reticule before

handing it back to her. "I think we'll have great fun in the future."

In the future?

"So...does this mean we can be friends?" Maleen asked softly, daring to peek up at him.

He grinned. "Friends."

"Your Highness."

They turned to see a servant addressing the prince.

"Your father wishes for you to join him. You'll be returning home soon."

"Thank you, Gregory," Prince Roburts said. Then he looked back at Maleen. "I'll see you at the Tennison Estate Ball next month?"

Maleen nodded shyly. "Most likely."

"Until next time, then." He bowed and grinned once more. "Friend."

LETTERS

To the Princess Maleen of Ertrique,

I hope this letter finds you in better health than when we said goodbye. I'm not used to writing many letters, so I hope you don't mind this one if it seems incredibly silly. You're probably wondering why I'm writing you a letter at all since we just met.

To be frank, my mother recently discovered a letter I'd written to a friend, and she was so scandalized by what she called its "appalling brevity" that she has assigned me the task of writing more letters in order to hone my skills. They have to be at least two pages long. And as most of my friends are males and dislike long, varied prose, I thought perhaps you wouldn't mind trading letters with me. You seem as though you know how to have more fun than most of the girls I know, so I'm guessing you'll have enough to write about to make the letters enjoyable.

I don't mean to be rude about girls, of course. But I just don't know what to do with them. I once got a letter from Lady Priscilla. She mostly stayed with the older girls, so you might not remember her. Be glad you don't.

She's about my age, and once, she invited me to her birthday ball. I was out with my father, thankfully, and couldn't go. Then she wrote me three pages of very small print about the party and all I'd missed when I was gone. And while I'm glad she enjoyed the party, I didn't really want to know the color of every guest's dress in attendance.

In other words, I really don't want to trade letters about party gowns. If you let me write you letters so my mother will leave me alone, I'll make sure to stand next to you the entire gala the next time we meet. Just please don't make me trade letters with someone like Lady Priscilla. Please.

(There. I made this one last at least one and a half pages by using my biggest loops. Hopefully, that will satisfy Mother.)

Gratefully yours,

Prince Roburts of Metakinos

To Prince Roburts of Metakinos

To answer your question, I am much better, thank you. Unfortunately, my uncle is very displeased with me. He says only silly, senseless girls fall into streams and half-drown. Because of the accident, he says I may not play with the other children at the Tennison Estate Ball next month. I can, however, eat at the refreshment table, which means I have a chance of at least seeing some of the others if they choose to eat there, too. I'm hoping someone will be hungry.

And I would be delighted to trade letters. I've never had a friend before. At least, not one my uncle would approve of. Brandon Tate, a local pig farmer's son, often works at the stables here. And there's Chelsea, the seamstress's daughter. But my uncle won't let me play with them either. At least, not where he can see. He says they're beneath me, which is strange because they're actually both taller than I am. When I pointed this out, however, he said that's not what he means.

I must ask, though. Do you really not mind that I'm from Ertrique? My uncle doesn't like your kingdom, and he tells me your father doesn't like mine. I don't see what all the fuss is about. Not that Uncle Perseus tells me anything. Not really. He says one day I'll inherit all my parents' duties. But right now, he says, I need to stay alive and learn to be a lady. I just hope you don't dislike it when I tell you of goings-on in our kingdom.

I also hope you don't dislike reading my letters. I've practiced writing letters, of course. Mistress Emille says I'm rather skilled at it, actually, for my age. But I've never practiced writing letters to a boy. Always to a queen or another princess or a lady. Imaginary ones, of course. It would be unlikely that Uncle would let me write letters without his permission.

Which brings me to another confession. If you could please address your letters to a man named James Wickson, it would be of great help in keeping this a secret. I'm probably not supposed to be writing letters at all, and especially not to you. It must seem like I disobey my uncle a lot. I really don't try to, but I'm afraid I'll go mad if I must stay here, cooped up without any friends for years to come. And galas, balls, and parties are interesting enough, but they only come every so often. Especially if Uncle never lets me play with the other children again. James Wickson is our steward. If you direct your letters to him, he'll give them to my governess, who will give them to me. In return, when I sent one to you, look for letters from the same James Wickson. That way, if my uncle asks, no one will be able to say there are any letters addressed to me.

I'm afraid you'll think me a rather talented sneak after this. And you'll probably be annoyed at my letters' length, too. Just another girl who talks too much. I promise to try to have more interesting things to say after this one. I must confess that some-

times, if I get too bored, I liven things up around the palace. Perhaps by the time your next letter comes, I shall have thought of some new way to do this. I've been wondering what would happen if I put one of my uncle's robes on one of the horses.

Thank you again for writing. I know I write an excessive amount for someone who is only eight years, but when you're not allowed to do anything, you must find ways to occupy the time.

Always yours,
Princess Maleen of Ertrique

CHAPTER 2
THE DUKE

D o we have to serve pickled oysters?" Maleen wrinkled her nose at the parchment Gretta had handed her. The kitchen staff bustled around them as Maleen continued to read the week's meal choices.

Rather than being offended by Maleen's rudeness as she should have been, the palace cook just grinned. "You'll thank me after this is all done and King Quinton of Ombrin sings your praises because you served his favorite dish."

"Oh, I trust *you* completely." Maleen made another face at the meal list and handed it back. "But you're a better person than I am for putting up with the smell long enough to cook *that*."

"Your uncle probably didn't tell you this," Emille smiled, "but Gretta cooked for King Quinton's nephew for a brief period of time."

Maleen laughed. "As I said, I trust you completely. I'm not even sure why you bother to share the details with me at this point. You've been doing this longer than I've been alive."

Gretta studied the paper, her smile fading slightly. "Whether or not I need this, Princess, you do."

"Everyone needs this." Mistress Emille glanced around at the kitchen servants. "They need to see that the throne is yours in every way."

Fear flitted through Maleen's stomach, but she shooed it away as she forced a smile. Now was not the time for such fear. Even if the entire staff seemed to be dripping with it. "Well, you have me convinced. Pickled oysters it is." She shook her head slightly and turned to Emille. "Where next? Do I have bedsheets made of butterfly wings to confirm for some anointed guest in another part of the palace?"

A young serving girl who was chopping potatoes nearby snorted but sobered quickly when Gretta gave the young girl a glare. At least *she* thought Maleen was funny. Maleen shot the girl a wink.

Emille just rolled her eyes. "Every time I think I'm about finished with you–"

"I tease, I tease." Maleen laughed and turned to go up the stairs. "To the dining hall we go."

The entire palace bustled with life as servants ran to and fro, preparing for the kingdom's greatest gala of the year. Tapestries depicting the beauties of everyday life hung from the walls, so many that the walls themselves could barely be seen. Color flooded the floor, the walls, and even the ceiling as Ertrique prepared for its grand Dye Festival—a week of Ertrique's merchants all descending upon its capital city to sell the hand-crafted dyes they'd worked hard to prepare all year. Other merchants from nearby cities would join them as well.

This event brought thousands of travelers through the city gates to purchase the renowned Ertrique colors every year. There were songs, performances, food, and even dances in the square. And to crown it all was the great gathering of the realm leaders for their own celebration of Ertrique's good fortune at the palace gala, where they tasted of the little kingdom's food, experienced its hospitality, and were graced with gifts of goodwill and, hopefully, newly struck up business deals that would benefit everyone who came to attend.

And now that Maleen was seventeen, she was responsible for it all.

"You're sure this isn't too much?" Emille murmured as they climbed the steps. She frowned slightly as they rounded the corner. "I'm not sure it was fair of your uncle—"

"I'm going to prove to my uncle that he can trust me with this and more," Maleen interrupted. Then she gave Emille a saucy grin. "Besides, you were my governess. If this all falls apart, I can just tell him it's your fault."

"You're unusually cheeky today, even for you."

Maleen beamed. "Why thank you."

Emille glanced around and pulled Maleen into an empty hallway. "I'm serious, Your Highness. Hosting the gala is no small feat. And your uncle hardly gave you time to prepare."

Maleen took her old governess's hands. They were strong and familiar. "Thank you, Emille. Truly." She looked out at the busyness in the main dining hall as servants rushed to fold and place napkins and the chamberlain squabbled with James Wickson about seating arrangements. It was honestly quite close to chaos, but then again, this was exactly what Maleen had been looking forward to for years. How did she explain this?

"I've been trying to convince my uncle—"

"That you're old enough to take on some responsibility." Emille gently touched Maleen's cheek. "I know. But I also know that..." She glanced furtively around and leaned forward to whisper. "I have little doubt that he wishes for you to fail."

"Of course he does." Maleen played with the tassel of her reticule. "Or perhaps, to be fair, he expects it. Which will make it all the more impactful when I prove him wrong."

Emille studied her a moment before chuckling softly and shaking her head. "You are your mother's daughter." She looked back out at the dining hall and took a deep breath. "Just remember. You have the support of your people. If you need us, please don't hesitate to call just to prove a point. You're not alone, and you won't be when you ascend to the throne."

Maleen was about to answer when Willard the chamberlain popped his round head around the corner. "There you are, Your Highness!" he cried. "We have a problem. Prince Karim of Hedjet is assigned to sit beside Princess Monique of Ombrin."

"Is that a problem?" Maleen blinked back at the man.

"It is, Your Highness." He adjusted his spectacles. "They hate each other."

"I'm afraid," said a tall, uniformed man as he joined them, "that we have an even bigger problem." His brown eyes locked onto Maleen's. "It involves the border."

"Oh!" Willard, the chamberlain, stepped back. "That is certainly important indeed." He gave Maleen a weak smile. "Do not fret about this, Princess. We'll handle it somehow."

"Of course, Willard. I leave it in your capable hands." She turned to the tall man. "Where to, Captain Dominic?" This was obviously not a discussion for the servants' ears.

"This way, if you please." He turned and made his way to one of the side entrances.

Maleen's confidence in her planning went up in smoke as she followed the captain out to the soldiers' quarters. If there was one swift way to lose her uncle's confidence, it was with the soldiers.

"I'm not sure," Captain Dominic said softly, "if you're aware that this year's gala was nearly canceled."

Maleen faltered slightly then had to hurry to keep up with his long strides. "Nearly canceled. But why?"

The captain's jaw tightened. "Your uncle," he continued in an even lower voice, "has somehow become convinced that Metakinos is determined to attack us in the very near future."

"Does he have anything to support such a claim?"

Captain Dominic nodded at a small stable and indicated for Maleen to enter first. When she did, he pulled the stable door shut behind them. There were several grooms tending to the horses, but Maleen quickly realized that they were all some of the palace's oldest and most trusted workers. Clearly, the captain did not wish for their words to reach certain ears.

Instead of remaining where they were, however, he led her to one of the empty stalls. The old stablehand went to the back of the stable and grabbed a saddle hook on the wall. To Maleen's amazement, the whole back of the stall swung open to reveal an empty room beyond. The wall was a door.

She knew better, however, than to make a scene about it. Following the captain's lead, she walked inside, and when they were through, the door shut noiselessly behind them.

There were several lit candles inside. Barrels just the right height for seating had been set up around the room, which was about the size of Maleen's very large bed.

The captain faced her, his expression grim. "I apologize for the secrecy, Your Highness, but your uncle has ears everywhere. And what we're about to discuss could get us both put to death for treason."

Maleen nearly protested that the princess couldn't be put to death for such a thing. But the look on Captain Dominic's face kept her mouth shut.

"Prince Roburts," he said, "was spotted on a military exercise near the southern border several weeks ago."

"Yes, I know." Maleen nodded. "He and his father run the same exercise every year. He's told me this himself."

"Generally, yes. But this year, the prince himself led his men closer to the border than they have before. We were assured officially that there was no crossing."

Maleen sighed. "But Uncle doesn't believe them."

The captain's mouth tightened.

Maleen took in a deep slow breath, pulling in the smell of

manure and hay. It helped ground her as she ran a hand nervously down the front of her dress. "Then I suppose the remaining question is whether you believe them." She met his brown eyes. "I trust your judgment on this." She frowned. "My uncle once did as well."

"I think," Captain Dominic said in a surprisingly gentle voice, "the question is whether or not *you* trust the Metakinos prince."

Panic flitted around Maleen's stomach, and she had to work hard not to let the surprise show on her face. Before she could answer, however, the creak of a door sounded, and she looked up to see another door opening from the wall opposite the one she and the captain had entered through. Only this time, Emille and James Wickson, the steward, came through.

"And where does that tunnel come from?" Maleen asked, leaning over to see a poorly lit stone-lined tunnel on the other side of the door.

"The kitchens," said Emille, dusting herself off. "Where are Alistaire and Tobias?"

"Coming," said Captain Dominic. "I advised them to come separately."

Sure enough, a scratching sounded from the door James had just shut. Alistaire, the palace physician, came through. Ten seconds later, Tobias, the palace priest, entered through the stable door as Maleen and the captain had.

Alistaire was a tall, broad shouldered man, a heavy contrast to Tobias, a short, wiry fellow whose red hair seemed incapable of being combed to lay flat.

"Sorry," Alistaire said, brushing himself off as Emille had. "I'm rather sure the duke is having me followed. I had a blasted time shaking the mutton-head he sent after me."

"Alistaire!" Emille said disapprovingly. "The princess is here!"

The physician looked up and bowed his head. "My apologies, Your Highness. I didn't see you there."

"I couldn't care a fig for all that fuss," Maleen scoffed. "Now what's all this about?"

"We don't have much time," the captain said. "Alistaire, why don't you tell her what you told us?"

Maleen stared at the physician in amazement. Were they meeting like this often? Why hadn't she ever been told?

"Before we delve into that," Alistaire said, running a hand through his graying hair, "I need to explain, Your Highness, what we're all about."

"I can only guess you're hiding something from my uncle," Maleen said. "Not that I blame you."

Alistaire flinched. "It is true that those of us from your parents' reign have...met from time to time," he said slowly. "At first, simply to remember the good days and to toast their memories. Unfortunately, though, it wasn't long after their deaths that we realized your uncle wasn't as fit for the throne as Ertriquen law assumes the king's young siblings to be in the case of the king's death."

"After your father died," Emille said, glancing at Alistaire, "we began to notice a change in your uncle's behavior. He became even more rigid than he had ever been. You noticed it from a young age, but we've been watching him since before you can remember."

"I've known something was wrong for years," Maleen said, looking at all of them in turn. "Why tell me now?"

The others looked at one another for a moment. Then Emille spoke again. "Two reasons," she said slowly. "First, because Alistaire has found something we previously hadn't known about. We couldn't. And there might be a way to use it to put you on the throne sooner."

"Or," Tobias broke in, "to at least replace the duke with a more suitable guardian."

"Second," Emille said, "because of the delicate nature of your...friendship with Prince Roburts, we thought it prudent to make you fully aware of the situation."

Maleen was struck with two thoughts. First, she was rather annoyed that they hadn't seen her fit to be fully aware of the situation sooner. Second, however, and more pressing was the sudden fear that gripped her.

"My friendship...it's not...common knowledge?" She looked at Emille.

"Not among the general staff," Emille said soothingly. "But as you've gotten older, people have begun to notice."

Icy fear held her frozen to the spot. "And my uncle?"

"Your secret is safe from your uncle," Captain Dominic said. "But it won't always be. And though everyone here believes you are the true monarch and would be capable of wielding the throne now, by law, I am required to follow your uncle until you're of age. And if I don't, there are a number of younger officers who would be pleased to oust me from my position and enact any order your uncle gives them."

Maleen swallowed hard then looked at Alistaire. "What... what was it that changed? You said something changed."

"Ah, yes." He cleared his throat. "I was doing an exam on your uncle two days ago when I confirmed that there is a growing lump on his head. Just behind his hairline."

Maleen stared at him. "A lump?"

"You can't see it yet," he said. "Not without moving his hair, at least. But it's my belief that the lump is the cause of his headaches. And possibly all of the ruinous things he's said and done."

"And you're sure it couldn't be Sortheleige-related?" Emille asked pensively.

"I can't be sure of anything," Alistaire said with a shrug. "Sortheleige is a dark power beyond my understanding. But..." He sighed. "I have been attending your uncle since he was a boy. And while he was never like your father—he was always meticulous, mind you—he was able for a long time to live and contend with the world as it was."

"He wasn't always this particular?" Maleen asked.

The physician shook his head. "No. There were certain colors he refused to wear, and he was rather particular about the fit of his shoes, if I'm not mistaken. But he didn't...struggle so much with needing everything just so."

"It became far worse after the king died," Emille reminded him.

"Yes," Alastaire grimaced, "but it was still nothing compared to what it is now."

"It is progressing then?" Captain Dominic asked.

Alastaire nodded. "Yes. I've been watching this lump for several years now, but only today have I been able to confirm that it is indeed growing. There might even be more, but I can't tell just yet. And...considering the duke's physical condition in that light, I'm of the belief that his continued behavior is due primarily to whatever malady is growing there. Not, as some have suggested, due to the dark influence of Sortheleige."

They were silent for a long while. Finally, Maleen drew in a deep breath.

"So...what do we do?"

Tobias answered. "I've been studying the law. It is my hope that there's a loophole that would allow us to strip him of his power and hand it to another." He glanced uneasily at the others. "We do not dislike your uncle, Princess. Far from it. Most of us here watched him grow up. But we fear that—"

"That he's going to bring ruin upon us all." Maleen nodded. "I understand. In the case you were able to remove him, who would take his place as the country's steward until I'm of age?"

"We're not completely sure just yet," Tobias said, "but it is my guess that either your cousin Topher or Captain Dominic would fulfill the law's requirements. Your cousin, though he doesn't live here, is your nearest relative of age on your father's side. And though Captain Dominic is not in the family, he was given his particular position by your father and legally holds an unusual amount of power for a captain because of it."

Maleen felt her body relax slightly. "I believe either of those possibilities would be good ones." She didn't know her cousin well, but he seemed in his right mind at least, which was more than she could say for her uncle as of late.

"While we get this all sorted out, however," Captain Dominic said, "you're in more danger than ever before, I'm afraid. If your uncle gets wind of this, I fear what he might do in retaliation."

"The servants are frightened," said James, speaking up for the first time since arriving. "I'm afraid if we don't address this soon, they're going to leave the palace in droves."

"There's another problem," Captain Dominic added. "While there are many soldiers who are loyal to you, your uncle has taken on the task of hiring the new recruits. Which means much of the army is now loyal to him rather than to me and your parents' other officers." His frown deepened and he shook his head. "Take care, Princess. And I suggest you warn your prince to do so as well."

Maleen nodded and swallowed. He was right, of course. She couldn't expect to have her friendship with Roburts kept a secret for so many years without at least a few rumors flying. But when they'd begun their friendship at the ages of eight and ten, exchanging letters over the years under false names, they'd never dreamed their link might determine the fates of those around them.

Maleen had only wanted a friend.

But she was no longer eight years, alone and frightened. She was seventeen years. Strong and ready to take the throne that was rightly hers the moment she turned twenty-four.

"Is that all?" she choked out, praying to the Maker it was.

Unfortunately, he shook his head.

"We need to be going before we're missed," Emille said softly. The others nodded and went their separate ways, some out through the stable and others through the tunnel door. Several minutes later, it was only Maleen and Captain Dominic once again.

"There *is* truly a border crisis," he said. "Your uncle ordered four squads of men sent out to keep watch on the part of the border near where Prince Roburts was training. This is in addition to all of the squads he'd deployed on other parts of the border. Even with so many soldiers gone, however, we were doing well enough until there was a small squabble in the square between merchants from the east this morning. I had to send another squad down into the village to ensure the rivals didn't attack anyone else. Which leaves me a squad short for tonight. And if the duke finds out..."

"He'll make a scene," Maleen finished. She put a finger to her right temple and rubbed. "Very well. This is what we'll do." Another deep breath. "Do you know of any men who formerly served? Men who could come and replace the missing squad just until the others get back?"

The captain's eyes brightened. "I could do that, yes. And it's a good choice. One I was hoping you would consider." He paused. "I'm supposing the crown is willing to pay them for their troubles?"

"No, not the crown. My uncle would see the expense." She rubbed her neck. "Tell them they shall be paid. It shall come from my allowance, though, and not the treasury."

The captain grinned as he crossed his thick arms across his chest. Then he bowed. "Your Highness," he said in another low voice, "seven years cannot pass quickly enough."

Maleen could not agree more, but for the sake of humility, simply thanked him and left the stable. She wasn't ten steps out when she was stopped again.

"Your Highness," a girl's voice called.

Maleen counted to three before forcing a smile and turning to face whoever was calling her.

A servant girl approached and bowed. "Your uncle has summoned you, Your Highness."

CHAPTER 3
MISSTEPS

Maleen straightened her shoulders and tried to prepare herself as she made her way to her uncle's study. The hair on the back of her neck stood on end, and she stretched and fisted her hands several times as she walked, hoping to release the tension that was quickly building. Her breath threatened to come too fast, but she refused to let it quicken or slow her step.

As she walked, she tried to guess why he had summoned her. Had he somehow gotten word of the meeting she'd just attended? Though this was her true fear, she was thankful to admit that it was unlikely. Not enough time had passed for word of the meeting to travel to him and then for him to have already tracked her down.

Had he discovered one of Rob's letters, perhaps? That was unlikely as well, though. They'd been corresponding for years under false names with the safety of not one but two other sets of hands receiving the letters before they were delivered to her by her own Mistress Emille.

Knowing these secrets were most likely safe should have

made her feel better, but trepidation still sloshed around inside her as she walked.

She did her best to look confident as she entered the palace and made her way to the set of winding stairs that led to his chambers. How she sometimes wished she could still see the world as she had when she was small. Back then, defying her uncle was something she generally avoided. But when she did, there had been little to pay for such indiscretions. She'd had no idea how hard the palace staff must have worked to shield her from his tempers.

Before she could dream up any more possible reasons as to why he'd called her, she was standing before his door, which was embossed with silver metal. Metal that looked decorative but was really thick enough to stop an axe. She nodded at the servant, who pulled a thin cord that ran up and through a tiny hole above the door. Maleen could hear a bell jingle on the other side. The door opened slowly, the way a portcullis might rise to admit visiting politicians.

Seven years. Seven years until he could no longer summon her as though she were five. Seven years until she no longer had to quake in his shadow. Still, she shuddered as she passed out of the bright hall and into the darkness.

"You're late," he said as the door shut behind her. The click of the lock was deafening.

Maleen drew in a quick breath and threw up a prayer to the Maker as she forced a self-assured smile and turned to face her uncle. "I made my way as soon as I was told you were looking for me."

He came closer, close enough that she began to make out the rigid lines of his face in the shadows cast by the weak fire-light. She knew better than to ask for more light. The room was dark. Always dark. At least, it had been since he'd ordered metal shutters be fitted to the inside of all the windows. There was a fire, but it was low, casting just enough light to cover the desk before it.

"You must have been far if it took you that long to get here." His frown deepened.

"I was with Captain Dominic in the stables." She willed her voice to be cool and smooth.

His eyebrows shot up. "Doing what?"

"Discussing the gala security." She could have said that the first time, but she'd learned long ago not to volunteer any more information than he asked for. It was a game they played, one of cat and mouse. He'd have it all out of her eventually, but if she gave it up too fast, he still would demand more.

"And did he send the squad to the border as I told him to?" He swiveled and walked quickly back into what had once been a bright, airy room for sitting and reading. One of her few remaining memories from before her parents died had taken place in that room. Now the study was as dark and cold as the rest of his rooms.

"He did."

"No doubt begrudgingly."

Her eyes were adjusting enough that she could see him run his hand across his sharp jaw in an agitated way. "The old fool didn't believe me when I told him I had intelligence of a possible breach."

Maleen held her tongue.

He turned back to her suddenly. "Never mind all that. I called you here for a reason." His voice fell to a whisper. "No one followed you?"

Maleen shook her head. "I took myself here."

"Good, good. Have a seat." He motioned to one of the chairs. Then he went and shut the study door and pulled the curtain over it that he'd demanded be installed last year. It dulled voices, he said. Though who he was hoping to hide his voice from, no one knew. Still, Maleen knew better than to bring any of this up. So she sat and waited obediently. Finally, seeming satisfied, he returned.

"I– Why aren't you dressed?"

Maleen self-consciously brushed a loose curl behind her ear. "I was seeing to last-minute details in the kitchen and didn't want to dirty my gown."

He studied her for a moment before nodding and then shaking his head, almost as if to clear his thoughts. "What I'm about to tell you cannot reach anyone else's ears." He turned and fixed her with a stare. "I know you were very much a child in your early years. Too much like your mother for my taste." He paused. "But, you've...surprised me recently. Though there are certainly details I would prefer adjusted for the gala, I've been tracking your organization, and it's not nearly as bad as I expected."

If Maleen hadn't possessed such self-control, she might have fallen off her chair from this praise. Surprise was immediately followed by suspicion. The last time he'd given her a compliment was...well, never. None that she could remember. Nothing was ever good enough for Perseus Summanus, Duke of Casia. She'd learned that when she was seven, the time she'd tried to braid him a crown of daisies.

"My governess," she said, trying not to choke, "says I look more like my father."

His expression softened slightly. "That, you do." For one long moment, they stared at one another, and Maleen wondered if she dared hope. Did he care for her? Was the love for his brother still there behind all the fear and anger?

He sucked in a deep breath, and in a blink, it was gone. His voice was all business once again. "I have just received news of the Metakinos throne's scheming."

Maleen remained silent, but her heart thumped dangerously.

"Ill-content to breach our borders with their military exercises, they've gone to Aldirnin and Cobren and have created an ambitious plan meant to suck our coffers dry and leave our merchants at their mercy, siphoning off traders who wish to come here, and sending them to our lovely neighbors instead."

Maleen frowned slightly. Rob hadn't said anything about such a plan in his last letter. But perhaps his father hadn't told him. Still, she waited. Her uncle was far from the most reliable source of information.

"What do they plan to do?" she asked, vaguely curious despite her refusal to let him excite her with his outrageous claims.

He motioned for her to join him at the small table in the room. Then he lit a candle so she could see a map laid out. "You see this tip of Cobren here? They wish to build a main highway that passes from the main trading port at Cobren into Aldirnin, up through Metakinos, and then up through several more kingdoms, all the way up to Starov."

"That passes through the corner of our kingdom," Maleen said, squinting at the map in the dark.

"Exactly. And you can guess what they want from us." Without waiting for her to answer, he leaned over the map again. "They want permission to cross through the corner of our southeastern border."

"The mountains," she said. "They must go around." Metakinos had several mountain ranges, but their largest crossed over their south-western border and skirted the edge of Ertrique's southern land as well. If they wanted to build a highway for merchants, the easiest way to avoid the dangerous peaks would be to cut through Ertrique's southeastern corner.

"Exactly." He began to smile. "The area is too mountainous to cross on their side, so they wish to go through ours." A strange look came into his eyes, making them glisten a little too brightly. "And we're going to refuse them."

Maleen's jaw dropped. "Why?"

"Because we're not going to give them that advantage! Without passing our border, they'll be stuck on their southern mountains. The way through is nearly impassable. People won't climb that mountain range, even to make a fortune. Metakinos and the others will have to give up!"

Maleen's carefully constructed facade faded, giving way to shock as she stared down at the map. "But...why not leverage this?"

His smile disappeared. "What do you mean?"

She pointed back at the map. "Look. If they're making offers, that means they're open to negotiations. We could suggest a few changes here to move more of the road into our territory. That way, we can set up travel posts–"

"Maleen."

She looked up. His eyes were darker than usual. "Yes, Uncle?"

"What are you doing?"

She looked down at the map. "Um... problem-solving?"

"No, I mean what are you doing, insulting me as if I didn't know the politics of my own people?" He sneered.

"I never said that. I was merely pointing out that we could create wealth this way. It could benefit everyone involved."

Her uncle yanked a bottle of ink off the desk and hurled it at the nearest set of metal shades. Maleen flinched as it shattered. Then he was beside her, so close he was breathing in her ear. "If I didn't know better," he whispered, "I'd think you were in on it with them!"

The discomfort of his whisper in her ear fueled her anger, and Maleen whipped around to face him. "Why can't we all benefit from this? Why is that so hard?" What had gotten into her? She was treading a line, and she knew it. Still, unable to quench her fury, she held his shocked, baleful glare.

"The king of Metakinos is a sniveling coward!" her uncle shouted, pointing to the east. "And he is our enemy! And as long as you are under my rule, you'll be challenging my enemy as well!"

"We weren't always enemies!"

"We've always been rivals!"

"Perhaps economically!" Maleen stood tall. "But I know for a fact that Mother and Father had nearly reached a trade treaty before they died."

"You don't—"

"I've read the documents, Uncle. They're still in the treasury."

"And that foolishness is the reason your mother and father are dead!"

The silence that followed roared in Maleen's ears. She'd already gone too far. Some small voice in the back of her head tried to call her back, begging for the sake of those around her not to put her uncle in one of his tempers. Not before the gala. She licked her lips to wet them and spoke slowly.

"That was never proven. We cannot place the blame of murder on mere conjecture."

"You would lecture *me* on the morality of conjecture?"

"If it is deserved!" That still small voice screamed at her again. But she was in too deep now, and fear warred with rage. Years of suppressed debate were now pouring forth from her mind, and she was having a hard time damming it up.

"Oh, you impish pup!" Her uncle ran his hand through his hair and laughed unpleasantly.

Father, why aren't you here?

He picked up a vase and looked at it, and she tensed, ready to run if he began to throw things again. He'd never hurt her, or anyone else that she was aware of. But his temper had grown worse as the years passed, and every hair on her body was standing on end, urging her to be anywhere but here. Instead of throwing the vase, however, after a long moment, he put the vase down, straightened his cloak, then cleared his throat.

"I was," he said, his voice cold, "going to give you oversight of the capitol as a sign that you're growing closer to your coronation. That was my reason for calling you today. But I'm glad I had a chance to recognize your immaturity before making that mistake." He turned and let himself out of the little room, apparently done with her.

Maleen was more than ready to be gone, but before she left his chambers as she should have, she paused once more at the main door. "I might not be able to take the throne now. But I will. In seven years. And—"

"As long as you don't give me reason to think your missteps are more than naïveté," he said in a smooth, hard voice. "Now get dressed. The guests will be here soon."

Maleen felt more words rising to her lips, so she clamped her mouth shut and forced her feet to carry her out the door.

CHAPTER 4
WATCH IT BURN

Mistress Emille fell into step with Maleen as she stomped back to her chambers. "I take it that didn't go as you'd hoped," she said in a low voice.

"He's worse than ever," Maleen snapped. "By the day, he–"

"Perhaps we should finish this discussion in your chambers, Your Highness." Emille's voice was respectful but sharp.

Maleen nodded sharply and took a few deep breaths as they made their way across the palace. Finally, when they were once again in her rooms and the door was locked, she turned and glared at her old governess.

"He grows worse by the day! If it's not one of his shoes or locks he's obsessing over, it's the safety of the food or the extra pennies the cook spent replacing spilt salt. Did you know that Kareem says he will now only wear the same outfit every day? They had to purchase enough material to make five of the same shirt and trousers!"

"Actually, that's been going on for two years or so," Emille's shoulders slumped.

"I'm not even sure how we're going to *have* the gala with

him present at this point. I'm afraid he's going to start a war if someone looks at him the wrong way."

"He's always had enough decorum to hold his tongue in the past," Emille said. "The staff paid for it after, but he did at least keep his thoughts to himself."

Maleen shook her head and began to pace. "He's getting more inflexible and paranoid by the day."

They were quiet for a moment as Maleen got lost in her thoughts. What was it he had been ready to hand over? Rule of the city? It wouldn't have been rule of the kingdom by any stretch, but if she had just kept her mouth shut, maybe she could have–

"Do you really think they will find a way to remove him from power?" Maleen asked in a low voice. When the others had suggested it at the meeting only an hour before, she'd been elated. But now Maleen felt the weight of danger they were dancing with as she recalled her uncle's words.

As long as you don't give me reason to think your missteps are more than naïveté.

The threat was subtle, but it was there. Her uncle, above all, feared betrayal. He was sure in his heart of hearts that their neighboring kingdom had betrayed them and killed his brother, even though there had never been conclusive evidence of such. And in the years since the king's death, he had become more and more suspicious, firing servants on a whim, subjecting others to intense castigation, while even more had been put in the stocks.

"If he realized we were doing this–" Maleen began.

"He could have us all arrested for treason," Emille said firmly.

Maleen groaned and fell onto the pink sofa beneath her window. "I don't know what to do. If I move too early, I risk losing it forever. But if I wait seven years, the kingdom may be too far gone for me to fix."

Emille gave her a sad smile. "I don't envy you, Princess. But–" Then her eyes lit up. "Oh! While you were with your uncle, something arrived that will cheer you."

Maleen shoved her face in a pillow. "Does it come with a side of cherry wine?"

Emille laughed and tapped Maleen gently on the head with something. Maleen sat up with another groan that stopped as soon as she saw what Emille held. "When did this come in?" She snatched it up and broke the gold-tinted waxen seal.

> *My Dearest Molly,*
>
> *I hope you're well. I'm sorry my last note was so short, and I apologize again for the brevity of this one. (Isn't it ironic that I'm now mourning the lack of words on a page? See, you have been a good influence on me.)*
>
> *My father has an assignment for me to complete immediately in the northwest forest. Unfortunately, it's going to keep me away for more than two weeks, so by the time you're reading this, you'll most likely be nearing the gala. Which means I have another apology to make.*

Maleen's heart fell into her stomach, but she forced herself to keep reading.

> *I'm so sorry. I truly am. I wanted to attend this event more than any other this year. I asked my father repeatedly to send someone else, but he's adamant that I attend to this concern personally.*
>
> *I wanted to see you in your gown with all those pearls magically strung through your hair. I wanted to claim you for the first dance and then spend the whole time spinning you in circles just to spite your uncle, as well as all the other unworthy sops who dared look your way.*
>
> *Promise me something? Dance with anyone you like–*

anyone but Cedric. One day, he'll make a comment obvious enough that I can justify planting a blow to his nose. But until then, can you wait for me?

As always yours,

Rob

"Maleen, what's wrong?" Emille's mouth fell open as Maleen unsuccessfully tried to wipe the tears from her eyes. She took up the letter and read it for herself, her look of alarm turning to one of understanding. "Oh, love. I'm so sorry. I– But what's this?" She picked a small slip of paper off the floor. "It looks like you missed something." She handed it to Maleen.

Postscript: I may not be able to come, but I'm sending a gift. Since everyone else is sending theirs as well, it should be decently hidden. It has no tag, but you'll know which one is mine.

The promise didn't erase the heavy feeling in Maleen's chest, but it did slightly lessen the weight of it.

He'd sent her a present.

"You didn't think he would really let you go so easily," Emille said with a knowing smile.

Maleen blushed a little as she brushed her tears away, laughing unevenly. "Being so far apart in enemy kingdoms makes one wonder in the dark hours of the night."

"Well, wonder no more." Emille's eyes brightened. "Now let's get you dressed. And then perhaps open your birthday gifts?"

Maleen did her best to contain her excitement as she was primped and readied for what felt like hours. Then the servants brought not one but three mountains of gifts into her room. She knew, however, from the way the servants returned her smile that she was failing miserably at containing any of her joy. It was streaming from her face like torchlight. She would be dying a little inside that night when she received her guests and he wasn't there. But a present...

He'd never dared send a gift before.

"Try not to glow so much," Emille murmured as the servants brought in the final gifts.

"I can't help it!" She waggled her eyebrows. "I have been on my best behavior, and I still had to wait for my birthday." Though Maleen's birthday had taken place a month earlier, they had made the decision—one her uncle was surprisingly open to—to wait to celebrate until the gala.

Emille rolled her eyes, but her smile widened as she shook her head. "You're seventeen. Are you still incapable of waiting for your presents?"

"Absolutely incapable." She paused as the final servant shut and locked the door. "Now, where shall we begin?"

An hour later, surrounded by piles of jewels, hairpins, shoes, shawls, pearls, and every other bit of finery imaginable, Maleen sat back and sighed.

"Unsatisfied?" Emille arched an eyebrow. She had been recording the sender of each gift.

"Oh, no. I'm very grateful." Maleen looked at the remaining piles. "I could start my own country with a treasure load such as this. I just..." She frowned slightly.

"You're only interested in one gift." Emille chuckled and shook her head. She stood and moved to the back of the second pile. "I suppose I can help you look if you're determined not to open any more."

It wasn't that Maleen didn't appreciate her gifts. She truly did. Her favorites were the books her aunt and uncle had sent her from the southern realm, two volumes on the histories of the greatest desert battles waged. She also loved all the home-made gifts her people had made. Hand-knitted scarves, vibrantly dyed silk blouses, hats with embroidered flowers. Not that her uncle would ever let her wear such in public. But they were gifts of love nonetheless.

"What about this one?" Emille emerged from the pile holding a small brown leather box. Maleen took it carefully, and taking a deep breath, opened the lid.

Sitting on a silk cushion was a thin silver coin with a hole at the top, through which was looped a leather cord. It wasn't encrusted with jewels, nor were there any details of beautiful artistry. Just the words stamped into the metal.

HOLD FAST.

"Oh!" Maleen traced the words reverently. Her voice felt as though it was caught, and all she could do was stare.

"That's their military cry." Emille frowned. "Is that supposed to mean something?"

In this moment, the little phrase meant more than it ever had. For the first time, it felt...almost like a promise.

"Yes. Yes, it does." Emille felt the tears threatening to fall again, and took a deep breath so her carefully applied makeup wouldn't smudge. Uncle would call that imperfection out for sure.

"Could you help me put it on?" Maleen held it out.

"Is that really wise?"

"If Uncle asks, I'll tell him there was no name on the box."

Emille pursed her lips. "He'll recognize the military cry of his enemy's kingdom."

That was a good point. Maleen looked around then bright-ened. "We'll put this on over it." She held up a necklace that had been cut to look like a garden of jeweled flowers. The assortment of small flowers was three fingers wide, large enough by far to hide the little coin behind it.

"You're playing with fire," Emille said. Still, she moved to help Maleen don both necklaces.

A bolt of rebellion streaked through Maleen's chest. "I've been playing with fire a long time." She smiled. "It's about time I get to see it burn."

CHAPTER 5
TIME TO BEGIN

Maleen made her way down to the entrance for the second time that day. This time, however, she was arrayed in a gown of pastel pink gossamer, sprinkled with small gems and glass beads that sparkled with each step she took. Her hair was pulled up in the latest fashion, one set by Queen Isabelle of Destin, as many of the latest fashions were, large curls tucked neatly at the nape of her neck, with a headband of more gems glittering beneath the candles in the chandeliers hanging from the ceiling. At her chest was the garden necklace, its own flowers reflecting their colors as well. But it was the little stamped coin beneath the necklace that added surety to her step.

In sending the necklace, he had asked her to wait. And though she hated waiting—and he knew it—she would wait for him.

"Was Mother really betrothed at her seventeenth birthday celebration?" she asked over her shoulder.

"Your father's seventeenth birthday, actually, as is tradition." Emille glanced at Maleen. "Why? What are you thinking?"

"Oh, nothing." Maleen stopped at the edge of the entrance hall. "I just wish they could have been here, too."

"As we all do, Princess," Emille said softly. "Now go and greet your guests with confidence. It is your birthright."

Maleen flashed her old governess a smile. "Thank you. For everything."

As she made her way toward his chambers, she glanced around, looking for any sign of her uncle. But he was nowhere to be seen, not even on his favorite banister that overlooked the entrance from above. This made her breathe a little easier, and suddenly, she was ready.

This was her kingdom. They were her guests. And no matter what he did in his madness, she would have what was hers.

She didn't have to wait long. Though she was early, carriages began pulling up just outside the palace's front steps.

"Prince Launce and Princess Olivia of Cobren!" the herald announced. Maleen let out a small sigh of relief. These guests were a safe place to start.

Princess Olivia and Prince Launce were opposites in every way. Olivia was warm and soft, with olive skin, laughing dark eyes, and beautiful curves. Launce, by contrast, was tall... extremely tall. His hair was brown, but it had shades of red, and he was one of the thinnest men Maleen had ever seen. His voice would be forever imprinted in her mind, as he was one of the first to help her after her near-drowning. Hopefully, when she took the throne, she would be able to get to know them better. She had a feeling their friendship would be one never to take for granted.

"Your Highnesses." Maleen nodded respectfully to the prince and princess, as they did to her. "I am so glad you could come celebrate with us."

"Not more excited than we are." Olivia's dark eyes danced. "I've been looking forward to this all year. I've been out buying every shade of dye your merchants have to offer, and I'm not nearly done." Then she put a hand on Maleen's arm and lowered her voice. "You look absolutely beautiful. Your parents would be so proud."

A lump rose in Maleen's throat and made it somewhat difficult to say thank you. But the princess seemed to understand and gave Maleen's arm a gentle squeeze before letting go.

"Just don't fall into any streams this year," Launce said. His face was serious, but his eyes smiled. "You're getting tall enough I'm not sure I could pull you out."

Olivia swatted her husband's arm. "Behave."

Launce laughed, which made everyone around them laugh, too. Then Maleen sighed.

"I'm sorry your sister cannot be here," she said.

"So is she. One of the children was sick, or she never would have missed it." He leaned forward. "Your gift from her is being delivered now, though. Courtesy of the Fortress's library."

Maleen gaped at him, somehow remembering to shut her mouth so she didn't look like a fish. But the couple just smiled knowingly and bid her happy birthday once more before moving on to make way for the next guests.

It wasn't long before Maleen began to feel truly comfortable. There were many politicians, of course, that she wouldn't trust farther than she could throw them. But there were also many kind and earnest guests as well. She'd invited more this year than usual, under the guise of bringing in more customers for the festival merchants in the city.

She was sure her uncle knew better, but she didn't care. Maleen simply liked people. If she'd learned anything from that first gala, aside from the fact that she couldn't swim, it was that she loved the company of others. Everyone had a story, a background, hopes and dreams, loss and sorrow. Everyone...even her uncle, was like a world to explore. And she wanted to know them all.

Well, perhaps not her uncle. She could safely study him from afar.

"I don't think we've ever had this many guests at the gala. And that's saying something, considering I've been attending the gala since my parents hosted it."

Maleen jumped a little at the sound of her uncle's voice beside her.

"My apologies, Uncle," she said, trying not to sound breathless from the startle. "I didn't hear you come down."

"I meant it that way." She gave him a strange look, but he simply examined the guest line. "I take it the Ashlandian king isn't coming this year?"

"I'm afraid not." Maleen smiled and addressed her next guest.

"The civil war." Her uncle's lips thinned. "Unfortunately, I'm not surprised."

"Uncle, do you think we might discuss this later?" Maleen extended a hand to the duchess who had just stepped up.

He frowned but nodded and seemed to satisfy himself with standing like a statue by her side. Well, at least he wasn't trying to take over. He seemed truly intent on letting her run the gala.

"Your Highness."

Maleen turned to find the castle steward standing at her elbow. "Yes, James?"

"It's time to begin."

Maleen smiled. "Thank you." With a glance at her uncle, she excused herself from the now dwindling line of guests and followed the steward to the dais. Her heart pumped so hard that she could feel it throughout her entire body as she forced one foot in front of the other. With each step, she was coming closer to the person her parents had wanted her to be. It felt like she was growing closer to them, too.

When she was at the edge of the dais, she nodded at the steward. James Wickson was a wiry man in his early sixth decade, but he had the energy of a man in his thirties. He had served under her parents before their deaths, and even her grandfather before them. He'd also served her these last nine years in assisting her continued correspondence with Rob. And Maleen was more than grateful for his guidance tonight under her uncle's watchful eye.

"I present, Her Highness, Princess Maleen Aretha Silvius of Ertrique."

Maleen forced herself to walk to the front of the dais. When she reached the front, she momentarily froze. There were so many people! So many faces staring up at her. She took a deep breath, wondering if she ought to feign feeling ill, when her necklace shifted, and something cool touched her chest.

HOLD FAST.

Unbidden, a smile spread on her face, and Maleen stood tall.

"I want to thank you all for coming to our gala. For those of you who have never attended the Color Harvest Gala, it's our ages-old celebration of the time of year when our dyes are harvested, prepared, and ready for use. Our farmers spend all year tending to the different flowers and herbs that we use to create our many colors. Our dyers then take those flowers and treat them, carefully preserving the color as they make them into the powders you most likely saw in the market today.

"Two hundred years ago, King Amadeus declared that there would be a celebration once a year in which the hard work of our people would be heralded. A week was dedicated to feasts and entertainment, something which quickly became a destination for outsider merchants and travelers who hoped to acquire the new dyes as well."

She paused. They seemed to be listening. Very few even looked bored. Encouraged, she continued.

"Now we are thankful to have you here as well. We hope to build bridges of friendship and to practice good trade to the benefit of all who are here. Throughout the week, we will have activities for the children, hunts for all of our distinguished sirs, and dyeing demonstrations for our ladies' enjoyment, just to name a few. If you have any needs, please see my steward, James, or another staff member, and we will do our best to accommodate you. You will be shown your rooms tonight when you're ready to retire. Supper will be served soon, and after will come dancing."

She glanced up long enough to see Emille at the back of the crowd. She was smiling as tears ran down her face.

"Um, one more thing." Maleen clasped her hands in front of her. "I also want to thank you for attending this particular year. Many of you were kind enough to send very generous gifts, and your notice and care have made this year's celebration even more special to me than any before."

She took another suddenly shaky breath. "In our kingdom, Seventeen is a special year, one of coming-of-age. You see, twenty years ago, my father celebrated his seventeenth birthday at the gala as well."

Breathe, Maleen.

"It was that year when he became betrothed to my mother." Her voice wavered, and she immediately knew that it was high time the speech came to an end. "So I want to thank you again for celebrating with me when they cannot."

Applause broke out, and as Maleen exited the dais, trying discreetly to dab at the corners of her eyes, she realized many in the crowd were doing so as well. When she reached the ground, she saw her uncle coming toward her.

"That was well done," he said, his eyes looking slightly reddened as well.

Maleen blinked at him. "Truly?"

He gave her a tight smile. "He would have been proud."

"That he would have."

Maleen's uncle stiffened, and Maleen turned to find King Damon standing before her.

"Your Majesty!" she stuttered, hastening a late nod to the king of Metakinos. "I didn't see you come in."

"I apologize for my lateness," he said, glancing at her uncle before returning his gaze to her. "But I wanted to bring you a present, and I had to wait until it came home."

Maleen stared up at him, but that only made him laugh as he stepped to the side. Behind him was a young man in a military uniform.

Maleen was painfully aware that her uncle was on the edge of apoplexy. But she couldn't help the ridiculous smile that came to her face.

The young man bowed. "Princess Maleen." Then he took her hand, and as his lips caressed her skin, a shiver traveled up her spine.

"Hello, Roburts," was all she could say.

CHAPTER 6
DIDN'T LIKE IT

Maleen's uncle was incensed, and she knew somewhere in her mind that he was glaring daggers at the king of Metakinos, but Maleen felt frozen in place.

It really was him. He had somehow grown another inch since she'd seen him last. And though she'd seen him in his forest green uniform before, he filled it out this time. His dark curls were more obedient than ever before, and he moved with a new kind of grace.

But those green eyes...she knew those. And now, as he gallantly held her hand in his, they betrayed the stern perfection of his military persona, dancing as though he were about to let her in on the grandest of jokes. That look nearly always got them into trouble.

She loved that look.

"I thought you were out on military reconnaissance," her uncle said stiffly.

Rob straightened and bowed his head out of deference, though Maleen knew it must kill him. Rob harbored hard feelings against her uncle for more than one past incident, and they all had to do with her.

"I wasn't sure I would make it back in time, so I thought it would be best to send my father in my stead." He met Maleen's gaze again. "I hoped it wouldn't be too unwelcome a surprise that I finished earlier than I expected."

The way he looked at her sent goosebumps up and down her arms. She wanted simultaneously to melt into a puddle and to throw a stick at him to remind him who was watching. But he simply continued to look at her with the intensity of her uncle's falcons.

What was he doing?

"Your Highness." James appeared at her elbow. "The dancing will soon begin."

"Perfect." Her uncle's voice was icy. "Let us go, Niece."

Before he could pull her away, though, Rob lifted her hand once again to his lips. "I know it is customary for the princess to dance her first dance with her father, but I'm hoping you'll save the second dance for me?"

Maleen's uncle's face turned bright red. "Certainly–"

"Certainly I will." She smiled brightly at her uncle. "Are you ready?"

Her uncle gawked at her, and she knew he would make her pay for this later. But something inside of Maleen had snapped that afternoon in his study. She felt as though she'd set some great wheel in motion and couldn't turn it back. Instead, she'd sent it rolling down a steep hill. And yet she realized, as she stood between the man she must submit to and the man she adored, she had no desire to turn it back. What she had set in motion would be.

Still, she knew better than to fight her uncle in public, so she allowed him to lead her away. They walked to the center of the large stone floor and waited as the crowd cleared a space around them. For one long moment, the room was silent, and Maleen wondered if the heavy pounding in her ears belonged to her own joyful heart or her uncle's enraged one.

Finally, the music began. It was a traditional song, full of quick crescendos and decrescendos that built and fell accordingly. Simple and sweet, the dance had been handed down from father to daughter for generations, the commoners and nobility alike celebrating this rite of passage. She tried to ignore the way her chest squeezed tightly when she remembered that this dance should have been shared with her father if all had been as it ought to be. Not her scowling, suspicious uncle.

"I hope you're not about to do something foolish."

Maleen gave a little start. "I'm sorry?"

Her uncle jerked his head to the right. "That boy. You looked like a lovesick turtledove when he took your hand. I hope you're smart enough not to do something that can't be undone."

Maleen heard the warning clearly enough, but against her better judgment, she burst into giggles. "Turtledove? I didn't know birds could look smitten, Uncle."

He squeezed her hand so tightly it hurt. The smile on his face no longer looked false, but menacing. "You heard me, Maleen. Follow the laws of this kingdom, and you will have your throne soon enough. Break them, though, and I will make sure you never do."

Maleen's face flushed hot. "Be plain, Uncle."

"My parents and brother worked too hard building this kingdom up for me to let it fall to some headstrong, lovelorn child." His grip on her hand made her wince. "Or worse."

"If you believe I would do something to put my kingdom in jeopardy, then you've failed to know me at all." Maleen gritted her teeth.

The music around them wafted to an end. Gradually, her uncle relaxed his grip on her fingers, and Maleen resisted the urge to flex them as she dropped his hand. The room around them was silent in spite of the great number of guests watching them. Still, Maleen did not drop his gaze.

"Your Highness. I believe you promised me your second dance," came Rob's voice, breaking the silence.

It was her uncle who broke their staring contest first, and when he did, he simply scowled harder. Rob stood beside them, his hand outstretched. She smiled at him and placed her hand in his, though it still pulsed from when her uncle had squeezed it. "I would be honored." She flashed her uncle another defiant grin before recentering herself on the dance floor. Anger still pumped through her body, but it was quickly being replaced by something she couldn't name.

Tendrils of music floated into the air, and Maleen shivered as Rob took her hands firmly but gently in his. She counted the seconds until they would begin to move. Time seemed to slow as he gently spun her out and the dance began. And though there were hundreds of people watching them, the world suddenly felt as though it were theirs.

"What are you smiling about?" he asked, a smile playing on his own lips.

"Just remembering the last time we danced." She flashed him a rebellious grin.

He groaned as he turned them slowly in time to the music. "I wish I could forget it."

"Oh, I haven't forgotten." She wriggled her eyebrows. "Nor do I plan to for a very long time."

"Molly, that was two years ago!" he laughed.

"I know! And I shall use it until it's all worn out." Her breathing hitched as his large hand wrapped around her waist and he pulled her close against his chest.

"So I must pay penance then."

She swallowed, trying to maintain her saucy look, rather than getting lost in the warmth of his eyes. With a little shake of her head, she took a deep breath as the dance bid her pull back a step. Perfect for clearing her head. "You wrote me, gloating that you were of age to dance, and I was not."

"Molly—"

"And then, to pour salt on the wound, you asked me how to catch Lady Priscilla's attention." She tossed her head triumphantly. "You'd known me for seven years by then, sir. What did you expect?"

He pulled her close again as the dance called for a slow spin, though in Maleen's recollection, she'd never performed this dance with anyone quite so close in all her very extensive practices. When he spoke again, his voice was a whisper.

"How was I supposed to know you wanted me to save my dances for you?"

For once in her life, Maleen struggled to think of an answer. His lips were inches from her face, and as the music slowed, she realized in a panic that the dance was nearly over. "Two years is a long time." She swallowed. "I didn't think you'd want to."

She was unable to tear her gaze from his until they were interrupted by a roar. Startled, she looked around and was reminded that powerful people from nearly every kingdom in the western realm had just watched them share the most intimate conversation they'd ever had. If her uncle had been ignorant of their friendship before this, there was no way he could be now.

She turned to look for him, and sure enough, he looked as though he might pass out.

"Come with me."

She looked back to see Rob's face trained on her uncle as well. His grip tightened on hers. But it wasn't painful. Never painful. Rob would never hurt her.

"Where?" she whispered.

"Just come." He nodded at her uncle again. "Look, Prince Launce is giving us our chance. Let's go."

Sure enough, Prince Launce had stepped between them and the kingdom's steward in a way that could only be intentional. He was chatting away about something with great animation and volume, something she had never seen him do before tonight. So she nodded at Rob and allowed him to lead her from the dance floor as other couples began to fill it in their place.

They were slowed slightly by well-wishing admirers who seemed to have read as much into the dance as Maleen had...if she'd interpreted correctly. And yet as she followed him, she had to wonder.

They'd never really claimed affection for one another. Not outright. But since the disastrous gala two years before, Maleen had often wondered at his intentions. Slowly, slowly the words of his letters had become more focused. And sometimes she dared hope, as she had when she'd received his gift, that he truly desired something more. His gift of the necklace was the boldest message ever exchanged between them. Nearly a promise.

She couldn't be misreading his intentions...

Could she?

He led her to the gardens, but they didn't stop where all the other guests were mingling. Instead, he continued to a secluded spot beneath a trellis, where roses climbed the posts and covered the crisscrossed planks above their heads. Moonlight painted the night in soft silver and shadows, making drops from an earlier rainfall glisten like gems on the flowers' pink petals.

"I love this place!" She smiled. "But I've never been allowed to see it at night! How did you find it?"

He gave her a sour smile. "Believe it or not, some of our parents don't follow us around into adulthood."

Maleen stepped away from him and spun slowly, taking in the magic of the moment. The air smelled sweetly of soil and water, and her closest friend was standing just an arm's length away, watching her, that strange expression in his eyes just as intense it had been before the dance.

Well, her friend and not her friend. The boy she remembered was gone. In his place stood a man with a slight shadow at the corner of his jaw, his head and shoulders towering over her like he never had before.

"Molly," he began, but she laughed.

"You can call me by my name here. This isn't a letter you have to fear falling into my uncle's hands." Not that her uncle wouldn't read *everything* after this.

Instead of laughing, he looked down at his hands. "I know." Then he looked back up at her again, that same strange intensity in his eyes that he'd worn on the dance floor. "But Maleen is the shy princess at the ball, fearful beneath her uncle's watch." He drew closer and took her hands in his. She sucked in a deep breath as he ran his fingers over her knuckles. "Molly is free. She doesn't hide things from me out of fear."

For the second time that night, Maleen felt her words stick in her throat, and as she looked up at him, was unable to utter a sound.

"When you danced with Cedric two years ago," he said softly, "why exactly did you do it?"

"You know why." She fixed her gaze on the golden buttons on his fine coat. "I wanted revenge."

"Revenge for what?" He lifted her face gently.

She hesitated. Did he truly want to hear this? Two years had passed. In some ways, she was mortified by the memory of what she'd done that night. It was the one and only time she'd truly done anything scandalous in her life, daring a public dance when she was two years underage. She'd been in trouble for months following the gala and had been conveniently in another kingdom, visiting a distant cousin during the gala the following year.

But, in all fairness, she'd gotten exactly what she wanted, and that was Rob's attention. They'd never spoken of that night in any of their few in-person exchanges after her daring act, though. Until now...here...tonight, washed clean in the light of the moon, where she, alone, was under his gaze.

"You said you were jealous." He took a half-step closer. "What were you jealous of, Maleen?"

"You were getting to dance. I wanted to as well." There. Better to be vague and make him hunt. If he really wished to know, he would ask.

"So you picked Cedric."

"I can pick anyone I want." She raised her chin slightly.

He gave her a knowing smile, and it took all of her willpower not to shake as he ran the back of his fingers down her cheek. "You hate Cedric."

"I hate being left out."

"Maleen," he said quietly, the teasing no longer in his eyes. "Tell me. Why did you sabotage my chances with Lady Priscilla? Was it the same reason you danced with Cedric?"

His lips were just inches from her face, and his breath tickled her temple as his chest rose and fell. Squeezing her eyes shut, she tried to focus. "I didn't like it."

"Didn't like what?"

Her eyes flew open, and a surge of reminiscent frustration washed through her like a wave. "That you weren't mine!"

There was a long moment of silence as she glared at him. He watched her with a strange look on his face, his head tilted slightly to the side. Silence? Truly? After he'd just gotten her to admit—

He leaned forward and whispered in her ear. "Do you know what I realized that night?"

"What?" she snapped petulantly.

"I didn't like it either." Then, before she could speak, he'd taken her face gently in his hands and was pressing his lips against hers.

CHAPTER 7
SAY YES

Maleen had often wondered what it would feel like to be kissed. Specifically, to be kissed by Rob.

And it was beyond any sensation she'd ever imagined.

His strong fingers cupped her jaw with one hand while the other hand moved around to her back and drew her closer. She was falling, floating down toward the earth with no idea of when or where she might land.

Maybe she would never find the ground. She would be fine with that.

He pulled back just enough that their lips brushed as he spoke in a breathless voice. "Marry me?"

Maleen froze then stepped back so she could see his eyes. They were wide and cautious.

"Do you...really mean that?" she whispered.

He gave her a nervous chuckle. "I wouldn't have asked if I didn't."

Maleen shook her head and stepped back so he was no longer holding her. Then she shook her head again and took a deep breath. He watched her carefully.

"I mean it, Rob," she said in a warbling voice. "Marriage is...

well, it's for the rest of our lives." She took a deep, shuddering breath. "You're young—"

"I'm older than you by two years," he said somewhat resentfully.

"But what if you decide you want someone else?" She put a hand up and rested it on her carefully coiffed hair. She'd loved the elaborate style when Mary, her maid, had done it earlier. But now it mocked her, making her feel like a little girl playing dress-up. "I'm seventeen, Rob," she said, holding her hands out. "I'm not as refined as all the great ladies in that hall. I'm still under the thumb of my uncle, and..." She suddenly felt very much like crying. "What if you decide I'm not worth the trouble? What if you change your mind?"

Rob had been turning redder by the minute, but as soon as these words left her mouth, his look of anger melted, and he took her in his arms once more. She rested her head on his chest, trembling as he rubbed her back slowly.

"I've been putting up with your uncle for the last nine years," he said into her hair. "You don't think I can survive him for another seven if it means I get to keep you for the rest of your life?"

She pulled her head from his chest long enough to look up at him. He wiped the tears from her cheeks with his thumbs and gave her a smile that melted her from the inside out. "Maleen, I've been thinking of this day since the gala two years ago." The gold hints in his green eyes glinted in the silver moonlight as he looked at her, seeming to see into her soul. And all at once, Maleen felt like she'd never been so at peace before.

Embarrassed at her tears and her fear, Maleen sniffed and tried to straighten. "Nineteen is young," she said, busying herself with straightening his lapel. "That's not very much time to think, you know."

He threw his head back and laughed before tweaking her nose. "My kingdom generally allows its youth to think what they want without being thrown in the dungeon for it." Then he sobered. "Your parents were betrothed at seventeen, were they not? And everyone who knew them talks of little but how much they loved each other." He tapped her nose. "And you."

Maleen felt herself beginning to smile.

"So," he said, bending to whisper in her ear, "*now* will you marry me?"

Maleen turned her head so their mouths met once more, and she kissed him until she nearly saw stars. He pulled back and gave a breathless chuckle.

"I hope that means yes."

Unadulterated joy streamed from Maleen's heart. She felt as though she had swallowed the sun, and now she was the one bursting with golden beams of delight. One morning, she would wake up beside this man. She would no longer answer to her uncle. She could do what she believed was best for her people without quaking in her boots, and she could go to sleep beside her dearest friend every night. Thrill made her stomach weak, but it was the sort of weakness she could easily resign herself to. Unlike when she was with her uncle, she could be weak around this man and know she was still safe.

"What are you thinking?" he asked, playing with a curl of her hair.

She grinned. "Only that I'm going to have your babies."

His eyes slightly widened then began to gleam. "Mmm." He kissed her softly again. "Yes, you will. How many? Two? Three?"

"Oh no." She made a face. "At least four or five."

"That many?"

She lifted her chin defiantly. "My children will never be lonely like I was."

"My love," he said, taking her face gently in his hands once more as he looked into her eyes. "You will never be lonely again. I promise." Then he kissed her again and began to tell her all about wedding traditions in Metakinos.

"You'll get a jewel engraved with our names on it," he said, swinging their hands back and forth between them as they walked. "It's tradition for the groom to give the bride. And we'll walk in a parade to the church. Then we'll be taken back to the castle in a carriage and we'll go to the...well..." He paused, and his face reddened so much that Maleen laughed at him, which made him poke her, making her laugh harder.

Maleen could have stayed in his arms all night beneath the starry sky, but soon they heard the distant announcement that dinner would soon begin. So she satisfied herself with taking his hand and ambling slowly through the garden toward the palace. Unfortunately, the sight of the palace brought up other, less happy thoughts as well.

"You know we haven't discussed the most difficult part of this arrangement," she said quietly.

"Your uncle," he said matter-of-factly.

She nodded. "What are we going to do? If I don't tell him, he'll most likely pick some horrid duke and betroth us without my permission."

His hand tightened around hers. "I think you underestimate how many problems this arrangement will solve."

"Oh?" she said doubtfully. He sounded far more optimistic than Maleen dared feel.

"Our kingdoms have had a rift between them for centuries. What better to heal that rift than to join them in the Maker's most sacred union on earth?"

"That's...true."

"Imagine it," he continued proudly. "We can bring peace and happiness to our people as we find it ourselves! What better ending to a difficult story?"

"And you're sure your parents won't mind?" Maleen suddenly felt shy. His parents had always been kind enough to her, even when her uncle had been his most obnoxious. But extending kindness to a child and blessing their son's marriage to her were two very different things.

"They love you." He grinned. "Why do you think my father waited for me to come home before setting out for the gala here?"

Maleen couldn't help returning his smile, but then she sighed.

"My uncle–"

Rob stopped walking and took her hands in his. "Maleen, this is the best place to break the news. Everyone will be here to witness whatever it is that he decides to do. Overreacting could result in a war. Even he should know better than to do something too rash in front of so many allies."

"I know it's...logical," Maleen said, beginning to walk once again. "But I'm not sure I have as much faith in his logic as you do."

They were quiet for a moment, and for a long few seconds, Maleen wondered if he was beginning to reconsider his proposal. It really was ridiculous. This shouldn't be nearly as complicated as it was.

When he turned to her, however, his smile was gentle. "How about we wait until the end of the gala? You can spend the whole time proving to your uncle what a good job you can do. Then we can tell everyone on the final evening."

Maleen filled her lungs with clean night air and surprised herself by laughing. "You know what? I think that will work." She wrapped her arms around him and kissed him again.

"I suggest," he growled through the kiss, "that we go back inside for supper *now*, before I carry you away and don't bring you back at all."

Maleen laughed. It really was the most magical sort of night.

They made their way into the palace and were quickly ushered into the dining hall for supper. Despite her joy, Maleen's face flushed when she realized that everyone else was already seated, which meant all the guests had delayed eating for the return of their hostess. She quickly seated herself beside her uncle and whispered a quiet apology, trying not to let his scathing look affect her too deeply. If her uncle resented her for breaking protocol, however, the other guests seemed to find the situation amusing. Prince Launce and Princess Olivia were smirking at one another from their seats. Several other guests, including Rob's father, looked just as smug.

The palace holy man was called upon to say the blessing, and the eating finally commenced. Maleen did her best to look contrite and small as she listened to her uncle and several of the other men, including Rob's father, continue the discussion they must have begun while they were waiting for her.

"Have some sense, Perseus," a fat man was telling her uncle. "The road would only benefit your kingdom. Why, you could build a new village at the foot of the mountains, where the travelers would be happy to find a warm bed and good food. And trade! Straight out of Cobren and Aldirnin, which have countless ports! Think of the resources you could acquire!"

"Or," Maleen's uncle smiled unpleasantly, "they might spend as little as possible, saving their coin and goods for the larger cities farther up the road."

"I've already told you," Rob's father said, shaking his head. "We plan to split the road. Half of it will go through Metakinos and half through Ertrique. I don't know why this is such a difficult concept for you to grasp!"

While Maleen had no desire to listen to her uncle make a fool of himself in front of the other sovereigns, she smiled smugly at the veal on her plate. Her idea from earlier that day wasn't so far-fetched after all.

"So *now* you're willing to split the road." Maleen's uncle sipped a spoonful of soup. "That wasn't in the plans that last time you sent them."

Maleen had to work to keep a frown from her face. Not only was he being an arrogant mule, but she was once again subjected to being aware of his eating. Watching her uncle eat had always annoyed Maleen. He was just so incredibly perfect. When she was little, she'd made a game during meals to see whether or not she could ever spot him miss a crumb or spill a drop.

Even now, she could only recall any such disasters happening twice.

Her uncle shook his head and smoothed the napkin down on his lap. "No, I think I know better than to throw in my lot with those who don't even recall what they proposed to me only days before."

The fat man rolled his eyes and sat back in his chair. "Oh, for the love of Destin. What is wrong with you? We're offering you the opportunity that other kingdoms begged for! Why can't you forgo your pride and take what we're offering?"

Maleen's uncle carefully dabbed the perfectly folded napkin around his lips before smiling serenely at the other men. "And if I don't?" he asked in a soft, pleasant voice. "What will you do then?"

The hall quieted. Most of the attention had somehow come to rest upon her uncle's quiet response. Maleen prayed quietly for the Maker to intervene. If her uncle wasn't careful, he was going to start a war. Then the horrible truth hit her as hard as the swollen stream had all those years ago.

Her uncle didn't fear starting a war. He *wanted* to start a war. And no one could intervene. Well, no one but the true heir to the throne.

Before she had time to talk herself out of the insanity of the idea, Maleen stood so fast her chair toppled over behind her.

"Prince Roburts and I are betrothed!" she blurted.

The stunned hall stared at her silently for a long moment. Then it erupted into cheers. Rob himself looked stunned for about three seconds before scrambling to his feet as well.

"It's true," he said, sending her a small nod of what she knew was approval. "We've been friends for a long time past." He fixed his green eyes on hers. "And now that she's of age, we wish to honor the tradition of her people and pledge ourselves to one another and our people in peace on this momentous day."

The cheering only grew louder. Men came to slap Rob on the back, and the women gushed to Maleen. Rob's father stood and hugged his son so hard he picked him up off the ground, laughing as tears streamed down his cheeks. Then he turned toward Maleen and stretched out his hand to her over the table. With a hesitant smile, she took it. His large fingers enveloped hers with a fatherly warmth she'd never received from her uncle.

"I couldn't have found a more lovely daughter if I'd searched myself," he said, his eyes twinkling.

"No!" someone screamed.

The merrymaking quieted as Maleen's uncle stood. She could see his thin frame trembling. When his eyes met hers, they seemed to have emptied of color, their depths like a chasm that threatened to swallow her whole.

She swallowed hard. Rob had been right. This was a conversation that needed to happen in the presence of many witnesses. There was no telling what his retribution might have been if she were alone.

"Why not?" She forced a smile. But when she spoke, her voice shook. "You should be happy for me. I'm sure my parents would have been. This is the answer to our troubles. An alliance—"

"An alliance with the kingdom that *murdered* your parents?"

"That accusation was as false then as it is now!" Rob's father shook his finger at her uncle. "Man, think of what you're doing! Why would you stomp out peace where it blossoms? These children," he put his arm around Rob and held the other out to Maleen, "have done what generations of politicians could not do in bringing—"

"In conspiring with the enemy and seeking the downfall of our own kingdom?" Maleen's uncle turned to address the rest of their guests. "I know most of you are guests and aren't familiar with Ertrique's law. If you are ignorant, know that our inheritance law states that I, not the princess, am the steward of this kingdom until she comes of age." He turned to Maleen, his face twisted in anger and misery. "That also means," he said haltingly as tears began to run down his face, "that I am the enforcer of justice. And by duty, I'm sworn to deal with traitors."

Maleen looked desperately at Rob. Whatever she had imagined her uncle's reaction to be to their news, this was not it. Rob had his hand on the hilt of his sword and looked ready to leap over the table. But his father's hands were on his shoulders, and he was whispering rapidly into his son's ear.

"Guards," her uncle called, weeping now as he spoke. "Arrest the princess." A shudder rippled down his body as he squeezed his eyes shut, his hands shaking as he covered his eyes. "Lock her in the scholar's tower."

"Uncle!" Maleen screamed. "What are you doing?"

He had to raise his voice to be heard over the shouts that were being hurled at him from all sides. "For seven years you will remain there until you are of age. There you will live and breathe and contemplate your actions." Then he made a slight choking sound and gestured to James, who was standing, white-faced, nearby. "Fetch a maidservant of the princess's age. Bring her to the tower as well." When he finished speaking, hands still shaking, he turned and took her hands, looking into her eyes as tears poured from his. "May the Maker soften your heart so that you repent of your rebellion."

As Maleen stared at him, open-mouthed, she felt cold metal chains slide over her wrists. They clamped down hard with a click so loud, Maleen was sure the entire realm had heard.

CHAPTER 8
TREASURES

Pandemonium broke out in the dining hall. Rob was trying to leap over the table, restrained by his father's arms as he continued speaking into Rob's ear. Everyone was shouting and arguing. Guards appeared from the shadows but seemed unsure of what to do, as nearly every guest was royalty or nobility from other kingdoms. Maleen had the nagging feeling in her heart that she should try to run, but she could only stare in horror at her uncle, who was staring back with a sadness of his own. There were also the chains now binding her wrists.

"Steward of Ertrique!" A voice rose above the others.

The noise quieted somewhat as everyone turned to find the speaker. Prince Launce of Cobren was standing on the table. When all eyes were on him, he looked at her uncle.

"First, I will begin by acknowledging that I have no authority here."

"You are correct," her uncle said, turning to face him. "You don't."

"But what I can tell you is that this action will not be viewed kindly by my wife's father, your southern neighbor. And it will be received with even less welcome by King Everard and Queen Isabelle of Destin."

A flicker of hope threatened to ignite in Maleen's chest. Could the queen of Destin save her once again?

"Do you wish to end your trade agreements with our two kingdoms? Or our allied protection? Think of what you would be sacrificing in treating your crown princess with such contempt."

"Aye!" a few other voices called out.

"We would do the same!"

"No more trade with our merchants either."

"Free the princess, and we'll keep our agreements."

Maleen felt a deeper gratitude than she'd ever felt before as those around her took turns pledging their friendship and loyalty to her. Rob was no longer fighting, but his eyes burned as he watched. Clearly, as dangerous as it had been, their union would be viewed as a blessing for the entire realm. Such a joining could do nothing but benefit Ertrique.

Surely her uncle would not jeopardize everything their kingdom had to put her in a tower.

When she looked at her uncle again, however, her hopes went up in flames. He listened, but the fire that sparked in his eyes was one that Maleen knew wouldn't be quenched by reason.

"Honored guests and allies," he said once the crowd had said its piece. "I thank you for coming today. It has opened my eyes to what poor friends we have." Then he gestured to the nearest guard. "Please take her to the tower."

The crowd roared more loudly than it had before. Two of the guards, including the one who had shackled her, took hold of Maleen's arms.

"Please!" she begged them as they began to gently pull her away. "You know he's insane. He has a sickness in the head! Ask the physician! Please!"

The guard at her left elbow lifted his helmet's visor to reveal Captain Dominic's face.

"Be still, princess, I beg you," he whispered, glancing nervously around them. "Allow yourself to be taken."

She stopped struggling and stared at him.

"I'll do my best to speak sense to him, but you know he cannot be reasoned with in this state," Captain Dominic said quickly. "Provoking him will only make your situation worse."

"But I'm–" Maleen tried to speak through her trembling lips, but he shook his head.

"If I let you go now, he'll relieve me of duty, and the one who will take my place won't be kind."

Maleen looked back at Rob. A look of agony had washed over his pale face, his sword hanging limp at his side. Whatever his father had said was staying his hand. She allowed herself to be taken away, the will to fight lost as she stared into her love's hopeless eyes.

The pain that hit her chest as they began to walk would have knocked her over if the captain hadn't been holding her upright. She sagged in his arms as they slowly made their way toward the entrance.

A procession, not unlike that of a funeral, followed Maleen, her uncle, and the guards out of the palace to the tower. Women wept, and more of the royals shouted threats at her uncle. But he ignored them all, facing the tower stoically as they walked.

The tower loomed above them as soon as they made their way out of the palace, colored orange by the light of the soldiers' torches. As a child, Maleen had often wished to go inside and explore. Now she wished she'd ordered the thing burned to ashes the moment she'd turned seventeen. It was three stories high, and the large rectangular stones with which it had been built were covered with all sorts of moss and ivy. Maleen couldn't remember ever seeing anyone go in or out.

One of the guards produced a long metal key and handed it to another guard, who opened the door. Then he whispered something to the young man, who disappeared inside.

At the same time, a young woman, about Maleen's age, was also led by guards toward them. Her eyes were as wide as tea saucers, and she carried a small, shabby bag. But when she saw the open mouth of the tower, she began to kick and scream and beg to be released.

"What are *you* doing here?" her uncle asked.

For a moment, Maleen wondered who he was talking to, when Emille appeared, grim-faced and holding two bags. One of them was Maleen's traveling bag. The other Maleen recognized as Emille's.

"I am here to join my princess," Emille said in a raw tone. "She may be stuck in this tower, but I can tend to her and fetch her whatever she needs." She arched a brow. "It would be a cruel thing to lock up your brother's daughter alone for seven years, don't you think?"

Maleen wasn't sure if she saw correctly, but she almost thought her uncle winced. Still, he shook his head. "I know how close you are. I also know that you've been poisoning her against me since my brother and his wife were killed."

Emille gaped. "Where in the—"

"I also know that my niece is clever, and I'm not about to give her the chance to escape and raise up our people in rebellion to the crown."

"It isn't rebellion when the crown is *hers*," Emille snapped.

Her uncle began to grow red, but just as Maleen wondered if his own anger might drive him to collapse, he closed his eyes and took a deep breath. When he opened them, his eyes were calm but determined. "My final answer is no. This maiden has already been brought to be her companion. Whatever they need will be delivered to them here."

Emille began to shout at him, but with a flick of Perseus's hand, another guard dragged her away.

Maleen looked up at the crowd for help one more time. She knew why no one had truly interfered yet. Making an act of war on behalf of a princess that wasn't one's own would be considered utterly foolish. War was expensive, and lives would be lost. And yet she had hoped that someone...

Her eyes rested on Rob. He still stood beside his father at the edge of the crowd. But instead of standing tall with his proud, fiery gaze, his shoulders slumped and he stared at her with dead eyes. The distance between them was only twenty paces or so. He could so easily cross the divide. He had saved her when they were children and had been ready to give up his own life. But now, he only watched.

A man who had gone inside the tower with girls' supplies came back down. He ran immediately to the duke and Captain Dominic. Maleen couldn't hear what was being whispered. Whatever it was made Captain Dominic frown. He left Maleen where she was and headed into the tower himself. Maleen again considered running but knew better before the thought was even finished. There were guards everywhere, and she was shackled. Running would do no good.

Captain Dominic emerged a minute later, coughing. "You'll have to delay it," he told her uncle grimly. "The air in that tower is as stale as a graveyard's. It needs to be cleaned and aired before those girls can breathe properly."

Her uncle nodded. "Put them in for now. We'll send up a clean supply of linens later."

Captain Dominic gave a start. When the captain didn't move, however, her uncle, who had begun to walk away, turned around again. "Did you hear what I just said?"

Instead of obeying, Captain Dominic removed his helmet. "I'm sorry, Your Grace. But I cannot."

Her uncle crossed his arms. "You *cannot*?"

The captain grimaced and looked down at his helmet. He rubbed at the insignia engraved into the side, an intricate symbol of his rank. "I...I cannot in good conscience lock this child up for the crime of falling in love. Especially not in squalor such as that." He stood slightly taller. "She is a princess and deserves a home befitting someone of her rank."

To Maleen's surprise, her uncle bowed his head. "I understand, Captain," he said softly. "I thank you for being so honest with your allegiance." He turned and addressed the circle of guards surrounding them in a clear, calm voice. "Captain Dominic is now relieved of duty and shall be charged with insubordination at a later time."

The crowd writhed with anger, but her uncle continued, unruffled.

"I will grant his position to the first man to carry out the orders that he refused to obey."

The guards looked at one another. Captain Dominic's face was gray, but he watched them with a grim air of resignation.

Maleen, however, was very close to throwing up. She half-expected to be trampled in the stampede of young soldiers lusting after the power her uncle promised. But to her surprise, most of the guards just stood there. Several laid down their weapons and shook their heads.

"Sorry, Steward," one of them said, a young man by the name of Titus. "But we must follow where our captain leads. And locking up the princess..." He swallowed and shook his head. "We just can't."

Maleen watched in awe as more and more laid down their swords. But just as she was beginning to hope that her soldiers might be her saving grace, a burly man, one of the newer soldiers whose name she couldn't recall, came forward.

"Sorry, Highness," he muttered as he took hold of her wrists with his meaty hands. He unbound her then turned her around so she faced the tower's open door.

"What? No!" Panic surged, and Maleen was tempted to kick and scream. The tower's dark mouth exhaled putrid air, and she realized with a shiver that the tower looked hungry.

The guard gave her a gentle shove.

Only pride kept her from falling on the ground and protesting like a spoiled child. Pride, anger, and the determination to prove to her uncle and all the rest of the western realm that she was the true royal here drove her now. She wasn't a pretender like her uncle. She took a step toward it. Then two.

The servant girl was still squawking and fighting the guards who held her as they pushed her toward the tower as well. The burly man sighed and followed her to do the same, but Maleen yanked her arm away from him.

"I can take myself, thank you," she said coldly. Then once more, she turned to look for Rob. But when she searched the crowd this time, he was gone.

Hope drained out of her as the guard gave her one more small shove. Three stumbled steps and she was in. Trembling, she turned around, staring out the open door at the agitated crowd until the door was shut in her face. And over the screams of her maid, who was lying on the floor, Maleen heard the heavy click of a key.

Fear tried to claw its way out of her chest as Maleen touched the door, trying to grasp the fact that she truly was a prisoner in her own kingdom. Tentatively, she pushed on the door. When it didn't budge, something inside of her burst. She turned and darted past the weeping maid, up the stone stairs, all the way to the top. Torches the young servant must have lit showed her the way.

The air was even worse than she'd supposed, but that was the least of her worries right now.

When she arrived, breathing heavily from the run and her fear, she looked around. She was standing in a circular room, the one visible from the top of the tower. There were four windows, one facing every direction. One bed sat beneath each window, with bookshelves lining the wall between each bed. A large writing table the size of a dinner table stood in the center of the room with four stools spread around it.

Maleen ran to the nearest of the four windows. Its wooden shutters were tightly shut. Maleen tried unsuccessfully to pry open the lock. When that didn't work, she rammed her elbow against the latch that connected them but only succeeded in bruising her arm. Giving up, she ran to the next window and did the same. But every single shutter was shut tight and seemed to have been that way for a while.

Complete terror threatened to overwhelm Maleen, the kind that was coming from the maid down the stairs. She did her best to close her eyes and breathe slowly in and out in shallow breaths, so as not to gulp down too much of the stale air.

No. She wouldn't panic. She was a princess, trained to lead her people in peace and in war. And though she wanted nothing more than to throw herself on the nearest bed and scream, one of her citizens needed her now. Besides, falling into hysterics would do nothing to fix this situation. If anything, it would make it worse.

Trembling, Maleen descended the stairs again. Anger tinted the edges of her vision. Anger at her uncle. At her guests for not intervening. And though she knew she shouldn't direct it at him, anger at Rob.

The girl was sobbing piteously on the bottom steps. Maleen knelt down beside her and took her hands. But when the girl cried out, Maleen realized her fingernails were bleeding. She sucked in a fast breath when she realized the girl must have been clawing at the wooden door.

"Come," she said, doing her best to sound soothing. How she wished Emille had been allowed to stay. "Let's fix your hands."

The girl, seeming to have run out of energy, allowed Maleen to duck under her arm and lift her from the side, leading her carefully up the stairs.

Maleen wasn't sure how she managed to do it, as the girl was heavier than she was, but she somehow got them to the top of the stairs. She gently laid her down on one of the four beds in the room and found an old rag to soak up the blood on her hands. She looked for water as well, and a new kind of panic threatened to strip her of all sense.

But no. The scholars who had once lived here had to have had a way to get water, and she doubted they'd gone out to fetch it themselves every day. It had to be here somewhere. Sure enough, there were several pulley systems strung up near the entrance to the stairs. Each one had a bucket attached. One of the buckets already held water. Maleen sniffed it. Mercifully, it was clean.

She removed the bucket from the pulley's hook and took it over to where the girl lay. Carefully, she dipped the wet rag into the water and began cleaning the girl's hands. When she finished, the girl lay still on the blanket, her eyes shut. She must have fainted.

Maleen looked around, and for the first time, she allowed herself to think.

What had just happened?

For want of something to do, she went back down the steps. Her legs were already aching from the continuous climbing, but she embraced the pain. It kept her tethered to reality, rather than allowing herself to sink down into blissful unconsciousness the way the maid had done. She put her ear to the door but heard nothing. Either her uncle had threatened everyone enough that the crowd had gone away already, or the building had been designed to block out sound, which wasn't an unreasonable consideration, as the tower had been built for scholars who wished to be alone.

"They're not going to let us out, are they?" a tremulous voice asked. The girl was standing at the top of the stairs.

Slowly, Maleen climbed back up.

"Not tonight, I'm afraid." She did her best to smile, but it felt more like a grimace.

The girl began to shake, and Maleen reached out to take her hands again, but the girl yanked them away.

"How can you be so calm?" she snapped. "We've just been imprisoned!"

Maleen swallowed. If only the girl knew just how close to breaking she was. "I'm aware of that."

"No." The girl shook her head, her voice trembling. "I don't think you are!"

"I beg your pardon?"

"No offense, Highness," the girl said, "but *you* don't have a family. Your parents and brothers and sisters don't rely on you to keep them from starving!" She turned around and ran her hands through her red hair, her voice growing louder and louder. "Seven years! And for what? I haven't even been told why I was snatched from my duties and told to pack!"

"I'm sorry!" Maleen raised her hands, palms up, then let them fall helplessly. "I never meant for any of this to happen! I did what I did for the best."

"What *did* you do?"

"I..." Maleen took a deep breath. "I accepted the hand of Metakinos's prince."

The girl's eyes widened. "So why am *I* here?"

"I suppose...my uncle believed I ought to have a servant in my exile."

The girl's mouth fell open, but no words came out as she sank back down onto the bed Maleen had put her in.

Maleen sighed. "What's your name?"

"Jalyna." She glared up at Maleen. "I was a chambermaid. Forgive me, Princess, for speaking out of line, but like I said, you don't understand. My parents work at the palace as well. I'm the eldest, and I was *supposed* to help support my younger brothers and sisters."

"I'm sure my uncle will make sure your family is compensated," Maleen said wearily, sinking onto one of the other beds.

"So...I really am a prisoner...for the next *seven* years?" She looked back down at the stairs again, and Maleen hoped she didn't make a mad dash for them only to fall and hurt herself.

"No." Maleen stood and shook her head. "No, you won't be. Not for that long, at least. And I won't either." She marched back down the stone steps, resolve blooming inside her with each step.

"How do you know that?" Jalyna called after her.

"Because I have friends who will not see me treated like this. And while they're searching for a way to get us out, I'm going to search this entire tower, every nook and cranny until I find the weakest piece." She looked around, realizing for the first time that the inside of even the circular lower wall surrounding the winding stairs was actually covered in shelves and shelves of books and scrolls. Her heart lifted within her chest. "And when my hands are too tired to search any more, I will read *every* book in this tower if I must to find another way out."

"You think *reading* will save us?" Jalyna asked doubtfully.

"I don't think *reading* will save us." Maleen ran her hands over the leather covers of the books on the first level. "But knowledge and resourcefulness might." She pulled out a book and opened it up. "If I'm not mistaken, this tower holds many of the crown's most treasured books. This place was created not only for scholars, but to keep their collections safe." She put the book back and pulled out two more.

"And what about your prince?"

Maleen stopped, and her heart squeezed so tightly it hurt. But no, she couldn't think that way. Rob might have been outnumbered tonight, but he wouldn't leave her like this. He was resourceful, too.

"He will hold fast," Maleen said softly. "And so will I."

THE SEVEN YEARS LETTERS

D*ear Book,*
Writing on such crisp, clean pages in such a beautiful leather binding seems nearly criminal, but no one has touched you for a long time, as I can tell by the fine coat of dust I blew off your cover, so I suppose you're not sorely missed elsewhere.

I'm writing here because I need to speak to someone. Anyone. Even if it's only empty pages. I haven't spoken to a single soul (who will respond to me) in two weeks, and I'm beginning to feel the need to slam things just to hear some sound.

My companion, Jalyna, isn't speaking to me. Or perhaps she's simply not speaking at all. I understand that she's angry. It's my fault that she's locked in here, away from her family and friends for the next seven years. I'd be angry, too. But my uncle is truly the one to blame, and I'm not sure how helpful it is for her to take out her anger on me. All she does is mend and sew and wash all day long with the supplies they've sent up the pulleys, glaring at her work and occasionally, me. She doesn't hum or sing or even whisper to herself when I'm not looking.

I'm frustrated, too. I've been through the entire first two levels of books, and I haven't found a way to escape, a book that might tell me how to do so, or even a mouse hole. It's as if this were the stoutest, safest tower in all of the western realm, protected even from little whiskered creatures. Honestly, if one were to pop out and speak to me, I'd probably be tempted to talk back.

I thought for sure we'd only be here a few days, or maybe a week at most. My servants cannot be in agreement with this. Then again, they have no power to stop him, especially if he's been replacing the military with his loyal soldiers in the stead of mine. Surely political pressure then, I thought. But no. It seems my uncle is too afraid of betrayal to even keep his trading treaties with the most powerful kingdoms in the realm. I worry that if someone doesn't change something soon, not only will I be stuck here, but our kingdom will crumble. He's destroying our military and our economy, and I can't do a thing about it.

My greatest hope is Rob, who is the most resourceful person I know. He's skilled in military strategy, and he has a will of steel when he's put his mind to something. Surely he will save me. He said he loved me, and I believe him. For Rob will do many things on a whim, but offering his heart would not be one of them.

I wish I could have heard what happened the night we were thrown in, after the door was locked. But I've found with much regret that our building seems to be doubly reinforced. There's wool between the inner and outer walls. I know because while I was searching the writing desk, I found an old drawing of the plans for the tower's construction. Apparently, according to the small handwritten note in the corner, the scholars wanted complete silence when they stayed here, so they had an extra layer of material put in to protect it from the sounds of the outside world.

The only interaction we have with the outside world are the three pulleys that raise and lower what we need and what we no longer need to the ground. (And yes, Book. I've considered openings as a means for escape as well. But as neither Jalyna nor I am the size of a bucket, I'm afraid we won't be leaving that way either.)

What would I have heard? Would Rob have found his tongue and challenged my uncle? Would the rest of the military have arrived and stood by him? Unfortunately, I'm afraid I'll not know until we escape. I can't hear a single peep from the other side of the wall, and the door is nearly as bad. Not the soldiers practicing their marching or the children laughing or sheep bleating or anything of the normal day-to-day sounds.

And yet I must believe he will hold to his promise to make me his. And I will hold to mine.

Dear Book,

I fear my plan to teach Jalyna to read might be misplaced yearning.

It seemed like a good idea at the time. We'd been in the tower for a month at that point, and Jalyna's anger was beginning to fade. I realized quickly I would need to find a replacement for it.

I know that sounds strange, to mourn the loss of her anger, but it really wasn't good. You see, the first few days we were locked up, Jalyna would wake up in hysterics, and I'd have to give her a cup of tea to calm her, as Emille did for me when I was little. Then, about a week into our imprisonment, Jalyna became angry with me. So angry she wouldn't speak. She just went about her chores, slamming things and throwing things when she had the chance. Every so often, she would look up at me and glare.

I didn't particularly enjoy this, but then again, I didn't know it could get worse. Then about three weeks after we'd been locked up, I noticed that her glares were beginning to fade. And in their place came the nothingness.

She stares blankly at her work now. Blankly at the walls. Blankly at the ceiling before she sleeps. There's no flame in her eyes, hardly an ember. Every time I make eye contact with her to smile or nod or ask a question, she simply seems to look through me.

For some reason, that look frightens me tenfold compared to how her anger did.

When it began, I tried to think of some reason to keep her hoping while I continued to search for a means of escape. But what could I give? I really do feel terrible for what she suffers. Though my uncle is awful, I have no doubt he'll pay her family for her services rendered to me. Probably double, considering that she's with me all the time. But I can't convince her of this. I think she really does believe I'm making it up to comfort her.

Then one day, as I looked around at all the books, I realized with great sadness that she most likely thinks them worth little more than a chunk of fire fuel. She cannot use them for learning or adventure. To her, they're just stacks of paper sewn together.

This wouldn't be unusual. Most of the commoners in our kingdom cannot read. I'm told that after she married my father, my mother attempted to hold classes to teach any little ones whose families wished to learn, but few attended or sent their children to attend. When she made inquiries as to why, she was told that it was simple: servants have little to no use for reading or writing. Best to keep their heads down and the floor shining. Or at least, that's what Emille told me the servants told my mother. Reading doesn't feed hungry mouths.

(And yes, Book. I have also considered sending notes asking

for help down with the buckets. But most of the servants can't read. And even more importantly, I'm convinced my uncle will station only men who are loyal to him at my tower. So I've come to the conclusion that such an attempt would be pointless. If it hadn't been, Emille would have sent me a message weeks ago.)

Our mouths aren't hungry, though, so in desperation, I told Jalyna that I was going to teach her to read. I did really hope that she would find it intriguing. I can't imagine not knowing how to read. So much wisdom and knowledge are all around for the taking! Like plump, juicy fruit, wasting away on the vine. I was sure this might pique her interest, even if only enough to briefly chase that slump from her shoulders and brighten her eyes with interest.

Her response was hardly enthusiastic, but I was relieved when she wearily consigned herself to sitting beside me so I could bring out the list of letters I'd made on some blank parchment from the writing desk. And for two or three days, she really did try. For though she didn't talk to me voluntarily, she did mimic my sounds when I made them and pointed to the letters. She even reached out and reverently touched her name when I wrote it in ink for her to see.

I only hope her interest lasts. I'm beginning to feel despair attempting to sink in, and I find myself wondering as I drift off to sleep at night if we'll really get out of here sometime in the next seven years.

To keep my mind occupied, I imagine what it will be like when Rob comes for me. At the moment, I'm imagining that I hear the scratching and clicks of the lock being picked. I'll gasp as the door opens slightly to reveal a hooded figure, hunching against the rain. He'll push his way in and throw his hood off as he grabs me in his arms and kisses me senseless. Then he'll tell me that we need to hurry. We only have a little time before the guard wakes up from the sleeping powder Rob blew in his face. Although if it's raining, perhaps he'll have to put it on a rag and cover the guard's mouth and nose with it. Anyhow, then we'll ride away on his horse, me sitting in front of him, the warmth from his chest on my back as I hold his cloak wrapped around us against the rain.

Every night I imagine this as I fall asleep. But for some reason, I can't imagine what happens beyond that. I thought I could at first. But each night, the story grows slightly shorter, as if his plan is less and less successful.

This doesn't really matter, though, as it's only a dream. I only pray that somehow, he does get us out soon. It's not fair to steal so much of Jalyna's life from her. This is between me and my uncle. And if Uncle Perseus thinks I'm going to forget this when I take the throne, he's sorely mistaken.

Dear Book,

This entry officially marks the one-year anniversary of the last day Jalyna spoke to me. One year I've gone without hearing another human's voice. One year and four and a half months since we were locked in this tower.

I speak to myself, of course. I sing. I read the books aloud. But it's not the same. How naive I was to think I was lonely back in the palace, even before I met Rob. I may not have had peers, but I had Emille and servants, and even my crotchety old uncle to speak to me.

What I wouldn't give to have a good shouting match with him now.

I know I've mentioned it in past entries, but I really am worried about Jalyna. I no longer offer her hope of escape. It's been a while since I've been willing to fill her with a promise I cannot deliver. But every day, a little wisp of her humanity *seems to blow away on the wind we can't feel. She still sews and darns and washes, but she has no conviction anymore. She simply goes through the motions.*

And do you know what worries me even more than Jalyna?

Me. I worry about myself giving in to the cold, oozing apathy that has taken her. Like a shadow, it sits quietly until the sun begins to fall. And with less light, the shadow grows, and it threatens to overcome me. And to my horror, before I shut my eyes at night, I find myself wondering what it would feel like to give in. What would it feel like not to get up in the morning, or to open my eyes and simply lie there, letting the world do with me what it wishes? For the first year we were here, every time the apathy would creep up, I would fight it with noble hope. Rob would come and my people would rise up, and all would be set to rights, I would assure myself. All things would be as they should be once again. The Maker would not allow such an injustice to reign.

I also have begun to understand the seething hatred Jalyna would send me in glares over her work for all those months, before her carelessness set in. The hope I clung to is no longer a weapon I can use against the shadow because the shadow simply eats it, too. But anger...anger is like a lump of burning coal I can wave in the apathy's face. It's not the cheery light of the sun, but it has a light of its own to ward off the darkness.

I always thought my anger would be at my uncle. I was angry enough at him when I was first imprisoned. He's the reason I had no friends as a child, and he was the reason I lost everything. But to my surprise, the anger now that burns in my chest is for the one who promised me all...and gave me nothing. I always expected nothing from my uncle. He fulfilled my expectations. What hurts more than his betrayal is the betrayal of the one who should have saved me.

I'm writing now what I haven't had the heart to say before. Prince Roburts has failed me. I knew it in my heart the night I was taken, when he stood there and watched them lock me up in the tower. I gambled my people and my position for him. I gave him my heart. And it seems the man who I believed could do anything has chosen to do nothing. Because I know him well enough to know that he could have scaled this tower barefoot, had he chosen to do so. But he didn't.

If anyone is going to get me out of this tower, it's going to be me.

Dear Book,

Jalyna stopped getting up today.

She's been later and later out of bed recently. I've tried coaxing, begging, pleading, and shouting. I even dumped a bucket of water on her head. But she simply refuses to get out of bed. She won't even look at me.

I should also mention that our food rations have grown smaller. I thought at first that I was simply hungry because I've been doing all of the chores recently, but out of curiosity, I decided to measure the rations when they arrived today. Sure enough, my meal is approximately a third smaller than it used to be. Is this some sick game my uncle is playing in his madness?

Someone needs to inform him that jokes are only funny if your victim is able to fight back.

Also, not greatly noteworthy, but I realized today that I've been incorrectly counting our time in the tower. It hasn't been thirty-three months, but thirty-four. We're only two months away from beginning our fourth year in the tower. I should probably admit that I'm not going to find a way out. But if I did that, I might go mad.

Dear Book,

As I was getting Jalyna out of bed this morning for her forced morning walk about the room, my foot slipped, and I dropped her. She hit the floor like a limp doll. The gash in her head was small, but I think I treated it well.

If nothing else, the hundreds of books in this tower cover a great many topics, and in all my time here reading, I've gained a considerable amount of knowledge on simple healing practices. I'm wondering now how much knowledge I've gained in other areas. I think I shall test myself tomorrow and write it all down to see just how much I can recall on every given subject. If Uncle ever releases me from this tower, my people might find they have a brilliant leader. Even if she does talk to herself like a madwoman out of habit.

As I was dressing myself today, I also realized that I've grown an inch since Jalyna made my last dress. That was over two years ago, though, so I'm not sure where I shall find a new one. They haven't sent up new fabric in over a year. I've also grown thinner, due to the continually smaller rations. I'm glad there's no mirror in this entire tower. I like to continue to imagine myself the way I looked at my birthday gala. But sometimes, I wish Rob could see me in all my gaunt waste. It would do him good to see what his cowardice did to the woman he claimed to love.

He probably wouldn't care, though, as I'm sure he's got himself a lovely, plump wife who can give him all the curves and delight he desires. He has no need to be haunted by what might have been. He's twenty-four now. A thought to the girl who disappeared five years past would be nothing more than a dream.

Dear Book,

The rations are no longer regular. And nothing but the barest of necessities is delivered. Perhaps Uncle has realized that when he lets me out, I intend to have my justice. He could be intending to starve us before that happens. If this is so, he's in for an unhappy surprise. I may be thin, but I'm strong, and every day, I feed Jalyna and force her out of bed, making her walk around the room with me, even if she leans on me all the way.

We may not escape, but we will see this through.

Dear Book

I haven't been good at tracking the days these last few weeks. Or months, rather. I don't know. My head is often fuzzy, and when I stand up, I'm dizzy. But when I dragged myself down the steps today to the door, where I scratch in the daily mark, I discovered that today should have marked exactly seven years. But since I've missed so many days recently, we've been here at least three or four weeks past.

No one is going to let us out.

CHAPTER 9
ALIVE

Maleen stared stupidly at the candle in her hand.

It was their last. After this one went out, there would be no more light in the tower, just whatever was cast from the measly fire Maleen had built by burning books after the wood ran out. More than seven years and five weeks, and all she had to show for it was an unresponsive servant, a pile of book ash, and one last candle.

With a sigh, she raised her tired eyes to the door again. How many times had she attempted to get out? It was marked with scratches and dents from all the times she'd gone at it, sometimes in anger, sometimes sobbing, sometimes with great scheming and high hopes. But always, the door had held.

Unless...

Maleen stood and looked at her last candle. Countless times, she'd considered using it on the wood, but the fear of fire had always stopped her. As it was, she'd been dreaming she smelled smoke every night as nightmares of fire and agony had overtaken her along with the biting, aching hunger. Every time she'd awakened, she was shocked that the dream hadn't been real, and she'd sworn again never to entertain the scheme, wishing it had never crept into her mind in the first place. But she couldn't very well ask Jalyna if she was smelling anything. Jalyna hadn't uttered a word in years.

The building was made of stone, but it was lined with wood and wool. If she missed even one tongue of flame, the whole thing would go up in a blaze to remember. Surely, she'd always reasoned, dying quietly of hunger would be better than that.

But as she glared at the hateful wood, she felt that conviction crumbling. Nightmares be hanged, she couldn't die here. Not, at least, without trying every last way to escape. To die free would be better than to die without hope.

Wouldn't it?

But she would have to be careful. She had no desire to suffer death by fire, even if she was desperate. And in her muddled state of thought, it would be far easier for her to make a mistake than it would have been even several weeks ago when her food was more regular.

Help me, she prayed. It was the first prayer she'd uttered in a long time to the Maker who had abandoned her. She should say something else, she was sure. But she had few words left in her mind. They seemed to be gathering dust, along with her memories of what the world once had been. And yet...

She looked at her hands. She had those. And two working legs. And a will to survive.

Determination surged, and she started back up the steps to fetch the bucket of water.

Ever since they'd been shut in the tower, food had been passed up and down in the buckets on the pulleys. Food had been more and more irregular, but their water, at least, had continued to come with slightly more regularity. Even that, though, had begun to falter in recent days. Their most recent bucket was only half full, but Maleen couldn't wait for the next. Because this...existence...wasn't living. This was a slow, painful death.

She grabbed what she needed and climbed back down the stairs with a renewed energy, as if she'd just had a full meal for the first time in months. She carefully set the bucket on the step beside her, dropped an old blanket inside to soak, and examined the door. The easiest place to break through would probably be the part with all the gashes from the times she'd gone at it with one of the fire pokers. Running back upstairs, she grabbed the poker once more and lit the candle using the fireplace. She placed the poker next to the bucket on the steps and then picked the candle up once more.

Carefully, carefully so as not to burn herself with the flame or the wax, she tipped the long, thin candle until it touched the bottom of the wooden door. For a moment, nothing happened.

Then the flames spread fast. Too fast. Maleen dropped the candle, stumbled backward, and threw her bucket of water at it, forgetting the blanket inside. The wasted water fell uselessly to the ground with the blanket. Maleen scrambled for the blanket and yanked it up, beating the flames with it as they spread up the door like starved, ravenous sprites. For a moment, she feared she wouldn't get it all in time. This was it. They were going to die.

It would be a horrible death, but at least her endless imprisonment would be over.

Instead of death, however, she felt the satisfying hiss of the fire dying beneath her blanket. Breathing fast, she stepped back, ready to jump at any more flames. Before her, though, was simply a blackened door, hissing and squealing as smoke rose up from its face. She stared in a stupor. Was it possible? Was she really just moments from escape?

No. She couldn't let her hopes rise yet. First, she had to see if she'd been successful. But to do that, she needed to try. So she grabbed the candle from the ground, where it had fallen and sputtered out, and ran upstairs to light it again. Then she came back down, set the candle on the step behind her so she could see, grabbed the poker, and looked for the darkest spot in the wood. There. She held her poker tightly and rammed it against the door.

Nothing. In anger, she tried again. And again. And again. Tears ran down her face as she pounded uselessly away at the door. She would never again feel fresh air on her face. Or feel the pressure of an embrace. Or taste sugar. Or hear a song echo through an empty hall. Or—

Her poker caught on the brittle wood, its nose piercing through to the other side. Maleen stared in shock for a moment. Then in a near panic, she yanked it back until it was free. This time, with shaking hands, instead of hitting wildly at the broad expanse of wood, she aimed the sharp end well, and it sliced cleanly through to the other side.

After pocking up the darkened surface for a while, she was able to abandon the poker and instead used a large piece of wood from an old bookshelf to make larger holes. By the time she had made a hole large enough to crawl through, the gray of the morning was pregnant with the dawn.

Maleen ignored the pebbles and broken wood that stuck in her hands as she went through on her hands and knees, and she had just gotten to her feet when the gold of the morning washed over her.

Maleen wasn't used to bright light anymore, but even as she had to close her eyes, she could feel tears of joy streaming down her face and dripping onto the ground. She didn't even try to stop them, though. For the first time since she could remember, she felt alive.

She didn't know how long she stood that way, gulping down the air as the breeze danced against her skin. But eventually, the direction of the wind changed, and Maleen choked as she sucked in a lungful of smoke and ash. She opened her eyes and let out an anguished cry.

Not a single building was left standing. At least, not

completely. There were ruins standing everywhere, half-buildings that were still smoldering as smoke rose out of them. The palace...her beautiful white, shining palace was now crumbling, stained with soot as though some giant had come along and stomped on it and set it on fire just for fun. Even from where she stood, she could see the broken rooms that lay exposed to the elements, empty and yet left exactly as they had been. How many bodies were left inside?

Maleen closed her eyes and did her best to keep control, but the sobs were determined to overtake her. Falling to her knees, she let them come.

She and Jalyna had gotten whiffs of smoke in the tower on and off for the last few weeks, but she'd been too tired and hungry to take much notice. Her nightmares, though...

They hadn't been nightmares. At least, not the scent of them. She must have been dreaming of fire because she was smelling it. If the wind had blown in the other direction, she was sure they would have smelled far more when she was awake. Or maybe she had and was just too numbed by hunger to notice.

The sound of crunching gravel broke her solitary mourning, and she stumbled backward when a man rounded the corner of her tower. He, too, cried out and fell back, spilling the bucket of water he was carrying when he saw her.

At first, she thought it was Rob. He had come for her. Maybe he'd been the one keeping her alive all this time, unable to do more as he schemed to free them...

But it wasn't. This man was too young. And not quite tall enough. She squinted in the bright morning light. He wasn't Rob, but he was the first human besides Jalyna that she'd seen in seven years. Doing her best to gather herself, she stood, trembling.

"What..." Her voice was dusty, and the words felt strange on her tongue. "What happened?"

"You're Princess Maleen!" he exclaimed, righting himself and the bucket. Then he blinked a few times and bowed. Maleen should nod, but she couldn't seem to remember anything except that everything she loved seemed to be gone.

He seemed to regain his voice. "Jalyna. Is she alive?"

Maleen stared at him. Why was it so hard to make her mouth move?

"My sister," he said, louder this time. "Does she still live?"

This woke Maleen from her dream, though speaking was still more difficult than she'd thought it would be.

"Um...yes. She's not doing well, though." She licked her lips and stared longingly at the bucket. "May I have some water?"

"Oh, yes!" He handed her the bucket. As soon as it was in her hands, he rushed to the front door and kicked a larger hole through the splintered wood before disappearing inside.

The bucket was only half full now, but Maleen tipped it and drank as though she'd never tasted water before.

Just as she was thinking she might have drunk her fill, the door was kicked open, its broken remains falling from its hinges with a crash. Jalyna was in her brother's arms, and he was looking at her as though he might cry.

"She's barely alive!" he half-choked.

"I think..." Maleen cleared her throat. "I think she just gave up."

He grimaced and hung his head. For a moment, Maleen wondered if he might be angry, but then he just shook his head at the ground. When he looked up, his face was haggard. "She never was one for stickin' hard times out. My mother worried for her because of it." He met Maleen's gaze again. "And you kept her alive, didn't you?"

Maleen nodded. "As well as I could." The words were coming more easily now.

He swallowed then looked around them. "I 'spose you're wonderin' what happened."

"I am." Maleen's voice cracked as she said it.

He nodded again, seeming to remember himself. "We can't stay here. There've been gangs of marauders about. It's why I've not been able to give you your food regular." He looked back up at the tower. "D'you have anything worth travelin' with?"

Maleen thought for a moment. When she'd planned her escape from the tower, it hadn't been with the idea of traveling through a wasteland. "I think so. I have a small knife. Our clothes, and a few cups and bowls you gave us. And I can pack some blankets as well." She considered taking the book she'd been writing in for seven years, but decided she couldn't carry it. As it was, she could see that Jalyna wouldn't be able to carry herself, much less anything else.

"I'm sorry to ask it, Your Highness," he said, readjusting his sister's weight in his arms. "But could you get them? Then we'll go." He looked around. "Not much use stayin' 'round here for long. The faster we go, the safer we'll be." She opened her mouth, but he nodded before she could speak. "Then I'll tell you everythin' I know. I promise."

CHAPTER 10

WHAT HAPPENED

Maileen ran back up into the tower, but not without trepidation. Fear that the open door would be closed again when she returned was ridiculous but strong. It was too much like her countless dreams where the door had begun to open and then slammed shut once again.

But she didn't have time to waste on such nonsense. Dreams were dreams, and this was very real. Her hands still smarted from the splinters she'd picked up while crawling through the opening.

And yet, she thought as she reached the top of the stairs, here was yet another kind of irrational dread, and if she stopped to ponder it, it was really worse than the first. A part of her—a very stupid part—wanted to cower in the tower and crawl beneath the thin, dirty sheets she'd slept in only that morning. In here, it was safe. At least, she felt that way now. There was no ruined palace outside. In here, she could pretend that her people hadn't been killed or run off and forgotten her.

In here, she didn't have to face the reality that she was a princess without a kingdom. The princess who should by now have been queen.

These thoughts circled in her head as she ran to the different parts of the room, gathering what little she could. She paused to stare longingly at the thick book in which she'd recorded her thoughts for the last seven years. But then again, maybe she was better off without them. She had delved down into very dark places within those pages, and she wasn't sure she wanted to go back. The thick volume was heavy in more ways than one. So leaving it on the writing table, she made her way back down the stairs with their clothes, shoes, and a few provisions in an old bag.

"I don't have much," she said, holding the bag up for him to see.

The young man nodded, still holding Jalyna in his arms. "All the better. We'll stay in my place today, then leave first thin' tonight." He looked around again, scanning the grounds behind them. "Dangerous to be out in the open like this as it is." He turned and made his way back toward the palace, and Maleen followed.

The closer they got to the palace, the stronger the air smelled of smoke, and Maleen soon had to cover her mouth with a wet rag.

"You get used to it," the young man said sympathetically, glancing at her over his shoulder. "'Sides, we won't be here too long anyway. Just enough time to eat and gather whatever rations are left."

"What's the hurry?" Maleen asked as they ducked through the smashed ruins of what used to be a kitchen door for the staff. "We were in the tower for a long time." The more she spoke, the more her tongue began to feel as though it were thawing out from a long, hard freeze.

"Soon as the army...or what was left of it...turned against your uncle, it started breakin' into smaller groups. They all think they're goin' to restore what was left of the kingdom, and they're fightin' each other to do it." He paused and held out a hand to help her down a broken step. Maleen did her best to keep her eyes on her feet as they crossed through the smashed kitchen. The stone floor tiles were shattered, shards sticking up everywhere, and many of the dishes were pulverized, recognizable only by their color and glint in the light. Maleen forced her eyes away from them as she was hit by a flood of memories in what had once been a happy place.

"I don't understand how they could do this, though," she said quietly. "Our soldiers were always loyal."

"Sure were," the young man said as they came to one of the far corners of the sprawling kitchen. "Trouble was that your uncle replaced them all with his own men who were all just as 'spicious as he was. No one trusted nobody else, and eventually, they quit trustin' him." He gently deposited an unresponsive Jalyna onto the floor and then walked over to one of the bread pantries. The bread was all gone, but he leaned over and studied the wood panels behind it for a moment before reaching toward it. He grasped something and pulled out a large rectangle of wood to reveal a tunnel behind it.

"So this is how they got in!" Maleen cried, quieting quickly when he put his finger up to his mouth. "Sorry," she whispered.

He was already lifting his sister again, and with Maleen's help, stepped over the bottom portion of the wall into the tunnel. Then he nodded for Maleen to enter as well.

A small lamp was hanging in the corner by the door, its light making the tunnel's floor visible.

"Can you get that?" he asked in a low voice. Maleen took it and held it up as they walked in silence. The tunnel seemed to have weathered the palace's assault better than the rest of the building. The walls were still sturdy, beams propping the sides and roof up, and Maleen felt comforted as she remembered that Emille had traveled this same tunnel seven years before. The walk itself was about five minutes long. It wasn't a difficult walk, but some of the bends were quite sharp, and several times, the floor's grade dropped off steeply so that they had to take care descending. But eventually, they made it to another wooden door.

He put his finger to his lips and opened the door just enough to peer through. After a few seconds, he turned and nodded. "We're clear." And he led her into the familiar room that Maleen knew stood behind the stable.

Barrels still stood on end in the corners, though there were several less than there had been the first time she'd seen the room. Now there was a rumpled pile of blankets on the floor on a thin layer of straw. A bucket hung from a peg on the inside of the trapdoor, and shelves had been tacked up on every wall. About a third of them were full of half-filled bags of seed potatoes, rice, wheat, barley, and an assortment of dried fruits. There were also weapons and a few random things leaning against the wall, and a few finer objects, such as silver candlesticks and jeweled goblets, on the shelves as well. These objects were nice enough that Maleen guessed they had come from the personal chambers in the upper floors of the palace.

She sighed. Not that it mattered anymore. A loaf of bread would do them more good than silver candlesticks now. And she was grateful for anything she was given.

"It just occurred to me," she said as he placed Jalyna carefully on the pile of blankets, "that I don't know your name."

"Name's Jim," he said, straightening. "Our mother worked in the kitchens. That's how I knew about this place." He went over to the shelf holding the food and began to rummage through it. "Won't be stayin' here much longer, though. We'll have to leave tonight, soon as it's dark."

"I remember. But you never told me why."

"The main militants that like to claim the palace as their own set out this morning to track down a smaller faction. They should be back in a few days, but I don't want to chance runnin' into them." He sent her a nervous glance. "I had to trick them into thinkin' you were dead, as it was. I overheard them talkin' about findin' the princess in the tower and marryin' you off to the captain so's he could rightfully claim the throne."

Maleen shuddered. "What did you do?"

"I crept up to the outside of their camp and pretended to be one of them. Was night, so they couldn't see me well, and there's 'nuff of them that they don't know everyone in their ranks. Told them the duke had ordered me to poison you before he died so's no one could claim the throne. The duke, beggin' your pardon, was mad enough that they bought it. But I still overheard a few of them sayin' they would check the tower when they got back to make sure."

"Well," Maleen said, swallowing, "it seems I owe you far more than I knew." She attempted to smile at him. "Thank you."

He looked down at his sister. "Won't deny it. Our family was right angry with you when your uncle took her from us. But the longer you were stuck in that tower with her, the more I realized what a wrong had been done to both of you." He let out a gusty breath. "They...those soldiers are why I couldn't feed you often. I couldn't cook until they were gone, and then I had to wait until they wouldn't see me bringing the food to the tower. Or they'd of realized you were still alive. I would'a liked to send you a message, too, but..." He shrugged. "Can't write, and I didn't want to shout. A few times, I tried whisperin' at the door, but you must not have heard me. Sorry I couldn't get you out faster."

Maleen gave him a wry grin. "We're still alive, aren't we?"

His brow furrowed as he looked down at his sister again. "I don't know about that."

They were quiet for a moment before Maleen sat on the floor beside Jalyna and covered her with one of the blankets. Jalyna immediately closed her glassy eyes and began snoring softly.

"So," she said, hoping her voice would stay steady, "what happened?"

"Hold on. I'll be right back." Jim exited through the trap-door once more and returned a few minutes later. In his hands was a steaming pot of broth and a bag of something tied to his belt. "They've left the laziest boy watching the fire," he said, grinning. "They leave him behind whenever they fight. I swipe whatever's on it whenever he's not looking. It's pretty easy to distract him. Simpler than cookin' on my own, I can tell you that." He spooned some broth out into one of Maleen's bowls and handed her a piece of bread from the bag. Then he knelt down and began spooning the broth into Jalyna's mouth.

"So..." Maleen began again.

"Not sure I can give you all the details you want." He flashed her a strange look as he handed her a piece of bread. "But I 'spose there's no other way to say it. After your uncle locked you in the tower, Metakinos attacked."

Maleen choked on the piece of dry bread she'd just bitten into. "*Attacked?*" What had Rob...? Or her uncle...? She stared at Jim, the bread in her mouth suddenly tasting like a sponge.

He shrugged. "Don't know who started it. Lots of people never trusted Metakinos. But then, lots of people were terrified of your uncle." He blushed slightly. "Again, no offense—"

"None taken." Maleen leaned forward. "But you mean to tell me that *Metakinos* attacked my kingdom? And set it aflame?"

"Well," Jim scratched his scruffy chin, "not exactly like that. The war went on a long time, see. It started on the border, and with each victory, they got closer in."

Maleen had the sudden urge to vomit. Instead, she climbed to her feet and looked around.

"Tell me what I can do to get ready after I'm done eating. I don't like sitting and waiting for things to happen." Anything not to think about how her once-beloved had been killing her people for nearly seven years.

Jim, seeming unaware of the effect this revelation had had on her, stood and brushed his pants off. "I need to start preparin' our supplies. We won't be able to carry much, so most of what we do take will have to be food." He looked at the candlesticks then sent her a guilty look. "These might help, though."

Maleen blinked at the silver candlesticks for a moment until she realized what he was saying. "It's fine. They're not doing anyone any good here."

"We can't take all of this with us, but we need to take as much as possible," he continued, almost seeming to talk to himself. "I don't know how many of the villages are still standin' since the war." He handed her a few small sacks. "Fill these with whatever grains you think we can still eat. Some of it's gone rancid. But whatever's left has to get us to Metakinos."

Maleen, who had been lost in anger and betrayal, nearly fell over. "But you just said they—"

"Attacked us? They did. But I can't say it wasn't unprovoked. Not that I know much of the politics of it all. I worked in the army kitchens, so I didn't hear all the things your uncle did or King Damon did." He shook his head. "Least, not directly. Knew better than to dig too deep there." He looked at her broth. "Why don't you finish eating while I tell you. Don't know how much time we'll have to eat once we start movin'."

Maleen did as he suggested, but not with any sort of appetite.

"Anyway, King Damon opened the border after the war ended. Said the people without homes and livelihoods could come into his kingdom. Guess they acquired some new sort of trade route. I don't know. He also built some new tradin' posts along the road, so lots of Ertriquen folk went to those to start new lives and such." He shook his head. "Anyway, my family is in the capital city, along with almost everyone else from the palace who wasn't killed. Most of the villages and cities 'round here are damaged, too. Lots of the crops were burned in the campaign's last push."

Maleen closed her eyes and leaned back against a barrel.

"I joined the army soon as I was old enough," he continued, seeming unaware of her angst. "Needed extra money to feed the family. The old commander—the one before this one—liked me. I asked if I could take over the duty of feedin' you and Jalyna. Took a risk and told him the girl stuck with the princess was my sister, and I didn't want her goin' hungry. Nice man, the commander was." Jim paused and frowned. "Probably why your uncle had him killed."

Maleen felt sick to her stomach yet again.

"Then a few months ago, like I told you, even your uncle's soldiers couldn't take no more. Decided your uncle was madder than ever, though I don't know how it took them so long to see that. Anyhow, after they killed your uncle and set stuff on fire 'round the city, my family left. Father had died during the war, and Mum had the younger ones. So I sent them to Metakinos and said I'd wait for the chance to rescue you girls." Then he paused. "'Pologies, Your Highness! I didn't mean to be gettin' too familiar—"

"It really doesn't matter," Maleen said with a sigh. "There's not much left to be a princess of anyway."

They finished the rest of their meal in silence. After she was finished, Maleen stood and began looking for grain that smelled decent. Jim seemed perfectly at ease with the quiet, but now that Maleen was free, she realized she was starved for information even more than food.

"Tell me," she said, trying to keep her voice at ease as she filled a small bag with rice, "I know you said you didn't hear much of the politics, but can you remember anything as to why Metakinos attacked us?" She nearly asked him to tell her what happened to Rob. But he probably wouldn't know. And she had no need to know anyway. Rob had abandoned her after all.

He shook his head again. "Sorry. I really don't. I know bad stuff started brewin' when your uncle locked you in here after that betrothal announcement. But I never knew all the details." He gave her a guilty smile. "I might have been a year too young when I joined the army. So it was best to keep my head down and my hands busy." He must have finally noticed her angst because he smiled more widely. "Don't you fret, though. My family was always loyal to you, and there's loads others who are still, too. They just couldn't say it to your uncle without gettin' killed. And it won't be the life of a princess, but Metakinos's big enough that if we get you some decent commoner's clothes, you should be left alone."

"It is the royal city." Maleen frowned. "The king lives there." As did his faithless son.

Jim shrugged. "True. But I doubt they'll be lookin' for you in the common squares right under their noses."

Maleen could object. She could insist on going her own way. She could traipse the countryside, trying to gather what was left of her people. To do what, though? She had nothing to offer them. No food or shelter or protection. Nothing but a title that had never come to fruition.

Or she could ask for asylum with one of her allies. She had no doubt the Fortiers would take her in. Or her distant cousins in other kingdoms. She would probably even be treated well and be given land or at least a respectable marriage.

But before these thoughts had even finished running through her head, she knew they were impossible. While her people were still suffering here, she couldn't leave them behind.

"Very well," she said quietly. "We'll make our way to Metakinos." She looked at Jalyna, to whom Jim was again carefully feeding spoonfuls of thin broth. Jalyna had been imprisoned for Maleen's sake, even if not by her command. And Jim had remained at his own risk to keep them both alive. If the time came when she needed to leave, there would be nothing and no one to stop her. But for now, she owed it to them to help along the journey. Even more importantly, she owed it to her people to discover if there truly was nothing else she could do for them.

She had survived seven years of solitude and near starvation. She could...*would* survive a journey to the doorstep of the enemy.

CHAPTER II
BEHIND

Maleen felt as though she'd only just closed her eyes when Jim was shaking her gently, telling her it was time to go.

"They're comin'!" he said as he frantically began shoving sacks of food into his bag, which was larger than Maleen's. "They weren't supposed to be back for a few days!"

Maleen was on her feet in an instant, grabbing her own pack, which was, to her great relief, already tied shut. "What time is it?" she mumbled.

"An hour until midnight," he said, stooping to lift his sister from the floor. Jalyna opened her eyes briefly before letting them fall shut again. "We need to get out of here before they get settled. Or we'll be stuck until they leave again, and there's no tellin' when that'll be."

Maleen helped him get his sister out of the tunnel once they reached the kitchen, then she brought up the rear. This time as they ran through, she didn't bother attempting to look away from the ruined room. It felt foreign and hollow as she ran through it, as if it didn't recognize the princess who had spent happy stolen hours there when she was little, when its ovens were warm and the air smelled of bread.

At this moment, she probably wouldn't recognize herself either.

They came to a halt at the same back door through which they'd entered the palace. Jim motioned for her to stay back. After putting his ear against the door, he cracked it open and peeked through. Then he nodded at her, and she held it open so he could carry his sister through.

A hedge that had once been small and well-kept had grown out in every direction. It was tall enough that they were able to hunch slightly and stay in its shadows. Maleen's heart sped when she heard the first sound of men's voices. Jim stopped so fast that she bumped into him from behind.

"...think they were warned," a man was saying, his steps crunching loudly on the gravel as he passed on the other side of the hedge. "They seemed to know they were coming."

"Doesn't really matter," his companion said. "Captain says tomorrow he's going to break the tower door down and see if the princess really is dead."

"Wasn't she poisoned?"

"That's what someone said. But a few people have sworn they've heard sounds sometimes."

Maleen bit her tongue so hard it hurt.

A hand grabbed her wrist, and she jumped. But it was only Jim. He nodded to their left, and she followed as he cut through a break in the hedge wall and into the shadows of a blackened orange grove. They had gone a little way, long enough for Maleen to feel as though they just might escape the palace grounds undetected, when at the edge of the forest, they ran straight into a pair of men holding torches.

The men wore tattered soldier's uniforms, and they seemed to be examining the river. But they turned when Jim and Maleen stumbled into the clearing. For a long second, everyone stared at one another. Then the older one blinked a few times and gave a start.

"It's the princess!" he shouted. They started toward Maleen and Jim.

Jim had his sword out already, but Maleen knew it wouldn't do him any good. He was carrying his sister over his left shoulder, and his bag was heavy on his back.

"Run!" Jim shouted. But Maleen wasn't about to leave them. So Maleen did the only thing she could think to do. She darted behind him and yanked at the bag on his back. Reaching inside, she felt around until she found the silver candlesticks.

"You don't need him!" she shouted at the soldiers as she yanked the candle holders out, her heart pumping faster than it had in seven years. "You just want me!" And she took off toward the stream.

It worked, and they both gave chase. At first, she was afraid they would catch her, their steps were so close behind. While she was taller than she had once been, her legs were nowhere near as long as theirs. But she reached the edge of the stream just in time, leaping gracefully from one side to the other, suddenly grateful that she'd continued trekking up and down the tower steps all those years. Her legs had stayed strong. She heard the satisfying yell and splash of a man falling into the water and the swearing of the other. She turned left and looped around, searching the dark bank as she ran until she saw the familiar outline of a wooden bridge.

Maleen made another sharp turn and climbed under the bridge, scraping her already sore hands and knees on the ground as she ducked below the wood.

The water level was half of what it had been when she was little, the day she'd nearly washed away. Now she listened carefully, trying to ignore the memories nagging at her as she listened for the footsteps of her pursuers.

Sure enough, they came thundering out of the forest.

Instead of continuing, however, they stopped there, and Maleen heard them whispering. Part of her hoped they would simply go away, but she also knew that if they lost her now, they would simply run back to their captain, and soon the whole country-side would be chasing after her.

She bent slowly and with a prayer, she tossed one of the silver candle holders to the ground just at the edge of the stream, where it caught the moon's rays.

They stopped whispering and came to peer over the edge of the bank.

"What's that?" one asked the other, coming closer and bending to pick it up. The other followed.

Maleen didn't wait. If she did, she would never move for fear. So she jumped out from beneath the bridge, took her second candle holder, and swung hard. The silver stick came down solidly on the back of his head. Then she rounded on the other man and hit the side of his leg as hard as she could. He fell to his knees with a cry of pain, which allowed Maleen to then reach his head.

Seconds later, they were both slumped on the ground, motionless. Maleen stared at them, hoping grimly that she hadn't killed them, while at the same time wondering if she ought to. What would happen when they woke? Then she and her friends would have the same problem as if the men had simply returned to the castle. They would eventually awaken and report her escape to their captain.

The men both stirred. One tried to stand, and the other groaned and began to roll onto his elbow, but before Maleen could even choose whether to run or hit them again, two short arrows made soft whooshing noises, thumping quietly in the night. Both men let out cries as their heads fell back. Then they were silent.

Maleen stared at the men for a long time before slowly

turning and looking to her right. Jim was standing there, his crossbow in his hands.

"I'm sorry, Your Highness," he said, his voice shaking nearly as much as her hands. "But they would have brought the whole army with them." His voice cracked as he looked back down at the bodies. "And I can't defend you girls from all of them." With that, he dissolved into sobs. "I never killed anyone, Princess. I'm sorry. I'm so sorry."

As he cried, Maleen was reminded of how young he really was. Hardly more than a boy, trained in the kitchen rather than for war. His sister, the girl who should have been the one to comfort him, was on the ground behind him, her eyes open and trained on him, but making no move to go to him or even get up. So Maleen, despite the shock of seeing death for the first time herself, went to him and hugged him. He hugged her back, crying on her shoulder like a small child.

"You did nothing wrong," she whispered, trying to keep her own tears at bay. "You saved us. And that's more than anyone could have asked for."

After a little while, he quieted, and once again, they had to decide what to do. Maleen would have liked nothing more than to set up camp there and not walk another step that night. But once his tears had dried, Jim argued that they needed to keep going. And so into the night they continued as Maleen left everything she knew behind her.

CHAPTER 12

NOT THEIRS

The journey was long. There was no other way to describe it. They traveled through charred fields, waded across rivers, cut through forests, and sometimes chanced walking around the edges of a few surviving villages that dotted the way. Maleen never actually went into the towns. The risk of being recognized was too high. There were soldiers everywhere, and Maleen guessed that most of them weren't standing around to preserve the peace.

Other factions, like the ones that had taken over the palace, had sprouted up all over the countryside, and it made Maleen's chest hurt to see that so many of her soldiers were either gone, dead, or had chosen to leave their true fealty behind.

The soldiers weren't their only trouble. At first, Maleen's feet hurt so badly that after the second day she had to bite her lip so as not to cry out with each step. But just when she was sure she couldn't go on, they stumbled upon an abandoned cart that had been loaded with household goods. Jim rummaged through the items in the cart until he let out a triumphant cry and held up a pair of women's boots. Maleen was hesitant to take them and would have refused, except that it was clear the cart had been there for a long time. Most of the goods had been ruined by rain, rust, or mold and were covered in a thick layer of dust. The boots were only still useable because they'd been packed in a thick trunk.

After that, the walking grew easier. Maleen felt herself growing stronger again. She'd never been as still as Jalyna in the tower, but one could only go up and down the stairs so many times a day without feeling insane. The longer they walked, the more she could feel her muscles regaining the strength they'd once held.

Food was their next problem. They worked quickly through their supplies and were soon near to running out. So many of the fields had been ruined by the war that Maleen refused to eat from any fields they passed. She would only eat from the wild places on the sides of the roads, or the fields if the houses were completely destroyed as well.

Jim objected to this often. "We have to eat if we're goin' to survive, Your Highness," he said on the third day. "The folks here won't be missin' a few bites."

"I think they will," Maleen said, frowning at the ramshackle house on the next hill. A thin string of smoke rose up from the chimney. "You can eat if you want. I'm not going to stop you. But I'll wait until we find something else."

"Or until you drop from hunger," Jim grumbled. "And I can't carry both of you."

"It won't come to that."

And it didn't. Jim sold the silver candlesticks in the first town they reached the next day, and with the money, they were able to buy not only food but a small cart for Jalyna to ride in. There were more people here, and they weren't all so gaunt and thin as most of the travelers Maleen and Jim had passed, which meant, according to Jim, that they were getting closer to the border. Maleen could only guess she looked gaunt and hungry, too. But there was nothing to be done for it. It probably made her look less like herself, which was what they were hoping for anyway.

Jalyna, however, was their greatest concern. Maleen had hoped that as they made their way to freedom, her old companion would find her words again. But all speech seemed to have passed forever from Jalyna's tongue. Three weeks after they'd begun their journey, her eyes were still dead, and her mouth remained closed, opening only for the food her brother fed her.

This began to wear on Maleen's nerves after the third week. Several times, she considered telling Jalyna that this was unacceptable behavior, but each time, she talked herself out of it. The brother seemed to have no objection to pulling his sister behind him, and she barely ate anything. Perhaps Jalyna's mother would know what to do. It wasn't as if Maleen had great experience in healing hearts and minds. She couldn't even heal her own.

After three and a half weeks of walking, they finally arrived at the largest of the border towns, one that straddled the kingdoms' border. Before the war, the city's official name had been Kotami-Lumen. Most travelers, however, simply knew the city as Two Rivers, for a river up in the foothills flowed down into the city and split into two parallel ribbons within before leaving its gates. The river on Ertrique's side was named Lumen, and Metakinos's, Kotami.

Maleen had never been to Two Rivers, but every child living in Ertrique knew about Two Rivers. It was one of the greatest trade cities in the world. The river brought in barges of goods from up in the mountains where mining and logging took place, and both rivers left carrying even more.

Disagreements had always existed between Ertrique and Metakinos as to which kingdom the city had belonged to first, and not even the greatest historians seemed to know. All anyone could really prove was that the city had begun so close to one border that it had inevitably spilled over the other, and the kings, try as they might, had never been able to properly separate it since.

"How many coins do we have left?" Jim asked as they neared the city gates.

"Not enough for an inn, if that's what you're asking," Maleen answered quietly. "Not if we're going to feed ourselves all the way to the capital."

He let out a huff. "That's what I was afraid of." Then he nodded at the sky. Dark clouds were gathering on the horizon. "Are you sure there isn't enough?"

Maleen frowned. They'd made it through several storms so far, but as they'd been traveling through the countryside, there had always been some sort of cave or cove or abandoned building to hide in. But here in the town, there was nowhere for them to take refuge.

"See how much food you can buy for a copper," Maleen said as they made their way to the city gate. "If you can buy enough for that, I think we could afford something small." She hesitated. "Though you would probably have to sleep in the stable, as we can't afford two rooms." She reached into her makeshift reticule and pulled out a copper. It was one of their last few left over from the sale of the candlesticks.

"I think you should come inside with me this time," Jim said. Usually, Maleen kept Jalyna and her cart somewhere outside the city gate where they would wait for his return. "I get the feelin' you'll gain more attention out here than in there." He nodded at something behind Maleen, and she turned to see a large group of soldiers on horseback making their way down the distant road Maleen's little party had traveled just an hour before.

Maleen frowned. "I think you're right."

Jim picked up the cart's handles again, and they made their way into the city.

Maleen had no memory of what it was like to be in a city. Her uncle had been very careful with where she was allowed to go, even in her older years. Even when they were traveling to other countries, she wasn't allowed to open the coach's door or windows to see what was outside.

But now that she was in one, it seemed...overwhelming. There were too many colors and lines and people to count. The smells assaulted her. Sizzling meat, horse dung, ripe vegetables, freshly cut flowers, and sweat, all jumbled together. And the noise. So much noise. People shouting as chickens squawked and horses clip-clopped around the streets, and children screaming over one another in their games. Maleen had to resist the urge to run right back out and cover her ears, nose, and eyes for the rest of her life. Suddenly, she wanted to be back in her tower.

Thankfully, Jim seemed to understand her confusion. He guided her to a quieter corner of the market. Then he parked his sister's cart beside her.

"Stay here!" he called over the din. "I'll be back!"

Maleen felt ashamed as she stood there. Noise and people and colors had never bothered her before. She'd thrived on the few chances her uncle had given her to sample life in public. But after seven years of near-silence with low light and the same musty smells, she'd forgotten how to live in the outside world.

Well, no more. She stood taller as she reminded herself that she should, by all rights, be ruler of this city. And queens didn't cower from such assaults. Even if they did make her head spin.

As her senses acclimated to the busyness and confusion around her, Maleen began to notice smaller details as well. And one of the things she noticed now was a full-length mirror that stood beside a milliner's table.

Maleen hadn't seen a mirror in years. Reflective glass was expensive and difficult to make. She'd had mirrors in her old rooms in the palace, of course, but there had been none in her tower. Now, as she gazed at it, a thin girl with sunken cheeks, limp, dirty yellow hair, and eyes too big for her face stared at her. Maleen stared back, horrified.

She hadn't filled out completely by her seventeenth birthday. But she'd had the beginnings of some lovely curves, she'd once heard Emille whisper to the seamstress.

Now all those curves were gone. In their place were sharp, bony angles. Her skin was filthy, colored only by all their time walking in the sun. Her clothes were shamefully threadbare, too. They'd once had color, but most of the color had washed out of them or was muted by dust from the road.

A commotion from the other side of the square drew her attention from the mirror, and Maleen looked up to find the soldiers from the road riding through. They wore black, trimmed with gold and red. The colors of Metakinos. There were at least two dozen, and they congregated around a man in the middle. She couldn't see him at first, but after a few minutes, he rode out from the center of the circle to talk to a well-dressed man who was approaching them on foot.

"Alec," the young man greeted the older man from atop his horse.

Maleen nearly fainted. It was *him*.

"Your Highness." The man named Alec bowed so his robes scraped the ground. "Welcome to Kotami. Do you need lodging for your men and horses?"

Rob nodded curtly. "Yes. And a private place to discuss something with my generals. Can you accommodate us?"

"Certainly, Your Highness." Alec, who was most likely the city mayor or some other sort of local governor, gestured, and several men ran out to meet him. But Maleen couldn't pull her eyes from the prince.

She couldn't tell while he rode the horse, but he looked even taller than the last time she'd seen him. His shoulders were broader, and his chest had filled out. His curly hair, much to her sorrow, had been cut short so there wasn't any curl left to it. Stubble covered his chin and jaw, and his eyes were hard and cold. She must have stared too hard, though. Because those eyes eventually turned to meet her own.

His eyes widened slightly, and for a moment, she shook with the fear and thrill that he would recognize her. Then his gaze dropped to her holey, unwashed clothes, and he returned his attention to whatever Alec was telling him.

Shame and hurt flooded Maleen's chest. He didn't recognize her. Or perhaps he would have, except for her peasant's garb. She wasn't the blossoming flower he'd proposed to in the garden seven years ago. She was a starving peasant woman, unkempt and crass. Anger quickly followed her sorrow, however, and she ducked back beside Jalyna in her cart, peeking out from where she could see him, but he wasn't likely to see her.

His eyes flicked back to where she had been standing twice more, but they never searched for more than a second or two.

Part of her wished to march up to him and demand his attention. But that would be incredibly stupid. He was the enemy now, after all. He had destroyed her kingdom. Well, her uncle had done some of that, too, but her uncle hadn't fought a war with himself. And who knew? She was the last remaining heir of the Ertriquen throne. That was a dangerous title to hold in the enemy's territory.

Besides, as she looked down at Jalyna's limp form, she was reminded that she had promised to get her friends home. She could decide what to do after they were safe. Getting them caught up in issues of state would be the least helpful thing she could do.

And yet...

She looked at him again. He had always been kind, as had his parents. Would he really hurt or imprison her? She studied his eyes and was not comforted. They were piercing, like arrows, and everyone he looked at seemed to melt under their gaze. They weren't the eyes of the boy she had fallen in love with.

"What are you doin'?"

Maleen looked up to find Jim standing beside the cart. She pointed at the royal party, and his eyes widened.

"We have to get out of here!" she hissed.

He nodded and pulled the cart, not even bothering to let Maleen out. Then, walking away from the prince, he carefully made his way across the square. Maleen wanted desperately to peek out to see if Roburt's sharp eyes were following them, but she didn't dare. Instead, she huddled in the cart until they stopped in front of a small stable.

"It's not an inn," he said, grimacing, "but it'll keep the rain off our heads tonight."

Maleen let out a sigh of relief, though a part of her mourned that it would add yet another smell to their bodies and clothes by the time they were done. "It's perfect," she said, dredging up a smile. "Thank you."

They made their way inside and settled into the hay. It was admittedly warmer than any of their campfires had kept them since they'd begun their journey. There was an old horse in one stall and two cows on the other side, and a few chickens ran around the floor. Jim lit the oil lamp in the corner, and the room was flooded with a warm glow.

"So," Jim said after they'd unpacked, finally breaking the silence, "I know it's not my business, but I'm wonderin' why you were hidin' from the prince out there." He tilted his head. "Wasn't he your betrothed?"

Maleen drew in a deep breath through her nose. "I'm the only living heir of the kingdom they just crushed." She tossed her hair over her shoulder. "The enemy."

Jim frowned down at the bread he was tearing into pieces. "But if he saw you—"

"That's not why she won't talk to him."

Maleen and Jim turned to look at Jalyna, their mouths hanging open. Maleen had nearly forgotten what the girl's voice sounded like.

Jalyna, who had been leaning against the stable wall, struggled to push herself into a sitting position. Jim reached out to help her, but she slapped his hand away.

"You don't want him to see you because of what you've become! You're a penniless wench without beauty or power," she snarled. "And you can't stand letting him see you as less than you thought he loved!"

"Jalyna!" Jim stuttered. "You...you don't know what you're talkin' about—"

"Oh, yes I do!" Jalyna screamed. "I know because even though she may be princess by birth, she's no better than any other woman who lost a man!" Tears began streaming down her red cheeks as she turned a hateful glare back to Maleen. "Because Felix loved you! He said he would wait forever if he had to!" She had been trying to stay upright, but her next fit of sobs made her collapse into a heap of tears on the hay. Jim jumped up and immediately tried to comfort her, but Maleen couldn't move.

"Your vanity is the reason you can't face him!" Jalyna screeched over her brother's gentle murmurs. "Because you're not what you were! And you'll never be again!"

Maleen's eyes stung as she remembered the skinny, dirty woman in the mirror. She could do it. She could stand up and march into wherever Rob was staying and demand to speak with him. He shouldn't be difficult to find. He was the prince for goodness sakes. By birthright, she had every right to do so. And in her heart of hearts, she knew he would speak with her if she asked.

But then what? She had no army to threaten with. No goods to leverage. Not even a home. She barely had a basket of food to her name. Beyond all of that, though, she knew Jalyna was right. This steely-eyed prince was not the boy Maleen had fallen in love with. And she was not the girl he had fallen for either.

"I'm so sorry," Jim called over his sister's sobs. "Felix was the man we thought she was going to–"

"No." Maleen sat taller and swallowed. "She's right." And Jalyna was. No one remained the person they had been. And if Rob couldn't accept that, then she would accept the consequences, whatever they may be, and she would do so as queen. She would see him, and she would demand to know what he had done and why.

But not now. Not like this.

"I know what I'm going to do now," she told Jim when his sister had quieted again. "I'm going to help you get Jalyna safely to your family. Then I'm going to the palace."

His eyes widened. "But Your Highness, you just said–"

"I will also see that you're rewarded for all the care you have given me." She gave him a small smile. "I think I know enough of the Metakinos royal family to know they reward good service when given."

He raised his eyebrows, and she knew what he was thinking. The royal family would reward good service to her while betraying the trust she had once put in them? A small voice in her head accused her of foolish vanity, just as Jalyna had. But this was too much to think about after the events of the day.

She would go.

She would see him.

But she was doing it on her terms. Not theirs.

CHAPTER 13
UNAFFECTED

Their little group left the stable the next morning after Jim had assured Maleen that the prince's entourage had already gone. Unfortunately, Jalyna, despite her outburst the night before, was no more desirous of walking than she had been in weeks prior.

The farther east they traveled, however, the easier the roads became. The houses they passed now weren't empty shells of what they'd once been, and there was food readily available everywhere that they went. The weather was continuing to warm. Spring had lasted well into early summer, but now it was summer in earnest. This meant that while the days grew sweaty and miserable, at least the nights were no longer threatening with their cold.

They reached the royal city two weeks later. They would have reached their destination much faster, except that Jim had decided a few days after her outburst that Jalyna was capable of walking a little every day. She moaned and groaned and protested, but he was insistent and refused to put her in the cart until she had at least made an attempt to walk.

This meant that Maleen spent much of her days sitting in

the shade of a tree, staring at the clouds, while the brother and sister warred. Eventually, though, Jim always won, and by the last few days, Jalyna was walking more often than not.

Maleen's throat burned strangely when they crested yet another hill...and there before her stood the royal city. It was nearly...ethereal.

Rob hadn't been exaggerating.

The city's name was Kismina. She'd heard all about it, of course, but she'd never been allowed to visit. On the few occasions her uncle had grudgingly ventured there for a summit or trade discussion, he'd vehemently refused to allow her to attend – one of the many grievances Rob had once held against him. To make up for this, Rob had spent countless hours telling her of its wonders. And for most of her life, Maleen had been convinced he was stretching the truth. Nothing could be as beautiful as the shining city he boasted.

But it was. The city below the castle on the hill was neatly ordered in rows and columns, its cottages and larger buildings fitting squarely against one another in perfect order. The colors were brighter than they'd been in any of the cities they'd yet passed through, and there was no dark soot marring the buildings or streets from fires or casum ball explosions. Here, it looked as if there had never been any war in the world.

The city, however, was nothing compared to the castle.

The castle itself wasn't as tall as her own palace had been, as it only looked to be five stories high, but what it lacked in height, it more than made up for in ferocity. Thick walls surrounded the base of the castle, a portcullis gleaming at its center. And though the walls and palace were largely made of yellow stones, many of the sides of the towers and walls were difficult to look at because they were covered in mosaics made of colored glass. It gleamed in the sunlight—yellow,, green, blue, orange, and white tiles fitted on every side, all arranged into large, gleaming scenes depicting the countryside.

The foundation of the castle seemed to be designed in the older fashion, a large rectangular tower in the center with four smaller octagonal towers forming a square around it. Bridges and extended halls joined the towers in multiple places. Maleen knew from Rob's descriptions that the palace portion was in the large tower in the center, though it was more difficult to see than the smaller towers because of the surrounding outer wall that connected them.

And to think. By now, it could have been the place she called home.

Jim let out a low whistle. "First, the lot of us...the palace folk, I mean, were sore that so many were leavin' for this place when things got bad. Seemed like betrayal. But now..." He shook his head. "Makes their decision seem a lot simpler."

They reached the city late the next afternoon. The land had more hills here than in Ertrique, which made sense, as Maleen could see real mountains in the distance, so it took them longer to reach the city than she'd first hoped. But when they finally arrived, the city was just as charming as it had appeared from afar.

Of course, by the time they reached the town square, they were surrounded by the smell of animals. No one could ever escape that in a city so large as this. But this city had, they were informed, not one but four town squares, and the streets were the cleanest Maleen had ever seen.

"See those ruts?" Jim pointed to grooves on each side of the street. "My guess is they make the road higher, and the junk runs into those during the rain. Keeps the worst of the muck and runoff out of the road." Maleen nearly gasped when she saw boys running about with shovels and large scooping plates, picking up the animal refuse and dumping it into buckets. Not only had Metakinos won the war, but the crown still had enough money to clean its streets. Daily, it seemed.

For years, Maleen had wondered why Metakinos had made

such heavy demands of Ertrique. Negotiations had often been heavily in favor of Metakinos, and she'd never understood why. The two kingdoms were of similar age, history, and size. But now she understood. Ertrique, for all its beauty and rich culture, could never...had never compared with this. Militarily, monetarily, structurally...

If anything, Metakinos had been far more generous than they needed to be. A blush crept up Maleen's neck and cheeks as her uncle's presumptions washed over her again. Suddenly, she felt much smaller than she had moments before. Her kingdom was nothing compared to this.

Fortunately, she didn't have time to dwell on such unhappy thoughts. They were here with a destination, rather than just passing through.

"Do you have any idea where your mother is?" Maleen called over the noise of the smaller market they had just left.

Jim, who was pulling his sister's cart through the bumping, jostling crowd, looked over his shoulder. "She was able to get me one letter after arrivin'. They should be on the north side of the city."

Not exactly what she'd hoped to hear. Maleen looked back up at the castle. It was a little too close for her comfort. What if he discovered her before she was ready? Rob had often left the castle to visit the city. Or at least he had seven years ago. But then again, the streets were crowded, and as he'd so successfully proven back in Two Rivers, she had become unrecognizable to him. She should be safely hidden until she chose to be otherwise.

"What will we do if we can't find them by nightfall?" Maleen asked, hurrying to catch up with Jim after several sheep broke loose of their pen and separated them.

Jim looked around and his brows furrowed. But just as he opened his mouth to answer, a woman's shout came from somewhere nearby.

"Jim! Jalyna!"

They both turned to see a tall, thin woman hurrying toward them. She had a rag tied around her hair, preventing Maleen from seeing its color, but her eyes and face were unmistakably like those of Maleen's travel companions. She looked to be in her late fifth decade, and already had her arms open to pull them into a hug.

"Auntie!" Jim laughed, embracing the woman back.

"We were near despairin' of you both!" she exclaimed in a sing-song voice, not unlike Jim's. "We wondered what–" Her eyes moved over Jim's shoulder and locked onto Maleen. She clapped her hand over her mouth and fell back a step, eyes bulging. *No*, she mouthed, her hand falling away from her face.

Maleen stood very still. Slowly, the woman moved past Jim and took Maleen's face gently in her hands, as though Maleen might break. "Princess," she whispered, her voice getting lost in the sounds of the street. She took Maleen by the hands and stepped back, looking up and down Maleen's person several times. And Maleen's face burned as she saw the sadness reflected in the woman's eyes. Her own eyes pricked and threatened to spill over.

But no. This was who and what she was. And she needed to become accustomed to it sooner than later. Beauty was...well, not important now. What mattered was what she could *do*. What she *would* do.

The woman blinked a few times and seemed to remember herself. "Quickly," she said, motioning them to the side of the street. "This way. Leave your cart here. It should be safe enough." She pointed to an empty space beside the castle wall.

They followed her about a block down the street to a two-story building. The shop on the bottom floor was a bakery. Maleen nearly began to cry as soon as the scents inside wafted out to her. This struck her as absurdly funny, considering she'd just fought hard against tears over her changed appearance. But the air here smelled like *cinnamon*. Her mouth watered like it hadn't in years.

Instead of remaining in the bakery, however, which was crowded with women and children with baskets, Jim's aunt led them to a small, narrow set of wooden stairs in the back corner. Jim put his sister down, and he and Maleen helped her slowly climb the stairs.

The room they eventually spilled out into was simple but clean. There was one window over on the far side of the room. A hearth with a pot hanging above it sat to their right, stirred by a woman with her back to the door. Bed rolls were spread out all over the floor, and two wooden chests sat beneath the window.

"Phoebe," Jim's aunt called out to the woman stirring the pot, "look who I found wanderin' the streets."

The woman named Phoebe looked up and let out a shriek. Her ladle clattered to the floor as she rushed at Jim and Jalyna. She sobbed as she wrapped them in her arms, sinking to the floor with both of them, muttering about her babies making it home.

Maleen had never felt so out of place, nor so envious of people with living mothers. How she wished for Emille. After being locked in a tower for seven years, being abandoned by the one man who had loved her, and traveling across the barren wasteland of her home, there were no arms outstretched, waiting for her.

Her chest clenched, and she gritted her teeth, once again, willing the tears not to spill.

"What is she doin' here?"

Maleen looked back up at the woman, having looked away to give them privacy. The woman—their mother, she assumed —was glaring daggers at her.

"I want her out of my home!" She glared at Jim this time. "She took both of you from me, and you have the audacity to bring her–"

"Phoebe," the first woman said gently. "Look at her."

"She helped us, Mother!" Jim exclaimed, extricating himself from his mother's grasp. He stood and gestured to Maleen, who felt her face growing redder by the second. "She saved us several times along the way! We wouldn't be here if it wasn't for her!"

Whether it was Jim's continuing insistence on her usefulness or his aunt's pointing out that Maleen looked nothing like a princess, Phoebe's face finally softened slightly. She took a deep breath and nodded. "Come," she said, somewhat resignedly to Maleen. "We'll see what we can do with you."

There wasn't much space left in the room as there were seven bedrolls already spread out on the floor, but they managed to put Jalyna in one of the larger bedrolls with one of her little sisters. Jim had to have his own because he was too big to share with anyone else, and they managed to clear a corner enough to make Maleen a nest of blankets.

Supper was a joyous affair, one Maleen watched with constantly warring feelings of enjoyment and envy. The younger siblings were exuberant when they saw their older brother. They also loved on Jalyna, though it was with far more hesitant embraces and looks than they gave Jim. Jalyna wasn't particularly helpful in laying their unease to rest either. She would nod or shake her head when asked questions, and she would allow her younger siblings to hug her, but she never returned their touches nor answered their questions with words.

"So what have you found to do here, Mum?" Jim asked as he buttered a third roll of bread. "Can't imagine butter and rent are free."

"No." His mother gave him a wry smile. "They're not. I work in the palace kitchens. The pay isn't bad. Better'n I got at..." She glanced at Maleen and cleared her throat. "We'd have a nicer place than this if we didn't have so many people." She smiled fondly at her brood. "And your aunt and uncle and cousin stayin' here helps, too. We're all hopin' to one day buy a farm outside of town, but for now, this'll do." She tapped the nearest boy, who looked to be about fourteen years, on the head. "Jude is apprenticin' with a smith down the street. Julia is workin' at the bakery below, and little Jana is helping your cousin and aunt at the seamstress's shop." She paused to take a sip of her soup. "Now that you're here, your uncle will be happy to have another pair of hands in the nobleman's stables where he works."

Jim nodded and tucked back into his food. "Sounds perfect."

Their mother turned to Jalyna and gave her daughter a sad smile. "And you, Jalyna. What shall we do with you?"

Maleen had grown accustomed to Jalyna's silence, but it struck her as interesting that Phoebe did not seem surprised by her daughter's lack of words. Instead she seemed...almost to be expecting it.

"What about you, Your Highness?"

Maleen gave a little start when she realized that Jim's aunt was speaking to her. "I'm sorry. What?"

"What do you plan to do now that you're here?"

Was she asking Maleen to leave? Maleen opened her mouth and searched for an answer when Jim's aunt shook her head. "I don't mean to frighten you away," she said with a small smile. "Only that I was friends with your servants. And they always said that you were never one without a plan. Even as a small girl."

Maleen gave a small sigh of relief and smiled. "My...my hope is to seek an audience with the prince."

The table went silent, and someone dropped a spoon. Even Jim's uncle, who had been focused only on his food so far, looked up from his plate.

"Just...just like that?" Phoebe asked, sending her sister a glance.

Maleen swallowed and tried to sit taller. "He owes it to me. After leaving me in the tower and then making war on my people, I deserve an explanation."

The sisters shared another meaningful look, and Maleen found herself wishing they would stop.

"I'm...I won't deny that," Phoebe said with a slight frown. "It's your birthright, after all. But...Your Highness..." She took a deep breath. "You were raised with niceties and honor due your station. As you should have been!" She added quickly. "But...not to offend, but...you...you appear as though you belong with us now. Your clothes, I mean, and all that. I'm not sure the guards will just let you waltz into the castle and demand an audience with Prince Roburts."

"That," her sister added, "and...well, word has it that the prince has never been the same since the war. He's cold now. And hard. Not the gentle young man he was when you knew him."

Phoebe nodded and traced the contours of her clay mug. "It's true. I've only seen him myself a few times, but when he makes his way down to the kitchens..." She shuddered. "It's as if the room freezes over."

If Maleen's face had been warm earlier, it was blazing now. Her first instinct was to protest. He would speak to her. He *had* to. But as she looked down at the thin fingers that clutched her spoon, she knew the women spoke the truth. "I have to try," she whispered. There really wasn't any other way. She had to see Rob.

Phoebe sighed and nodded. "I suppose you do. You can start by washin' up with water from the well tomorrow. I'll give you a bucket, and you'll have time to yourself after the men go out to feed the animals. You can bathe and brush your hair, and perhaps you'll...feel more like yourself."

Maleen was fairly sure she had meant to say that perhaps

she would *look* more like herself, but she wasn't about to pick a fight over vanity.

"I'll give you one of my dresses," Jim's aunt added. "It's not palace-worthy by any means, but it's a far cry better than your travelin' clothes. I should be able to hem it tonight to fix the length."

Maleen did her best to nod and look grateful. Really, it was more kindness than she deserved, especially after what this family had suffered because of her. But as she lay in her corner that night, she couldn't get the dark ice of Rob's gaze out of her head. And if she was honest, her heart was breaking slightly. The prince they were describing now made Maleen feel almost as if he had died.

Jim and his mother stayed up late into the night, discussing all that had happened since they'd separated, but Maleen was awake long after they went to bed, the hard look in Rob's eyes ever at the forefront of her mind.

Maybe, she thought sleepily as she began to doze, her exhaustion lending her heart grace she couldn't find during the day, he hadn't been so unaffected by the war either.

CHAPTER 14
HOPEFULLY

Maleen didn't sleep well that night, so waking up with the others the next morning wasn't difficult. What was difficult, however, was the moment Maleen realized, bucket in hand and standing in front of the well, that she had no idea how to get water herself.

It had looked simple enough when the women in front of her were doing it. Put the bucket on the chain and lower it into the well. But when her turn arrived, she realized that she didn't know how to attach it properly to the chain itself. Panic drove her breath in short, tight bursts as the women and girls behind her began to grumble and complain while she fumbled with the chain and the bucket handle.

"Come on, already!"

"Did yer mother drop you on yer head?"

"What kind of idiot–"

"Here."

Maleen looked up to see Jim's aunt at her side. "It's this way, love," she said in a low voice, turning it to reveal a small hook that had gotten caught on one of the chain links. Maleen wanted to disappear as she watched Jim's aunt lower the bucket down quickly and pull it up nearly as fast. She was thin but strong, unhooking the bucket and holding her head high as they walked back to the little room above the bakery. Maleen just looked at her feet.

"I'm sorry," Maleen mumbled as they made their way up the stairs. "I...I've never had to do that before."

"Of course you haven't. It would have been a shame if the kingdom had been reduced to sending its princess to fetch water from the well." She pursed her lips and glanced at Maleen. "As it has now." Then she shook her head. "You're up earlier than I expected."

"I couldn't sleep."

"Well, if that's the case, here's a rag. Wash up as well as you can. The men will be back to eat breakfast in about ten minutes, so unless you want to wait until everyone else is gone, which you can if you wish, I'd be quick." She handed Maleen a dark blue woolen dress. "Not anything fitting your station, but...a good measure better than the rags you're wearing now."

Maleen thanked her meekly and set to washing as well as she could. The water was freezing cold, and she was shivering by the time she pulled the dress over her head. Not a minute too soon, either, because Jim and his uncle knocked on the door with firewood a few minutes later.

How good it felt to have clean hair! It wasn't anything like it had once been, silky and golden, tied up in ribbons the way Emille had told her servants to fix it. But at least it wasn't so oily or dirty.

Fixing it up, however, was another story. They had no mirror, and after Maleen twisted and rolled it this way and that for several minutes, she gave up with a huff. She had learned how to tie it back with a simple cord, but nothing appropriate for meeting with a foreign dignitary. How in the world would she survive in the common world if she couldn't even draw water or do her hair?

Larger hands pulled her hair back and began separating it. They were so rough in their yanking that Maleen nearly yelped but stopped herself just in time. Phoebe had come to stand behind her, and was already beginning to braid.

"Thank you," Maleen whispered.

Phoebe braided then pinned in silence for several minutes before speaking. When she did, her voice was low and rough. "I was angry with you for a long time, you know."

Maleen nodded, not knowing what else to say.

"But seeing you here, now..." She finished coiling the braid on Maleen's head and stepped back. When Maleen turned to face her, the woman's eyes were red. "Your mum would have wanted someone to take care of her baby the way you helped take care of mine."

Phoebe's words still echoed in Maleen's head as she made her way to the palace. She had often wondered what her parents would say if they could see what had happened to their kingdom and their daughter. Never in her life had she wanted her mother more. Or Emille.

She was soon distracted from her thoughts, however, when she neared the castle. It really, for all its beauty, was an imposing structure. A fierce beauty if she had ever seen such a thing. Forcing herself to walk with her head high, she made her way with the throng that was slowly moving toward the arched opening.

What would she say when she saw him? Her heart pounded violently in her chest as she passed through the gates with the others. Would she have to introduce herself? Prove that she was who she claimed to be? Or what if he refused to see her? What if he had recognized her the other day and had *chosen* not to acknowledge her?

"Name?"

Maleen jumped a little. Somehow, she'd been so distracted she hadn't realized the gate guard was looking at her. "Um," she paused. What she was about to do could be extremely dangerous. But it was for her people. Giving her true name was the least she could do for them. She cleared her throat and raised her chin proudly. "My name is Maleen Aelia Helena Valeria, Crown Princess of Ertrique."

A mild roar went up from the crowd around her. Some pushed their way closer to ogle at her. Laughter rippled up from others. Those closest to her tried to step farther away. But she didn't allow herself to meet their eyes to see what they thought of her. Instead, she kept her gaze on the guard.

His brow furrowed as he looked up and down her person. "*You* are Princess Maleen?"

Maleen allowed him one condescending nod.

"She can't be the princess." A second guard...no, a knight walked up behind him.

"Why?"

"Because the princess is dead." The man sniffed, giving Maleen a look of disdain. "The tower she was in? It toppled, crumbled to the ground." He waved a dismissive arm at Maleen. "Peddle your lies elsewhere, girl."

The first guard shrugged and called the person in line behind her.

"No!" Maleen took a step closer but stopped when he put his hand on the hilt of his sword. "I need to speak to Prince Roburts. He'll vouch for my identity if you only let me see him. And if I'm lying, you can punish me."

The guard's thick eyebrows rose. "You'd be willing to risk imprisonment to see him?"

Maleen nodded.

The man stared at her for a moment. "I saw the princess once. And I'll grant that you do look like her. But if Sir Vincent says no, I can't do anything about it." He shrugged. "I'm sorry, Miss." Then he looked again to the person behind her.

Slowly, Maleen made her way back toward the street. Last

night, she had wondered briefly if they would let her in. Fear of failure, however, had kept her from envisioning that outcome. And this morning, she'd been so overtaken with worry about what she would say and do when facing Rob again that it hadn't even really dawned on her that she might not get to speak with him at all. Now she understood Phoebe and her sister's hesitance the night before.

Not only was she failing as a princess, but she was, apparently, really bad at being a commoner, too.

For lack of a destination, she was nearly back to the little room above the bakery when she heard Phoebe's voice.

"Princess!"

The woman was standing in an open door that led through the castle wall which backed the line of merchants' tables and tents across the street from the houses and shops. Maleen walked over to her. "Quick! Before someone sees!" Phoebe took Maleen by the wrist and yanked her inside, shutting and locking the door behind them.

"They wouldn't let me in the front. Am I allowed to be in—" Maleen began, but Phoebe cut her off.

"The cook is lookin' for a new scullery maid. If you get the job, perhaps you can find a way to speak to him from there." She began pulling Maleen through the tunnel that ran through the wall, speaking in a rush and glancing over her shoulder twice.

"Are you sure?" Maleen asked, frowning slightly. "If it's going to get you in trouble, I'll find another way."

"Either you need to do this for your people or don't," Phoebe whispered fiercely. "But don't wallow in-between."

Maleen swallowed hard and nodded. "Right. What do I need to do?"

She soon found herself in a very hot, very crowded kitchen, facing one of the largest men she had ever seen. He was a head taller than Jim and at least twice as heavy. And by the look on his face, he wasn't impressed with her.

"She's thin." He shook his head. "How's she supposed to do any work if she's nothing but skin and bones?"

"Give her something to eat, Michail, and she won't be." Phoebe crossed her arms and glared at him. "You'd be skin and bones, too, if you'd just walked from Ertrique."

"Another one?" He ran a hand through his thick, black hair and looked back down at Maleen.

"Your prince invited us. We broke no laws." Phoebe gave him a sly smile. "Do you wish *I* hadn't come?"

He sighed heavily and rubbed his eyes. "Well enough. If you can vouch for her competence, then she can be a scullery maid. Sophia left two days ago to have her baby." He eyed Maleen unhappily again. "If she can fulfill her duties, she can stay."

Maleen and Phoebe exchanged a look. Maleen wasn't stupid. She'd been tutored by the best teachers her uncle could find. But she had never been trained in the art of the scullery maid. Hopefully, her wits could develop the skills her experience lacked because this time, it wasn't only her job on the line.

Hopefully, Michail's obvious like for Phoebe would be enough to save her from his disdain for Maleen.

Hopefully, she could soon find the prince.

CHAPTER 15
SCARS

Life as a scullery maid wasn't as hard as Maleen had thought it would be. It was harder.

They were all awakened by bells at four in the morning, though Maleen knew for certain that sometimes the cook awoke them even earlier, and she knew this because they would be deep into their work by the time the clocktower rang out.

She started every day with cleaning. And not dishes, as she'd believed the scullery maids were supposed to wash. Washing dishes had looked simple enough. Instead of dishes, she found herself scrubbing parts of the castle she'd never even considered, such as the chamber pot for the other servants. The newest scullery maid was always assigned that particular duty, she was assured, and as soon as another one was hired, that poor girl would take her place and she could move on. But for now, it was her job.

After she had cleaned that unholy object, she had to clean herself again in time to help prepare breakfast and tea for the higher servants, while Michail and his more favored assistants, such as Phoebe, prepared food for the king and his court. Then she really was assigned to wash not only dishes, but also walls, floors, kitchen hearths, and windows. Once the higher servants were finished with their tea, she and the other scullery maids would venture into their dining hall to clean the remains of the tea. This all took place before the kitchen flew into an uproar as it prepared for the royal luncheon. And so the day continued from before dawn until long after the sun set.

Maleen had never been so tired in all her life. Even heavier than her physical exhaustion, however, was the toll it took on her mind. The difficult, disgusting tasks might have been easier to bear if she only knew what she was doing. She'd only ever been allowed to wander her own palace kitchen when she was very small, before her uncle had realized she was playing with the servants' children there, and then later, when she was being trained in how to organize the kitchen staff. Emille would have died from shock had Maleen suggested she learn how to properly carry a stack of dishes, or worse, scrub them. Her months of poor feeding didn't help her either. Though her legs were strong from walking, her body as a whole had not yet recovered from its poor, irregular meals.

"What in the blazes am I supposed to do with you?" Michail bellowed after she dropped her fourth dish in three days. "Tell me, girl. Where were you trained? Because it can't have been a kitchen."

The entire staff stopped what they were doing to watch, and a few of the other scullery maids snickered. Maleen's stomach turned.

Ashamed, she kept her head down and started to pick up a shard of the dish she had broken, but he grabbed her wrist. "I asked you a question–" Stopping himself mid-sentence, he turned her hand over and examined it. Then he demanded the other one. Grudgingly, she let him have it.

"Your hands look as though you've never done a day of work in your life!" He looked up incredulously.

"I...I was trained in the upper palace," she whispered. "In

the way of the high lady." Perhaps not to serve them, but it was close enough, at least.

Michail rubbed his face with his hands. "A lady's maid. You were trained as a lady's maid. *Now* you tell me this."

"I'm sorry." Maleen tried not to look at everyone else. "I just needed work."

He let out a gusty sigh and shook his head. "Clean this up. But be warned that the first chance I get to ship you off to another part of the castle, you're out of these kitchens forever. Understand?"

Maleen nodded, a small ray of hope sprouting in her soul. The idea of having a job with the servants who worked in the main part of the castle was too good to be true. She would be closer to Rob.

Not as important, but still a relief, would be that she would most likely be able to adapt to their sort of work much more easily. Emille had ensured that she was far from a pampered princess. At least, not pampered as far as princesses were concerned. She could sew and do needlepoint quite well, and she knew exactly how tables should be set and in what order meals should be served. *If only*, she prayed to the Maker.

But the Maker did not grant this prayer during the first week of working in the castle. Nor the second week nor the third. Slowly, painfully, she began to learn her new duties. After several weeks, there were fewer accidents, and after a few more, the other servants stopped watching her in hopes of witnessing another exciting accident. Her fingers stopped hurting so much and developed callouses. And for the first time in years, she was no longer always hungry.

But the thing she needed to do...the whole reason she was living through such misery, she could not. She was so busy from before dawn until late at night that she never had time to sneak into the castle to look for Rob. Because she was the newest scullery maid, there was always someone watching her. Even during her mealtimes, she was constantly being told to finish up and do something else. And at night, when she might have searched for him, it was too late. He was assuredly in his bedchambers by then.

Bedchambers that might have been hers, too, had everything gone as it should have. This both quickened her heart and brought a sour taste to her mouth. If her uncle hadn't lost his mind.

If Rob had kept his promise.

But there were enough *ifs* to fill all the wells in the world, as Emille used to say. Oh, Emille. If only she could be there, all of this would have been easier to bear. Maleen didn't get to see Phoebe much, as they were both kept so busy. But she did request that Phoebe ask around to see if anyone had heard about what had happened to Maleen's beloved governess. After a month, however, she'd heard nothing.

Still, it wasn't all bad. As much as she hated to admit it, there were a few benefits to the horrid job. For one, as the scullery maids were given cots in one of the lower rooms of the castle, she was able to move out of Phoebe's crowded house. No longer would she be a burden to their family. Not if she could help it.

Second, there was the food. Three times a day, she was fed along with the rest of the kitchen staff. And the food wasn't bad either. It was nothing compared to what she'd once eaten in her own palace, but after nearly starving, she wasn't going to complain. After several weeks, she decided that her wrists no longer looked skeletal, and Michail quit throwing her looks of concern, as though he was worried she might simply topple over.

Good food or not, however, she began to despair of ever sneaking away to talk to Rob. But in the middle of her second month, she finally found her chance. Michail was sick, and the young man who had been training beneath him was in charge.

This young man was everything Michail was not. Wiry and worried, he fretted all day and night. Instead of bellowing at the top of his lungs, as Michail did, he was constantly peppering the kitchen staff with questions. Were the biscuits finished? Was Phoebe sure the tea was steeped enough? Did the meat have enough flavor?

He was distracted enough that while Maleen was supposed to be eating supper that evening, he forgot to look in on the scullery maids. Not that they needed looking after, but for some reason, Michail seemed convinced they might forget their purpose with full bellies. Or perhaps he was smarter than that and considered that someone might try what Maleen was determined to do.

Her stomach grumbled at her for missing supper as she snuck up the stairwell. She and the other scullery maids had worked unusually hard that day after the news had come that a royal party from another kingdom was arriving. Michail's protege had been in a full panic as he'd ordered every dish in the kitchen to be cleaned...even the ones that had just been put away.

Maleen told her stomach silently that it would indeed survive without supper for one night—she'd done it enough before—as she turned another corner. She was in the upper servants' dining hall now. It was the farthest she'd ever gone from the kitchens. She came up here daily to set and remove the teas and meals that the upper servants enjoyed during their breaks. The room was too dark to see well, but she knew where the staircase was that led from the upper servants' dining hall into the main castle, and she prayed hard now that it would be empty as she ascended into the darkness.

To her chagrin, when she reached the top of the stairs, the stone floor was polished and gleaming, even in the low light of the sconces on the walls. Her boots would tap with every step, and though she couldn't see how high the ceilings were in the darkness of the particular room she'd entered, what she guessed to be a lesser dining or meeting hall, the last thing she wanted was to be heard and shooed back downstairs by another servant. Or worse, dismissed.

In her stockings, shoes in hand, she made her way noiselessly toward the end of the hall, which showed a more promising light through the crack of the large wooden door. Peeking around the door, she found a hall which, though slightly better lit, was empty as well. Hesitantly, she rounded the corner.

I don't know why I'm here, she prayed silently, *but please help me find him.* Even as she prayed, she was reminded of just how large the castle had looked from the outside. How in the world was she to find him in all these towers?

She would find him because she was a princess, was she not? And not just the princess. She had at one time been the prince's closest confidante, the woman he had wanted to marry. His heart might have changed in the last seven years, but she doubted he had changed his habits as well. Maleen straightened her shoulders and walked toward the door.

In his letters, he had often talked of visiting the menagerie to see the animals there. But visiting the menagerie at night would be no good. The animals would all be asleep. He had also spoken of sneaking down to the kitchens to beg a treat out of the cooks and servants. Unfortunately, that habit *did* seem to have changed, for she knew she would have seen him or at least heard of it had he come since she'd been employed. So what was left?

As she stood in a dark corner pondering, she heard several sets of footsteps. She looked around, but the only place to hide was behind one of the tapestries hanging from the dark ceiling. There was no time to wonder whether or not this was a good idea because the footsteps were growing closer. So she dove behind the tapestry and pulled it over her, trying to hold it still to keep it from fluttering at whomever was passing by.

"...should hear soon," a man's voice said. "You sent the offer a full month ago."

"If we don't hear anything in another week, we'll send a second rider to see if something happened to the first," his companion replied.

Maleen clapped a hand over her mouth and put her other arm around her stomach to keep herself from falling to her knees. That voice. Yes, she'd heard it in the market, but here it seemed to be magnified by the empty halls, and she couldn't get used to it. It was just so much deeper than she was used to. And yet it was *his* nevertheless. Cruel and beautiful, it carried her back to the night when she had been happy, and for one brief moment, everything had been as it ought. Silent tears ran down her face as she pressed her knuckles to her mouth, forcing her sobs to stay quiet.

Unrepentant, the voices and footsteps continued to walk, as though they hadn't just shredded her heart to pieces. "I can't imagine her having any second thoughts," Rob continued.

They stopped walking.

"And...and you're sure about this, Your Highness? That you're ready, I mean?" The words were respectful but kind, and they made Maleen hurt anew, but this time, for Emille, who had asked such questions of her.

"It's a little late for that, isn't it?" Rob asked in a hard voice before resuming his walk.

Maleen waited until they had rounded the corner in the next hall before following them. She wiped the tears from her eyes as well as she could, hoping they wouldn't show too well in whichever room she found to confront him in. Because she was going to chase him wherever he was headed, improper or not. For her people, he had to hear her. He had to answer.

Thankfully, the man who had been walking with him was

gone by the next time she caught sight of him. Her heart lifted slightly in her chest when she realized his destination. It was a library. She'd been prepared to follow him into his personal chambers, but this was much more proper. At least, she told herself that.

She waited outside for a moment before peeking through the door. He had his back turned and was looking out the dark window, so she stole inside and quietly locked the door. But just as she was about to step into the light and demand his attention, he began removing his shirt.

Horrified, Maleen froze briefly in place. Part of her knew she should turn away to give him his privacy. But she couldn't look away. And it wasn't because of his defined shoulder blades or the cut of his torso. She had seen him swimming once without a shirt, when she'd escaped Emille at age fourteen and had gone looking for him at some grand event. He'd been out with the other boys, swimming in only their trousers. She'd thought him incredibly agreeable even at such a young age. He was twice now what he had been then, muscles rippling down his back and through his shoulders and neck. The muscles weren't what made her stare, though.

Where his left arm had been, from the elbow down, there was nothing. Nothing but a stump with criss-crossing scars. Scars also cut across his back in jagged, uneven lines. Healed as the skin seemed to be, it still gathered and puckered angrily across his back.

The last seven years had left their mark on him as well.

Maleen's sense returned to her somewhat as he turned in her direction, and once again, she was forced to hide, kneeling behind a large, overstuffed chair next to a stack of very old books.

He sat down at the writing desk and stared blankly at the wall of books behind her. She felt her heart squeeze as she watched him. When they had been young, she had always loved looking into his eyes. They were green, like a spring day. She'd always felt a rush of warmth when they had landed on her, and his smile had been like sunbeams reaching out to draw her in. But now as he stared unseeing at the wall, they were no longer warm or inviting. They were hard and cold, and looking at them gave her the sudden urge to shiver. If she had not seen him before and heard his name announced, she would never have recognized the man who had been her beloved. And suddenly, she felt as though that man had died.

Shaking his head slightly, he seemed to recover from his thoughtful stupor and removed a small jar from one of its drawers. Then he dipped his hand inside, and when he pulled his fingers out again, they were covered in a white salve. He began to rub the salve on the end of his elbow, where his arm had been, grimacing several times as he did.

Maleen should speak. She finally had him alone where no one else could hear. She should open her mouth and demand to know why he had left her in that tower. She should make him tell her why he'd made open war upon her people.

Why he'd broken his promise.

But her throat was suddenly thick, and her eyes were blurring once again. Instead, she found herself with the foolish desire to run to him and throw her arms around his neck and trace the angry wounds with her fingers. Lost in her warring duties and desires, she nearly screamed when a knock sounded on the door behind her.

"Your Highness?" a muffled voice called.

"Hold on," he called back. From her position, she could see Rob sigh and pull his shirt back on. He buttoned it expertly with one hand as he walked slowly back toward the door. When he got to it, he stared for a moment at the lock, and she cringed as she realized he hadn't locked the door behind him. Instead of turning and looking for the source of the locked door, however, he simply shook his head and opened it. "Yes?"

"Princess Priscilla's reply has just arrived!" the man who had walked with him earlier said now in a hushed voice.

"And?"

"She has agreed to marry you. Her entourage will be here in no less than a fortnight."

CHAPTER 16
GOING TO THE BALL

Maleen didn't get a chance to seek Rob again for another two weeks. She'd been unable to follow him to his next destination that night because the messenger who had come to deliver the news of his betrothal insisted on staying with him in the library, and Maleen had been forced to cower behind the chair until they left together.

She could have followed them, she supposed afterward. But she'd lacked the determination. The indignation at all she'd suffered at his hands seemed to have melted as she tried to understand all she had just seen and learned.

Rob had not only left her behind, but he was now getting married. And his intended was not her.

The next two weeks were so busy that she didn't have time to sneak away. Someone was always ordering her around, it seemed, every moment of the day. And when she was finally able to go to bed, the scullery maids were even watched there by one of the kitchen matrons to make sure they didn't while away the time by gossiping as some liked to do. The approaching princess's entourage had Michail in a flurry, and he couldn't have the kitchen clean enough or stocked enough no matter how hard the staff worked.

Maleen would have been greatly annoyed by this before her late night escapade, but now she felt somehow disconnected, as though the only thing that grounded her in the reality of her life was how exhausted she was every night when she finally lay down on her cot. All she could think about was how cold Rob's eyes had become, and how now they would be for someone else.

For Princess Priscilla. That was another mystery Maleen pondered, though not always on purpose. It was just so strange, though. As a child, she may not have been taught the art of carrying a stack of dishes, but she had been made to memorize the names and family trees of every major royal family in the western realm. And there had never, not even as a baby, been a Princess Priscilla. That she was from the eastern or southern realms was possible, of course, but Priscilla was not an eastern or southern name.

There was, however, a *Lady* Priscilla. In fact, she'd been the same Lady Priscilla who had turned Rob's head when he was fifteen. But if they were truly one and the same, how had she gone from the daughter of a duke to the child of a king?

Well, Maleen thought, scrubbing a sticky plate particularly hard, if she was the one Rob had truly chosen to ally himself with, he deserved every ounce of misery he was marrying into. Because she had been one of the most conniving, scheming girls Maleen had ever met. She'd had a way of turning the head of nearly every boy she passed, and it hadn't simply been because she was lovely. She'd always had a way about her...not simpering, exactly. More that she knew what *would* turn a man's head. Flashing a dimple shyly with one while delving into higher conversation with another. She hadn't excelled at knowing exactly how to gain each man's particular attention. She'd mastered it.

A small voice in her head reminded Maleen that he was probably being pressured into such a marriage by his father or his advisers, as alliances between royal families were common. But Maleen decided she didn't care. Anyone stupid enough to marry Priscilla, no matter what resources she might come with, deserved everything he got.

The day of the mysterious princess's arrival dawned cold and rainy. But the chamber pot still had to be cleaned, and no matter how hard Maleen tried to stay under the cover of the awning outside as she cleaned the pot, she was soaked by the time she was finished. Once inside, she bent at one of the buckets of fresh cleaning water to scrub her hands, but as she bent, she slipped on the water from her own dripping hem. The bucket and soap suds went flying.

The entire kitchen was silent for a moment as everyone stared. Maleen looked up to see the walls, the floor, and even a few of the servants dripping with soap. Her hip hurt from where she had fallen against the stone floor, and her hands stung, but this was nothing compared to the heat that rose to her cheeks when Michail's voice rang out.

"What has happened? Why is everyone—" He rounded a table and laid eyes on Maleen. Her tongue seemed stuck to the roof of her mouth as she gingerly pushed herself up off the floor.

After a long moment of staring, he sighed and rubbed his eyes with his hands.

This was it. Maleen had lost her chance. She was going to be kicked out of the kitchen and the palace as a whole. She'd never get to speak to—

"Come with me," Michail said in a resigned voice, nodding at the stairs. The rest of the servants gaped as she hesitantly obeyed. Once they were in the relative privacy of the stairs, he clasped his hands in front of him and fixed his gaze on her, which she did her best to avoid. "You were trained as a lady's maid, were you not?"

Not trusting her voice, Maleen nodded.

"I thought so. You see, it was a good thing I was coming to get you because as of now, you have a new duty in the castle."

His voice was so strangely gentle that she dared to peek up at him. A new duty?

"Princess Priscilla is arriving this morning, and she has already requested a new lady's maid from our own staff, someone who will be able to get her whatever she wishes for."

Maleen stared. Was she hearing this correctly?

"So," he continued, "I have told Madame Amara that you would be perfect for such a position." He raised an eyebrow at her sopping skirt and the puddle that was growing beneath her. "I will take you to her now, and she will have you properly cleaned and attired in time for the princess's arrival this afternoon. Yes?"

Maleen could only nod and squeak her thanks as he motioned for her to follow him again. But inside, her mind was racing as though it were a thoroughbred colt. Lady's maid to Priscilla? If she truly was the Priscilla that Maleen was thinking of, this could be very bad. Rob may not recognize her, but she had a very strong feeling that Priscilla would.

Madame Amara was not appreciative of Michail's offering.

"She's hardly fit to stand," she said, glaring at him over the rims of her spectacles. "She'll surely faint before the day is over. I hear Princess Priscilla is quite particular."

"She's been working almost two months in my kitchens," Michail said, seeming unfazed by the older woman's disapproval. "Never fainted once."

"Hm." Madame Amara sniffed and looked back at Maleen. "Since I have precious other options, I suppose you'll have to do. Tell me, are you familiar with how to prepare a royal toilette?"

Maleen nodded. At least, she knew what one would require. And if this castle was so great as she assumed, surely there would be other servants to assist with the more difficult parts, such as the princess's hair and drawing water for baths and such. At least, she hoped.

But those became the least of her concerns as Madame Amara stripped her down and made her wash, then redressed her as a proper lady's maid. For Maleen was far more concerned about what she would do when she finally came face-to-face with Priscilla than what she might do with the other woman's hair. Ought she run now? She wasn't contractually obligated to be here. If she just asked for the chance to relieve herself, she could make her way back down to the street and–

"You might be fit to be seen with a week or two more scrubbings." Madame Amara interrupted Maleen's thoughts. She pinched her lips as she gave Maleen one final inspection. "But I suppose you'll do. You're not half-bad looking when you're clean and brushed."

Even if she had decided to make a run for it, Maleen never had a chance. For she was immediately led to the front of the palace, where she was put in line with about two dozen other servants. A few gave her curious sidelong glances, as they had been the ones she'd served tea and breakfast to only the day before. But their attention was demanded by the sound of carriage wheels on cobblestones outside.

Maleen bowed her head as all of the other servants were doing, but she kept it high enough to watch the scene that unfolded on the front steps.

Rob had been standing outside the open doors, but now he made his way to the carriage. The footman had jumped down and was pulling down the little foldable step when Rob jerked his chin. The footman looked up in surprise but skittered out of the way just in time as Rob opened the carriage door. Maleen couldn't help feeling annoyed at the prince as she remembered the warnings of Phoebe and her sister.

Has he really changed so much?

She could also see now why she'd missed the fact that he only had one arm. What was left of his arm filled the top of the sleeve enough that if one was far away, he looked whole. But closer up, she could see that the end of his left sleeve was tucked into the front of his coat, as if his hand was cold and he was warming it there. Once the carriage door opened, he held his good hand out and bowed low before the young woman standing there.

Maleen's breath caught in her throat. The woman who emerged might have been Lady Priscilla. But it was impossible to tell because the woman who took Rob's hand and stepped daintily out of the carriage was wearing a thin pink veil over her face. The veil was tight enough to make out the shape of a nose and cheeks, but nothing more.

From the slight shifting around her, Maleen sensed the other servants found this odd, too.

She was too far away to hear exact words, but Rob said something, and the new princess laughed. He led her inside, down the center of the rows of waiting servants, and they continued on through the entrance.

Maleen felt another stab of jealousy. She knew better than to lift her head higher than she needed to see. Servants, she had learned the hard way, were not to look their masters in the eye. This was strange, as she remembered no such rule in her own palace. Even her uncle, mad stickler as he had been, had never rebuked a servant for looking at him. Maleen wondered now if this had always been the case here in this castle, or if it was new, just like Rob's temper.

The entry hall was grand, and Maleen wished she could see it in all its majesty. But not now. Now, she was watching the man she had loved walk ahead of her with another woman on his arm.

Something sharp jabbed her in the shoulder blade, and Maleen glanced back to see another servant scowling at her. She'd been caught. Scowling back, she lowered her head slightly.

"...like a tour?" Rob was asking.

"I would love one," Princess Priscilla was saying, "but I'm quite fatigued after my journey. Do you think I might be shown to my room so I can refresh before supper?"

Rob didn't turn, but he snapped his fingers loudly. Seconds passed before Maleen realized he was summoning her. Indignation burned with embarrassment as she hurried to their sides. She should do it now, raise her head and look directly into his haughty eyes, demanding the attention that was hers by right.

And she might have done it if she'd believed he would listen. But they were in a public place, and something told her that the new Rob wouldn't take kindly to being challenged in front of his court. She would have to find a way to talk to him privately. Well, if serving Her Royal Highness hand and foot would earn Maleen that chance, then she would do it.

"Take Her Highness to her chambers," Rob said. "Help her prepare for supper with my parents."

Maleen nodded and curtsied before gesturing toward the stairs on the left, keeping her face down so neither would see. "This way, Your Highness."

Princess Priscilla also curtsied to Rob before following Maleen. They walked in silence all the way to the princess's chambers, but Maleen's heart thumped wildly the whole way. Was the woman beneath the veil really Lady Priscilla? If so, would she recognize Maleen? And if she did, what would Maleen do?

Maleen nearly sighed in relief when they finally reached the large, ornate doors of the princess's chambers. Several other of the lady's maids joined them. That was strange. If she had her own maids, why would she ask for another?

"If you'll make yourself comfortable here," Maleen said in her most subservient voice, "I'll call for the servants to draw the bath."

"No, not yet, thank you. I would like you to come here instead. Lock the door first, though."

Maleen froze briefly before slowly obeying. Two of the princess's guards stationed themselves just inside the door, but the princess didn't seem to mind. So she locked the door and came to stand before the princess, who was standing with her finger on her chin, watching Maleen thoughtfully.

"You wanted me, Your Highness?" Maleen whispered, trying to pitch her voice higher than usual.

But the princess didn't answer her. Instead, she walked slowly around Maleen in a full circle before coming to stand in front of her again. "I asked that they send me a royal servant because I need a particular service granted me. And my own maids are too frightened to try again."

Maleen went perfectly still. *To try what?*

"And since I'm not a cruel person, I've decided to let them be. Which means you shall now be in my employ." It was strange. The princess's voice was polite and cordial, as if she weren't discussing something that sounded...horrible.

"You're too thin," she continued. "But you're about my height, at least. So that's good. And your face shape..." She gently tilted Maleen's face up. Then she drew back as though Maleen had bitten her. Her calm tone was gone when she spoke again. "You're...Maleen!"

Maleen should run. There would be another way to talk to the prince. There had to be. One that didn't involve playing guessing games with a princess. But before she could make her

feet move, which suddenly felt as though they'd rooted themselves to the floor, the princess began unwrapping the veil from
her face.

This time, it was Maleen who fell back a step. "Oh!" she
whispered.

Maleen's guess had been right. For she was staring at Lady
Priscilla. Or at least, there were traces of the Lady Priscilla she
had known. For though they were close in age, Lady Prsiscilla
having been two years older than her, the youthful, flawless
features Maleen remembered were gone. Instead, Priscilla
looked as though she'd aged thirty-seven years instead of
seven. Lines edged her eyes and mouth, and she looked
exhausted, as there were discolored, sagging bags beneath her
eyes. Even more than her signs of aging, however, was the dull-
ness of her eyes. Eyes that had once sparkled were now...Maleen
didn't know how to describe them.

"We've both changed, haven't we?" Priscilla smiled wryly.
"And not either for the better, I'm afraid. No, I won't dance
around the changes my actions have wrought. To do so would
be stupid. I won't regret them either." She went to the bed and
sat down on it. "I do find myself immensely curious as to how
you came to be in your position, though." She patted the bed
beside her. "And, of course, I'll do the polite thing, and after you
tell me your story, I'll tell you mine."

Maleen stared at her. This was absurd. But did she really
have a choice? She wouldn't sit beside the woman. But she did
come to stand beside her. They stared at one another in silence
for several long moments.

"Very well, I'll tell you my story first," Priscilla finally said.
"Perhaps that will help you share yours." She smiled, and a hint

of the dimples she'd once charmed boys with showed. "Let's see, the last time we saw one another, I was…nineteen. And you were a princess, and my father was a duke." She paused. "Did you know my father was a twin?"

Maleen shook her head.

"No, I thought not. It wasn't well known even among our own people. Well, he was, but he was second born. Meaning my uncle was king because he was born six minutes before my father. My father kept quiet about it, but it always irked him that a mere six minutes separated him from the crown. He never let on, of course. That would have been beneath him. But as the years passed, and my uncle never sired a child, my father began to scheme. There had to be, he said, a way to secure my place on the throne."

"Wouldn't…" Maleen frowned. "Wouldn't it pass on to your father if your uncle died first?"

"It would." Priscilla nodded. "Unless my uncle and aunt adopted an heir, which they had begun to speak of incessantly. My father was desperate that I not be denied the throne the way he had been, especially now that I was of age. So he started to search."

"Search for what?" In spite of her strange predicament, Maleen couldn't help feeling relief at the momentary sensation of having a conversation with an equal, even if her sense screamed at her that this was a bad idea.

"A way to secure my place on the throne. Or some sort of throne, at least. Well, several years after he began searching, he learned of a magician or wizard or some sort of mage who had once turned his entire family into wolf shifters. They lived deep in a forest in my own country, and only recently were they freed–Anyhow, that is neither here nor there. What's important is that he learned that the ancient man had manipulated great power. And my father believed that if I could secretly utilize some of these powers, I might become indispensable to my uncle."

Maleen couldn't help reflecting on how different their positions were...and yet how similar. Only, her father had been the one to inherit the throne. But she had still wound up a servant. Whereas, somehow, Priscilla had managed to become a princess.

"Did you wish to pursue the arts of power?" Maleen asked uncomfortably. Such arts were forbidden in the western realm. To use power that wasn't yours by right, she'd heard Queen Isa say once, was toying with the Maker's wrath. But she did not think it wise to express such qualms at this moment, so she kept her thoughts to herself.

"At first, I was hesitant," Priscilla replied. "But when I met my teacher, a woman of power my father had tracked down and hired, I realized what kinds of things I could do for people. With her instruction and the information I read about in other sources, such as the book that was taken from the wolf people, I've begun to piece together a way to link different kinds of power." She looked down at herself and held up her arms. "Obviously, one must pay a price for such gifts. I didn't realize they would have such a heavy cost, perhaps, but..." She shook her head. "I don't regret it even now." And from the look of it, she was telling the truth. Even in her altered state, she seemed completely serene.

Maleen shifted. "I thought you said the magician was dead."

"Oh, he was," Priscilla said, smoothing her skirts. "But there are others, you see, who also know how to manage such... strengths. The kind that aren't acquired naturally."

"So how did you become princess, then?" Maleen asked.

"Well, when he was sure I was ready, my father decided it would be unlikely that my uncle would help me as long as he was alive. So my father...disappeared."

Maleen sat upright. "He *died*?"

"No. I don't think so, at least. I like to think he's still alive." A flash of discomfort played on Priscilla's face for a moment before it smoothed over again. "But I don't know. The main point was that he wanted my uncle to believe that I needed to be cared for. So not long after your war broke out, my father arranged for his disappearance, leaving in his will that, should something happen to him, his dearest wish was that my uncle would take me in and protect me as his own." She shrugged. "In short, it worked. I became crown princess and am now prepared to help my people in whatever way they need." Her smile widened. "In this particular instance, by uniting two kingdoms and securing possibilities we've never dreamed of before." Her voice was low and reverent.

Maleen swallowed, her heart speeding in her chest as she asked the question she dreaded most. "And...what do you need me for that your ladies-in-waiting won't do?"

"Yes, I knew we'd come back around to that." She took a deep breath and folded her hands in her lap. "Obviously, my appearance as it is now is rather altered. The effects of my new... abilities were rather immediate, and before my father left, we agreed that I couldn't be seen this way. At least, not until people became more acquainted with my new gifts. So my father recruited the daughters of his most trusted servants and gave them to me for my use."

Maleen swallowed. Her *use*. It already sounded inhuman.

"While I was studying, I learned how to make things... appear differently than they really are. Through a lot of trial and error, I've even discovered how to combine the powers, that of my teacher and that from the wolf-wizard book in the forest, for instance. Which means I've been able to alter—briefly, mind you—the appearance of a chosen substitute. For short amounts of time, I can have another act in my place, and no one but us knows the difference."

Was she saying what Maleen *thought* she was saying? Maleen swallowed hard. "So you...you make them look like you?"

Priscilla nodded once. "Precisely."

"But...didn't their mannerisms give it away, though?"

"See, that is the genius of it all!" Priscilla stood and walked to the vanity, where her personal things had already been unpacked. She searched for a moment before lifting a small, ornately carved pale pink jar and opened it. Inside was a black salve that reflected the light of the room. Maleen felt her muscles seize as soon as the lid was open, and she stumbled backward as Priscilla held it out to her. Stomach threatening to lose its breakfast, Maleen drew back. Whatever was in that jar was dangerous. She could feel it in every fiber of her body.

"What is that?" she asked, pressing her back up against the wall. "Is it..." She couldn't get herself to utter the word.

"Sortheleige? Yes, but not in its most potent form. I've mixed it with a fair number of herbs and aloes and such. But it is the main source of all my gifts."

Maleen stared at her. "You mean changing people's appearances?"

Priscilla just smiled. "You'll see. What we need to discuss now is how you're going to help me."

"I respectfully decline," Maleen said, glaring at the pink jar.

"Unfortunately," Priscilla said, her voice still cheerful, "I don't think that's going to be a choice you can make."

"And why not?"

"Because this salve doesn't just change your appearance." Priscilla's smile grew. "Have you ever seen a marionette show?"

Maleen didn't dignify her with an answer, but Priscilla continued on patiently as if she had. "While the salve is in effect, I will have control over your body. You can see now why my servants don't wish to play this game anymore. Which is perfectly acceptable, considering how many times they've played it for me." Her eyes briefly lost their dull look and gleamed. "At first, I wasn't sure this was going to work, but I really think it's best this way. A welcome surprise, if you will." She put the lid back on the jar and laid it down again. "I honestly don't care how you've ended up in my lap, but you know Roburts better than almost anyone, myself included. This marriage is entirely political, but having you here means you'll be able to interpret his words and reactions for me better than I would be able to myself."

"If you can really control people against their will, I'm not sure why you need me," Maleen snapped. "Can't you just... change your own appearance? Or tell him what to do without my help?"

"Good questions, for sure. To put it bluntly, while I can manipulate people somewhat, such as what I'm about to do to you, the level of power I will need to exercise over Roburts and his family is of a... particularly intimate kind, one that can only be performed from within the confines of marriage."

"Which means," Maleen tried to press her shaking hands against her sides, "you want to use me to take control of him."

"A simplified explanation, but yes."

"Why can't you simply alter your own appearance?"

Priscilla sighed. "Unfortunately, I'm not able to juggle too much magic at once. Not yet. But if you're bearing the weight of the magic by wearing the disguise, I am left free enough to do as I need while maintaining my focus on what's going on with you."

"No." Maleen shook her head, pressing herself back into the wall. "I won't do it."

"I'm afraid, love, that you have no choice." Priscilla held up her right hand, which was covered in both wrinkles and the black salve. She darted forward and grabbed Maleen's wrist. Maleen twisted away quickly, but some of the salve was already smudged on the back of her hand. Priscilla smiled and raised her hand up high. Horrified, Maleen watched as her own right hand was lifted into the air and made a little flourish that perfectly matched Priscilla's. The hand itself had thickened slightly and sprouted two rings that matched the ones Priscilla wore. Maleen's fingers were slightly longer than usual, too. Unlike Priscilla, however, this hand was young and smooth, not wrinkled as Priscilla's real hand was.

"I can now feel everything you do. It's as if your hand is mine. And in return, your hand will do everything I want it to."

"I'll jump out that window before I allow you to use me like this," Maleen said as she tried to pull her arm down.

"I'm afraid you won't be able to help it." Priscilla snapped her fingers, which meant Maleen snapped her fingers as well. In response, several manservants appeared from the shadows and came forward. Maleen tried to scream as they cornered her and held her down. But one pinched her nose and covered her mouth until she was forced to gasp for air. As soon as the hand left her mouth, and Maleen was gulping down breath, Priscilla gently traced her fingers, once again covered in the black salve, across Maleen's lips. Maleen tried again to scream when they let go of her nose, but instead of screaming, her smile mirrored Priscilla's.

"Instead of fighting me, you should be glad," Maleen heard herself say as Priscilla bent to paint the salve across Maleen's feet. "Tonight, I'm sending you to a ball."

CHAPTER 17
MALEEN

Rob stared blankly ahead as his valet prepared his coat, not seeing the wall before him. On that wall hung a larger-than-life portrait of himself, one his mother had insisted on commissioning to add to the family hall someday. The day it had been finished and presented to him had embarrassed him more than he could say. Having a picture of his own person that was at least as tall as he was...and possibly taller, felt like something an insecure royal would have done in order to accentuate his importance.

But he didn't care now. He hadn't cared in a long time, just as he didn't care what color his coat was or what buttons had been used or even how his hair was cut. What he did care about was undoing all the damage he had inflicted upon his father and his people. And if getting married to Priscilla was part of that, then so be it.

"What do you think, Your Highness?" his white-haired valet asked, standing back to examine his work.

Rob straightened and actually looked at himself in the full-length mirror that had been placed beside him. After a cursory glance, he nodded curtly, but not without brushing his fingers over the empty sleeve that had been sewn into the inside of his coat. A small price to pay for his folly.

A ghost of shame rebuked him for not thanking the old valet for his hard work, but Rob had learned to ignore that voice long ago. Words were hard. He often felt with his words as though a pauper must feel with his money, beginning the day with little, only to run out before the day was done.

His new silences worried his mother. She'd mentioned it to him and his father many times, but nothing was to be done for it. How did one conjure something that wasn't there?

"Where is the princess?" he asked as he strode toward the bedroom door.

"She's been brought to meet you at the top of the stairs," Gregory, his personal servant, told him as he opened the door. "Just a warning, I'm told she's feeling a bit faint after today's ride. She nearly swooned before she'd made it out the door of her own chambers."

Rob's frown deepened. "As long as she can remain upright for one evening, I shall be happy."

Gregory was too well trained to utter a sarcastic comment, but he'd served Rob long enough that the slight rise of his eyebrows told his master exactly what he was thinking. Nothing would make Rob happy, and they both knew it.

Rob caught sight of his betrothed when he turned the last corner and made his way down the hall. She stood waiting opposite him, and he was reminded of why he'd been infatuated with her, brief as it had been, as a young man. Even before she was a princess, back when she had been Lady Priscilla, she'd carried herself with a sort of confidence that could make the plainest of women turn a man's head.

Plain, however, she was not then, nor was she now, he noted, relieved that she'd not chosen to wear the veil to their engagement feast. Odd as her veil had been that afternoon, she had been traveling all day, and it wasn't unthinkable that she would wish to avoid looking weary and worn to her future subjects.

Tonight, her blond hair was piled on her head with little ringlets artfully escaping down her cheeks and neck. When he drew near, she turned to him and tilted her head in that familiar, coquettish manner that had first attracted his attention as a boy. Her cheeks dimpled as he bowed and kissed her fingers.

"It's been a long time, my lord," she said. "I apologize for my quick escape this afternoon. I was quite fatigued after such a long journey."

His first instinct was to simply nod and hold his arm out, but as she placed her arm on his, he was reminded that he was about to take this woman as his wife. His store of words was short, but then, it always was. He might as well attempt to make an effort.

"There is nothing to apologize for. I've been to Vaksam once, and the journey was tediously long." Largely because he had spent the first part of the journey begging and pleading for his father to invite Maleen to come along. He'd been thirteen back then, and she'd been eleven. But his father had been forced to explain to him the kind of strictures his little friend was subject to, and that even if they did stop along the way to ask, he knew for a fact that her uncle would say no.

Rob had spent the remainder of their journey contemplating ways to depose her uncle but had only gotten himself a headache by the time they'd reached Vaksam's castle.

What he wouldn't give to be that thirteen-year-old boy with a headache now. He might have been in pain. But at least he'd had hope.

Thankfully, conversation with Priscilla was not required now that they'd reached the stairs and the court was watching them closely as they descended.

She really was beautiful. She seemed to have blossomed in their time apart, and the six years since he'd seen her last had been kind to her. She had well-defined curves and she walked as though she knew it.

It was all playing out as his father had planned. And yet as they descended the stairs to roaring applause, he couldn't help but notice that something felt...off. The way she tilted her head now, for instance. Not in that coquettish way, but rather, as though she were curious. He couldn't ever remember seeing Priscilla do that. As if hearing his thoughts, her head snapped up, and she grimaced slightly as if doing so had hurt her.

His father and mother, who had been waiting at the bottom of the stairs, walked forward to meet them.

"My dear," his father said, reaching out with both hands for Priscilla's. "I am so grateful to you for taking such a long trip as this, not only to visit but to begin your new journey in life."

"Indeed," Rob's mother said with a nod. "It is difficult to start anew so far from home. And it's a shame your uncle wasn't feeling well enough to come."

According to Priscilla's last correspondence, just before she had arrived, her uncle had been suffering from gout and had been unable to make the journey. An unfortunate occurrence, but not unheard of for the older monarchs, particularly those who partook in far too much wine.

"I am honored," Priscilla said, dipping into a low curtsey. So low, in fact, that she fell over. The crowd gasped, and Rob, along with half the court, was at her side in an instant. But Priscilla just waved away their worry and dusted herself off, laughing as she allowed Rob to pull her to her feet. "I apologize. I've grown taller recently, and it's made me a bit awkward."

This time, it wasn't only Rob who frowned in confusion. He saw his parents exchange a glance as well. Rob had never known exactly how tall Priscilla was, of course, and asking would have been impertinent. But he was certain she was the same height she had been the last time they'd seen one another. That had been six years ago, however, so he could be wrong.

"Shall we make our way to supper?" the king asked, gesturing to the hall at their left. Everyone agreed and made way for the king and queen and then Rob and Priscilla. Priscilla brightly thanked Rob again for his help but continued to grimace slightly as they walked.

As soon as they made their way into the banquet hall, however, her mouth fell into a little O, and Rob, in spite of himself, was gratified. His home was his favorite place in the world. The palace's interior, with its eggshell tinted stone arches and matching floors, seemed to glow, even in indirect light. Ridged columns rose up around them, supporting higher arches between. The throne room wasn't nearly as tall as Maleen's had been. In fact, it had the lowest ceiling of any other grand palace or castle he'd toured. But the fine detail of the tiled mosaics made the room shimmer, and the carvings that had been chiseled out of the stone walls gave the place a distinctly ancient feel, as if the walls themselves were alive with days gone by.

"Do you like it?" he asked as she continued to stare around in wonder. At the sound of his voice, however, she startled slightly and the wonder disappeared.

"Oh, yes. Just as I remember." She smiled diplomatically, but Rob found himself wishing to frown instead. Something about her manner was...incongruous. The awe he'd just seen in her face was at odds with her careless words.

They were seated at the center of the long table which had been prepared for them. She stumbled slightly as she sat, once again seeming unaware of the length of her legs. Thankfully, she fell right into the seat, but when she wasn't looking, Rob's mother sent him a look Rob couldn't decipher.

Supper was less eventful. No one fell out of any chairs, but after a while, Rob almost wished someone would. Anything to break the tedious tête-à-tête he was forced to keep up as

Priscilla unleashed upon his mother a stream of polite gossip about every royal they shared acquaintances with.

Finally, she excused herself to go powder her nose, and Rob couldn't have been more grateful. Even this relief was short-lived, however, as it dawned on him that this wasn't a torture he would be free from after this evening.

This was going to be for the rest of his life.

"Roburts, come here please."

Rob looked up to see his mother pursing her lips. She was gesturing for him to join her, so he stood and knelt between her chair and Priscilla's empty one.

"Are you well?" she asked softly.

Rob drew in a deep lungful of air. He was tempted to say no. To beg his mother to find some creative way to get out of the betrothal while avoiding yet another war. But even as the words rose to his lips, he recalled all too well the stench of blood on the fields, the countless bodies slain around him. His father had looked so young for his age before the war. Everyone had always commented on it. But now the gray had chased the black out of his once-dark curls and beard, and his face was heavily lined.

And it was all Rob's fault.

"Yes." Rob tried to meet his mother's eyes but couldn't. "Thank you for asking, though."

His mother didn't smile, just continued to watch him. Then after glancing around, she leaned forward and whispered, "Something is wrong with that girl."

Rob's head snapped up. "You think so?"

"I've known Priscilla since she was born." Her eyes narrowed. "Call it a hunch, but something foul is at play."

"What makes you say that?"

"The way she walks," the queen said, still frowning in the direction that Priscilla had gone. "And some of her expressions. They're hers...but they're not."

Rob rubbed his eyes. Fantastic. This marriage had been painstakingly researched, and the terms had been meticulously crafted in order to bring about trade agreements that would benefit both kingdoms. The last thing his father needed was for the future queen to be hiding something.

The princess returned shortly after. Her smile was bright, almost overly so, but as Rob studied her, he realized that his mother was right. She looked strangely...almost disheveled. Her hair no longer lay smoothly beneath its pins. Strands were sticking out in several places. The left shoulder of her dress lay slightly higher than the one on her right, and her eyes had the slightest hint of dark circles beneath them that hadn't been there before. And somehow—impossibly so—she looked...thinner?

"Is everything well?" he asked.

"Now, don't you look serious?" she laughed. "I apologize for the delay." She played with the food on her plate for a moment and then set her fork down. "As delicious as this is, I'm afraid rich food sometimes makes me slightly ill." She flashed another brilliant smile at him. "Shall we dance instead?"

Their betrothal dance wasn't supposed to take place until the hour chimed nine, but Rob simply nodded and stood to offer her his arm. Something was amiss, and he needed to find out what it was. It would probably be easier to discover her secrets if he allowed her to relax, thinking herself to have the upper hand.

Their first dance was quick, too lively for talk, and so was their second. But these moments weren't wasted, for Rob used the time to study her, taking note of her mannerisms, her gait, even her smiles and laughs.

His mother was right. There were moments, particularly when she was speaking, where she seemed her old self, saying all the right things and never missing a step. Everything about her was practiced. Almost perfect.

A wave of sadness hit him so hard he nearly miscounted his steps. As a young, stupid boy, her shine had drawn him like a moth to a flame. She was perfect then, too...or at least, had seemed close to it. And he'd had the adolescent need to touch that perfection and experience it for himself. But the shine had worn off fast, and he'd soon seen, or rather, Maleen had made him see, that Priscilla's perfection was all learned. There was no spark within her. Not like Maleen had.

Grief threatened to cripple him, and he couldn't dance another step. Instead, he turned, unable to even excuse himself, and began to walk away. It was possibly the rudest act a prince could offer his betrothed, but all of the breath had gone out of his chest, and Rob suddenly wanted nothing more than to be alone.

"Roburts?" Priscilla's voice came from behind him, and he could hear her footsteps chasing him. Closing his eyes, he willed his voice to work again. He would have to be cold and curt. He simply couldn't stomach this conversation right now. If he did, he would likely start yet another war. But when he turned to face her, she didn't give him a chance to speak.

"Tell me the truth," she said, speaking through gritted teeth. Her face was taut, and she looked as though she were in pain. "How long did it take you to forget her?"

He stared at her.

"Maleen," she said, her voice cracking. "How long did it take you to forget Maleen?"

Rob's mouth fell open as she put her hand in her hair and seemed to grab a handful before yanking it hard. Her mouth opened, but she whirled around and stormed away, leaving Rob gaping behind her.

CHAPTER 18
AGAIN

Maleen's body was racked with pain as she walked slowly back to the princess's quarters. It was the last place she wanted to go, but the princess was forcing her on, searing Maleen's body with needling pain every time she tried to disobey. Even slowing her pace the way she was doing now hurt, but Maleen's anger kept her from acting the complete puppet. Her head rang with the princess's ranting, but this only made her smile even as she gritted her teeth against the pain.

She hadn't known how strong the princess would be until she'd touched nearly every part of Maleen's body with smears of the black Sortheleige salve. Hands, arms, shoulders, legs, feet...even her neck and eyelids had been touched. It didn't completely cover her like paint, but there were smudges everywhere. And every part that was smudged with the salve had become Priscilla's to play with as Maleen helplessly obeyed.

As she walked now, Maleen had to own to herself that she wished she knew more about Sortheleige. Emille had tried to teach her about it when she was younger, and there had been a few books on it in the tower. She'd never studied it in earnest, however, and now regretted her inadequate knowledge quite painfully.

The little that she did know about the dark power was that it took a number of different forms. Power, the books had said, that was either stolen from the Maker's intended recipient, or power that was used inappropriately. Some of it came up from the depths in the oceans. Queen Arianna of the merfolk had the job of keeping that evil contained. Similarly, the Fortier family of Destin protected the western realm and even beyond from such dangers. King Everard, Queen Isabelle, and Prince Henri were some of the few known individuals who had the power to destroy the dark strength.

Unfortunately, none of them were here now, and Maleen knew very little else about the darkness that Priscilla was using against her.

When Priscilla had touched her with the coal-colored salve earlier that afternoon, Maleen had stared in horror at the mirror as her reflection had changed from her own into a duplicate of the woman beside her. Except Maleen's new reflection had exceeded that of its origin. Her hips had taken on alluring curves, and her chest had swollen amply until the dress Priscilla had forced her to wear looked as though it might burst. Her limp, yellow hair had taken on a luscious, silky shine, and her lips had grown into a pout.

"Perfect," Priscilla had said. Except, it hadn't been Priscilla who had said it. It had been Maleen in Priscilla's voice, and then her mouth had turned up into the dimpled beam she had hated so much as a child. Her own slightly upturned nose had been replaced by Priscilla's straight, thin one, and her eyes had changed from deep brown to blue.

Living in the tower back at home had always been difficult, but walking around the castle as Priscilla was even worse. Maleen not only had to face the man who had left her behind, but she was expected to spend all evening watching him woo another. And in what felt like a cruel twist from the Maker, she would have to live it over and over again until Priscilla tired of her or they were found out. Maleen couldn't have imagined another scenario more painful if she'd tried.

And yet...then had come the moment when Maleen had needed to cough. It was just before Rob had arrived to escort her to supper. She'd been despairing of her situation when the cough had escaped her quite by accident. That little cough, though harmless as it must have seemed to Priscilla, had proved to Maleen that her defeat wasn't final. If she could cough without Priscilla stopping her, then surely Maleen had to be able to do something else.

And so she had spent the evening fighting with Priscilla as the woman screamed in her head for her to listen. When Priscilla had forced Maleen to briefly excuse herself from the feast, giving Priscilla a chance to mentally shout her into submission, Maleen had suffered great physical pain, pain so strong she'd nearly collapsed in the empty room where she'd hidden. However their connection worked, Priscilla seemed to be able to induce physical pain at will, and had done so throughout the evening every time Maleen had attempted to defy her. And yet...Maleen had caught both Priscilla and Rob by surprise when his strange moment of weakness had come.

And it had been worth it.

Unfortunately, she knew Priscilla would make her pay for her ingenuity. She was incredibly aware of this as Priscilla's door opened and she was yanked in.

"You idiot!"

The moment the door closed behind her, Priscilla's open palm slammed into Maleen's temple. Maleen stumbled, but even as her skin burned where Priscilla's fingers and rings had left their marks, she smiled wryly at her old nemesis. This smile grew as she felt her own face return to her body. When she looked down at her hands and arms, she was relieved to see that all of the salve was gone as well.

"I thought you were supposed to be talented," she said, fighting not to sound breathless.

Priscilla only clenched her fists, and Maleen was knocked to her knees as sharp, invisible knives seemed to stab at her calves.

"*I* combined the power of Fae and ancient wizard!" Priscilla hissed. "*I* taught myself what even that old witch wouldn't teach me. I read a *book* and gained power from mere paper! So don't act as though you're very clever because you're not." She kneed Maleen in the shoulder as she walked past Maleen to her vanity. "You are only alive now because I have use of you still."

When she spoke again a moment later, she still didn't look at Maleen, but her voice was more tempered. "I could rant and rave at you about how you've nearly ruined everything, but I won't. The fact that he's the one who left you during the dance is good. It will keep his parents apologizing and put us in a better position to negotiate." She turned around. "What I *will* say is that if you defy me again, I'll put you through more pain than you could have ever imagined possible."

She squeezed one salve-stained fist tightly again, and Maleen couldn't help letting out a whimper as her own hands felt like they might go up in flames. When the near blinding pain had passed, Priscilla spoke again, quietly this time.

"If you do this right from here on out, I will need to attend fewer events, which means I will need to use you less." She gave Maleen a saccharine smile. "I may even plead sick with a headache one evening." Her smile disappeared. "But try your tricks one more time, and I'll make sure you never walk again when I'm through with you."

CHAPTER 19
GROW

Maleen had been provided a small room off of Priscilla's for her own, but Priscilla wouldn't hear of her sleeping there.

"Private sleeping quarters are a privilege," she told Maleen as she climbed into bed that evening. "You may sleep on the couch there."

Maleen just barely restrained herself from sticking her tongue out at her mistress as the horrible woman fell asleep. Making a face at Priscilla would have felt wonderful and childish, but the price wouldn't be worth it. Priscilla was on to her now. If she wished to disobey, she would have to choose her battles carefully. Picking small, fruitless fights would gain her less than wise warfare.

Maleen kept herself awake for a long time after Priscilla's quiet snores began, searching for a way to escape and talk to Rob as herself, but it was no use. There were guards at the corners of the room, nearly invisible except for the gleam of armor in the low moonlight that came in through the balcony window. Their constant presence didn't seem to bother Priscilla, which would make sense if she took them everywhere, but they made Maleen particularly uneasy. Even when she'd been a small child with an obsessive uncle, she'd never been so closely observed at all times.

But the couch, which she was loath to admit, was worlds more comfortable than the cot on which she'd been sleeping with the other scullery maids, and eventually, Maleen could stay awake no longer.

The next morning, she was awakened by a blinding light as the curtains, which had been pulled shut most of the way the night before, were thrown open by the princess herself.

"Time to get up," she said in a sing-song voice, as though she were fond of Maleen. "I've had an invitation to go riding this morning with Rob, and you can't be late." She was already rummaging around in her wardrobe, her maids at her sides. She tossed a few dresses on the floor before pulling out a violet gown trimmed with white and black spotted fur along the collar. "Yes, I think this will do nicely." Then she held the gown out to Maleen.

Maleen considered throwing the gown on the floor and stomping on it. Doing so would have been morbidly entertaining. But as she had the night before, she bit her tongue and took the dress instead. If Priscilla wanted a docile version of herself to manipulate, she would get it.

Right up until Maleen decided otherwise.

Because the same determination that had gotten her through seven years of near isolation was well-practiced, and Maleen knew without a doubt that whatever mess Rob had become, thanks to the war, neither he nor his people deserved Priscilla.

Once she was painted up with the salve and dressed in Priscilla's clothes, she was shoved out the door, and none too soon because Rob appeared not half a minute later.

"Good. You're ready. Let's go."

Against her will, Maleen felt an irksome girlish giddiness

bubble up inside of her as she took his arm. *This isn't you he's escorting,* she scolded herself. *It's Priscilla. You're only here because you were stupid and were in the wrong place at the wrong time.* And yet Maleen soaked up every moment.

They didn't speak again until they were both in the carriage. But instead of sitting on the cushioned bench next to her, as she had expected, he sat across from her and stared out the window, seeming to forget she was there at all.

Priscilla seemed intent on studying him because she found herself studying him every time he looked away. Maleen grieved inwardly at how cold and hard his eyes had become. There was no light in them. Not anymore, at least. At one time, Rob had seemed like his own sun, one she'd warmed herself in whenever she'd had the chance. But now, he looked nearly as angry as her uncle used to, and that hurt her more than she could fully express.

"What do you think of it?"

Maleen gave a little start, as it seemed Priscilla had been lost in thought as well. "Excuse me?" She felt Priscilla stutter.

"My arm," he said, beginning to unbutton the sleeve. "You were staring at it."

Was she? Maleen cleared her throat. "I'm sorry," Priscilla said with her mouth. "I was in a daze. I didn't even realize where I was looking."

"You should look nevertheless," he continued in the same, hard voice. "If you're going to live with it for the rest of our lives, you ought to know what you're getting into."

"Oh no!" Maleen felt herself shying away as she threw hands up in front of her face. "I ask you, please. Not yet! I can't stand the sight of mangled flesh!"

Shame at the words she was uttering made her face hot. They weren't hers, but she had to suffer them all the same. If Rob's face had been cool and unreadable before, now it might as well have been carved from granite.

"I see," he said, buttoning up his shirt once more. He paused. "Then I suppose you'll be desiring separate rooms on all occasions then."

As mortified as Maleen was at the words that had just come from her mouth, and as thankful as she was that it was her enemy's face she was wearing, she couldn't help herself. No, this tall, moody man no longer looked like her Rob. In fact, there seemed very little of that person left at all. But this grown-up Rob...the one who was angry with Priscilla...was undeniably alluring. And suddenly, Maleen knew she wanted to get to know him more. She hoped stupidly that this would be a long ride. Because she might never have a chance like this again.

A horrible lapse in judgment, if she was honest with herself. But she wanted it nonetheless.

They were now traveling at the edge of town and heading out into the country, close to the orange orchards Maleen had seen from a distance when she'd first entered the city. A long, stony silence stretched between them as the carriage rolled over the cobblestones.

"I'm sorry," Priscilla finally said. "I don't mean to be rude. I just..." She sighed deeply. "I'm afraid I'm not...not practiced at seeing the effects of war. And after my father died, my resistance to it grew."

"That is understandable," Rob said slowly. Then he fixed his green eyes on her. "But you do need to understand that my kingdom has been at war. And there are many of our subjects who will not be able to conceal their injuries as neatly as I have been privileged to do."

"I understand that," Priscilla said, looking demurely down at her hands. "And I do hope to do better in the future." She widened her eyes and looked up at him again. "I'm sorry."

After a long moment of study, his gaze softened slightly,

and Maleen had to keep herself from ruining her rebellious plans with a gag.

Their conversation thawed after this, and much to Maleen's annoyance, their conversation was decently...pleasant, if she was honest. Priscilla was very good at using the kinds of tactics Maleen had been taught by her uncle for learning about one's political opponent, and her grace and education made Priscilla nearly impossible for Rob to resist.

Really, what red-blooded man could resist such perfection? Priscilla was the very niece Uncle Perseus had wished for, as conniving and careful as he was. Instead, he had inherited Maleen.

Maleen waited for a lull in the conversation, a time she knew Priscilla wouldn't be expecting an uprising. Oh, she was sure she would pay for it later. Her face still smarted where Priscilla had slapped her the night before. But it would be worth it. She could do it for his people. And hers.

And him.

"Can we stop here?" she asked suddenly as they passed a well. "I'd quite like a drink."

Rob stared at her as though she'd just sprouted twigs. "You...you want a drink here?" He looked doubtfully at the well. "I'm not sure it's safe water. It might even be dry. During the war, there were a few scoundrels who–"

"Here will do," Maleen forced out, wanting to pant for the effort. Defying her mistress was possible, but she was nearly dizzy with the effort. Time seemed to drag as they came to a stop and Rob leaned out of the carriage to give directions to the groom. But before he had finished, Maleen had thrown herself at the door and nearly fell out onto her face. Rob caught her just before she hit the ground. She stood and, unable to speak just yet, nodded her thanks before traipsing up the partially-over-grown stone steps that led up to the well.

"Are you sure you're well?" Rob asked, frowning as he kept

his hand on the small of her back. Maleen, who was nearly doubled-over with the effort to climb, finally gave up and stood still, panting. This was it. She'd needed a situation that would make more sense for what she was about to say. Something that Priscilla would not understand. But Rob would.

"I just..." she said, forcing the words through an unwilling mouth, "need to...hold fast."

Rob, who had been hovering, froze as their eyes met. For an eternal moment, he held her gaze.

"What did you say?" he whispered, his eyes narrowed.

"Do you know what?" Priscilla finally said, forcing Maleen into submission, "I think I'm better now. I just needed a bit of fresh air, that's all." She fanned herself and made a great show at feeling faint from the summer's heat, but Maleen's forced words couldn't be taken back. Maleen wished she could smirk.

Priscilla's punishment was swift. As soon as they climbed back into the carriage, Maleen developed a raging headache, and Rob's offer of little tarts and slices of fruit made her sick.

But, she thought to herself as the carriage moved back toward the city, the seed of doubt had been placed. And Maleen couldn't wait to watch it grow.

CHAPTER 20
HELP

Rob stared at Priscilla the entire ride home. To say that her behavior about the well had been bizarre would be an understatement. But the words that had come out of the princess's mouth...

Hold fast.

It had been a message. It must have been. But a message from whom?

Only one princess would understand the significance of those words to him. They could only be understood if the princess had studied Metakinos's military traditions and history. Which Priscilla could have done, of course. The military motto wasn't kept a secret. But then again, he'd never known any princess to take an interest in such a mundane piece of information. Well, perhaps Princess Genevieve of Destin. She was princess of what might be the world's strongest military, though, and that was beside the point because this wasn't Princess Genevieve.

Which, once again, only left him with one logical conclusion.

His clothes were suddenly stifling, and he was finding it

hard to breathe. Sitting upright as though his world hadn't been turned on its head was suddenly all he could manage.

Less than two months ago, he'd seen Maleen's broken tower with his own eyes. And the hope he'd secretly held out...despite all attempts of others to convince him of her death, had finally died. He'd mourned her loss for years, shouldering the blame for everything that had and might have happened to her and to everyone else in the wake of the war he'd caused. Her ghost had haunted him every time he closed his eyes, and often he had looked at his missing arm with a malicious satisfaction. Due payment, he thought bitterly, for his rash hubris and stupidity. This...this message, though. It couldn't be her. It couldn't.

But then, who else could it be?

Unfortunately, staring at the princess did nothing, it seemed, but encourage her conversation, which meant he had to continue to think up answers. No, there was nothing in her appearance that would suggest she was anyone except who she claimed to be. The way she casually leaned toward him, eyes shining as she spoke of their future together, looked every part the excited bride. But her strange lapse last night, speaking directly of Maleen, which broke protocol by omitting Maleen's title, had been incredibly familiar. And today's episode at the well...

The carriage jolted to a halt, and Rob had to call on all of his self-control in order to patiently help her down. Once she was safely on the way to her chambers, however, he was free to sprint toward the castle chapel.

Unlike many of the other chapels Rob had visited, the one on the castle property was nearly as large as the churches in the local communities. It was a part of the castle, but its soaring arches were magnificent of their own accord and still would have been without even the castle to add to its grandeur. Rob felt a little guilty as he ran toward it, very aware that it had been months since his last visit.

"Father!" he called as soon as he burst through the main doors. His voice echoed in the large room, but today he didn't have time to feel cowed by his inappropriate entrance. The hope that might break him in two threatened to stop his lungs completely if he didn't see someone soon.

A young man in brown robes had been lighting a reading candle beside a large copy of the Holy Writ, but at the sound of Rob's voice, he jumped, nearly dropping the candle.

"Your Highness! I'm...I'm sorry. I didn't expect–"

"Who are you?" Rob frowned at him. "Where's Father Petras?"

The young priest blinked at him. "Um...Father Petras died. I only came to replace him yesterday. I would have been here sooner, but I was on a journey to visit my..." He cleared his throat and took a hesitant step forward. "I'm Luca, if I can be of any assistance."

Rob stared. Father Petras had died, and he hadn't known? Or maybe, a voice in his head whispered, he had known. And he'd chosen not to listen. Had he really grown so cold that the kind old priest's death hadn't affected him?

But there was no time for that now.

"Father," Rob said, trying to sound more level-headed. "I apologize for the rude entrance, but I must know something."

"I'll be glad to help if I can." Luca clasped his hands twice before gesturing at the smaller door on the far end of the room. "Might we speak in a more private setting?"

Rob nodded, grateful for the young man's suggestion. When they were comfortably seated in the holy man's personal quarters, Rob on the only chair and the priest standing by his bed, Luca asked him kindly to start again.

"How..." Rob frowned, trying to find the right words. "How would one know whether or not dark powers were at play in the castle?"

Luca, who had been running a hand through his thick hair, froze briefly. "Dark powers, Your Highness?"

Rob just nodded.

"Oh. Well, um, that would depend. Some darkness can only be sensed by powerful people who are gifted with such sensitivities...such as the Fortiers of Destin or the Sea Crown of the merfolk. And some very experienced holy men can sense it as well. Which, unfortunately, I am not." He frowned, stroking his beginnings of a beard for a moment. "I do have, however, a way to detect cruder magic, or darkness that is being used by a less competent manipulator." He blinked at Rob. "And you...you think you have such an instance in the castle?"

"I have reason," Rob said slowly, weighing each word as it left his tongue, "to believe someone within is being manipulated against her will."

"That would be very serious indeed. And how, um, do you believe this has come to pass?"

So Rob related to him how oddly the princess had been acting, the way she had seemed to suddenly change her personality both today and the night before.

"Even my mother thinks there is something wrong with her," he said. "And she's known the princess her whole life."

"So..." Luca said slowly, "you believe someone is manipulating this princess?"

"No. Or possibly." He shook his head. "Or rather, it's more that..." He took a deep breath, knowing that what he was about to say sounded insane. "Princess Maleen is trying to get out."

"Princess...Maleen. You mean the dead princess from Ertrique?"

"That's just it," Rob said slowly. "I'm not so sure she's dead."

Luca studied him for what felt like eternity. Then his eyes lit up. "Wait a moment. Wasn't Princess Maleen the one you were in—"

"Yes, we were once betrothed," Rob snapped. "What does that have to do with anything?"

"And the princess you mentioned before is..." Luca waited.

"My newly betrothed."

Luca nodded and steepled his fingers. Pressing them against his mouth, he thought for a moment. "I hope...I hope I am not seeming disrespectful, Your Highness, but..."

Rob knew where this was going.

"...don't you think this could be your mind and your heart, wishing it were Princess Maleen?

That thought had occurred to Rob, yes, but it was utterly too depressing to take into account, so he had immediately discarded the idea completely. "No, it's not in my imagination," he growled. "As I said, you can ask my mother."

Luca nodded quickly. "I see." His voice was suddenly pitched slightly higher. "And...just so I know a bit more about your betrothed, where is she from? Staroz, isn't it?" Then he laughed a little. "I apologize for my ignorance. As I said, I only returned last night. I am not aware of the goings-on yet."

Rob stared at him. "No. No, my newly betrothed is from Vaksam." He peered at the young man. "Isn't that where you're from as well?" If he wasn't, he sure sounded as if he was. "What's wrong?"

Luca had gone white, and his steepled fingers fell limply from his face. "She is from Vaksam?" he whispered.

"Yes. What of it?"

"Are you telling me," he swallowed, "that your father betrothed you to Princess *Priscilla* of Vaksam?"

"Um, yes. That's exactly what I'm saying."

"Quickly!" The young man jumped up and began to run around, seeming to search for something. "We must go to her chambers and examine them!"

Rob stood, his heart beating faster. "We do?"

"Yes!" Luca continued to dash about, seeming unable to

find whatever it was that he was looking for. "I thought your betrothed was from Staroz, not Vaksam. I didn't realize..." He lifted a bag and looked beneath it. "Dark things have happened in our forests. One in particular. And not long ago, as I was training for my position, actually, reports reached us that an ancient magician's book went missing! It had been stolen. The rightful owner said it held notes of the darkest curses, curses that had wrought horrors for the magician's own children for decades!" He was talking animatedly as he hurried, still searching through baskets, under heavy books, and on the floor. "We...the holy men...were warned at the time to be on the lookout for such a book." He shuddered slightly.

What was in that book? "Could it allow one person to...use another?" Rob asked. He didn't know exactly what was being done to Maleen...if knowing such a thing was even possible. But he had to try to find out.

"Aha! I've found it!" Luca held up a green wax candle. Then he tucked it into a worn leather satchel and made for the door. "Come! We'll go now!"

Rob followed, praying a thanks to the Maker that the holy man believed him now.

"What makes you think the princess might have something to do with the missing book?" he asked quietly as they made their way through the halls.

"I don't know for sure, of course. But there were also reports of...of strange things happening at the palace in Vaksam not long after the book was taken. Dead chambermaids and ladies' maids. Servants who had been driven mad. Such awful things. The book itself was never found." He shuddered. "In truth, that is why I have not lived there in recent years. I was young when it happened, and my mentor, fearful for my life, sent me to train under a holy man in Ashland."

"I wonder why we never heard of such things," Rob said quietly as they walked.

"There wasn't much to hear. We only had one source. A servant who had escaped. She died not long after finding us, though we never learned the cause of her death either. When a few of the holy men went to enquire about her family, we were promptly escorted off the palace grounds. I believe the crown was desperate to cover it all up."

They were forced to stop talking as the number of people within hearing distance grew greater, but Rob used the time to attempt to stop his head from spinning.

Had he accidentally become betrothed to some sort of witch?

Was the real Priscilla even still alive?

Was the witch, whoever she was, abusing Maleen in this strange act of charades? The answer, as unlikely as it might be, spurred his feet on faster.

Only when they arrived at her door did Rob realize their predicament.

"What are we doing?" he whispered.

The priest held the green candle up. "I need to burn a few things."

The answer made little sense to Rob, but then again, he'd never studied Sortheleige at any length. He did know, however, that to get answers, he would need the room clear of all people who might interfere. And with the way things were going, he could find himself facing anyone.

His heart beat stupidly fast. *Anyone* could include Maleen.

"We could tell them that someone attempted to lay a curse on the palace, and I need to search to see if any of the curse's remnants remain," Luca whispered.

Rob frowned. "She'll probably want to do that herself. Or she'll know what we're up to, and it will tip her off." He took a deep breath and blew it out slowly. "We'll need to chase them out. All of them." Then he snapped his fingers. "I know!" He motioned for Luca to follow him and took off down the hall as fast as he dared. Unable to help himself, he grinned. This was going to be fun.

Several minutes later, he returned knowing full well the menagerie game controller was under the impression he had lost his mind. Because no one in his right mind would ask to borrow a feral wooly cat. In fact, the man had been so concerned that Rob had finally allowed him to come along with them on the one condition that he was to keep their exploit completely secret from anyone who asked.

The cat himself, an ill-tempered tom, made hissing sounds from inside the bag the animal controller had chosen to transport him in, and several times, at the sound of tearing fabric, Rob had whirled around, sure the animal had torn his way out. But the animal controller knew what he was doing, and soon they made it back to Priscilla's room. Standing just out of sight from Priscilla's door guards, the animal controller took a small spoonful of fish paste and spread it on the corner of the door. Then he took another spoonful and smeared it all over a little wooden ball.

Then, as they'd agreed, Rob strode confidently past Priscilla's two sentries and knocked on the door.

A timid-looking maidservant answered.

"I was wondering," Rob said in a loud voice, "if Princess Priscilla would be available for a walk. I was planning on visiting the orange orchard, and—"

Luca, who was walking behind Rob holding a tray of tea, stumbled and dropped it, smashing what sounded like every piece of china against the ground. The guards' heads swiveled toward the mess Luca had made. Likewise, the maidservant's attention was drawn to Luca as well, giving Rob the perfect chance to toss the little wooden ball into the room.

Now, Rob thought. As if hearing the command, a vicious hiss and growl filled the air. A ball of gray fur dove past Rob, who let out a loud yell of what he hoped sounded like surprise.

Whether or not Rob was convincing, the maiden screamed as the cat tore past her and into the room, and the guards pushed inside after the cat.

"Careful!" the animal controller yelled from down the hall, where he'd been instructed to stand. "He'll bite!"

"Quick!" Rob shouted. "Everyone out!" He ran into the room and tried to heroically shoo the remaining occupants out. Priscilla held a towel over her head as she darted out, sobbing as she lamented her wet hair not drying properly.

"Keep her safe!" Rob barked at the guards. The guards followed their princess willingly, and in two short minutes, the princess's chambers were empty.

Smiling smugly to himself, Rob sheathed his sword as the animal controller went in search of his cat. Luca was already busy going through the various objects on the princess's vanity.

"You said we need to burn something," Rob said softly. "What do we need to burn?"

"A few hairs from the princess's brush, perhaps. A dry flower she's handled. A piece of food she's eaten from. Anything that might have had close personal contact with her," Luca whispered back.

Rob didn't really understand, but for the first time in years, he felt useful. Doing something...being proactive made him feel alive again.

They didn't have to search long. Because near the door on one of the thick, plush carpets was a dull, sticky clump of black...something.

"Is it tar?" Rob asked, reaching out to poke it, but Luca pushed his hand away.

"I'm sorry, Your Highness," Luca replied, answering Rob's raised brows, "but you don't know what it is." Luca removed a small set of tongs and a pen knife from his robe pockets. Then he carefully cut out a stained portion of the rug.

"Would you please light this, Your Highness?" he asked,

handing Rob the green candle. "Only, do your best not to drip any on the floor. If there is dark magic being used here, its wielder would most likely recognize the wax."

Rob did as he was asked, careful not to let the wax drip on the floor. This earned him a burned finger, but it was worth it. He held the candle as steadily as he could while Luca used the tongs to hold the clipped piece of carpet over the flame.

For a moment, the flame merely sputtered and flickered. But after about five seconds, the fire turned as green as the wax itself. Luca's mouth fell open, and his eyes grew impossibly wider.

"I'm afraid," he whispered to Rob, "we're going to need help."

Rob's blood pounded in his ears so loudly he could barely hear Luca's whispered words. So he hadn't imagined it. Something was amiss. "The Fortiers?" he asked, trying to hear himself over the pounding of his heart.

Luca nodded, his eyes still on the flame. "As soon as possible."

CHAPTER 21

SORRY

An hour later, Rob was standing in front of his parents on their personal balcony. When Rob had first asked them to join him, his father had looked a little put out at calling off the hunt he had planned with a few of his favorite advisers, but when the queen had insisted that this conversation was of the utmost importance, to the king's credit, he had appeared without complaint.

Now that they were looking at him, Rob's hand felt clammy, and his voice seemed to disappear every time he opened his mouth. His parents stared at him with wide eyes as he tried a second time. But still, nothing came. Frustrated, Rob rubbed his face with his hand and walked over to look out at the garden below.

"How do I say this and not sound insane?" he muttered.

"I believe," his mother said gently, "you said this had to do with a concern about Priscilla?"

Rob nodded and turned back to face them. "It does. It's only...I know it will sound far-fetched the moment it leaves my lips." He gestured back at the holy man who was sitting behind him. "But I've already spoken to Luca—"

"*Father* Luca?" his father prompted.

"Yes, *Father* Luca." The man seemed far too young for anyone above the age of twelve to call him Father, but that was beside the point. "And he believes that there is something dark at play."

His parents continued to stare at him, and Luca didn't seem to be in any hurry to speak, so Rob took a deep breath.

"Mother, you said yourself the first night she arrived that something was wrong."

His mother nodded and glanced at his father. "I did. And I still believe something is off. Priscilla hasn't been behaving like herself since she arrived. What with the veil and then at the dinner–"

"What happened at the dinner?" his father asked. He frowned at Rob. "Besides you leaving your betrothed on the dance floor?"

"It's hard to put into words." The queen frowned slightly. "The way she walks, for instance. Her gait changes mid-stride. Not every time she walks, but enough that I noticed it three times. And the way she tilts her head. And sometimes, the way she talks...the expressions she uses as she's speaking."

Rob nodded emphatically. Maybe he wouldn't sound as crazy as he thought. "And not only those things. That first night, after our dance, she demanded to know how long it had taken me to forget Maleen." Her name still tasted bitter when he said it, but he forced himself to stay in the moment and not give way to the grief that had seemed to attack him anew these last few days.

"That's...not in the usual etiquette," his father said slowly. "But not completely unreasonable, considering you became betrothed publicly and then–"

"There's more," Rob hurried to say before his father could continue. "Today, while we were out riding, she suddenly demanded that we stop at a well because she was thirsty." His father opened his mouth, so Rob continued. "And when we got out, she stumbled around like she was drunk. You can ask the groom and footmen if you don't believe me. And when she had taken a few steps, she fell. I reached out to help her, and she told me she simply needed to...to hold fast."

His father blinked at him. "I'm sorry, but the significance of this is lost on me."

Rob swallowed hard. "When Maleen was hanging off the bridge, back when we were children, I shouted at her over and over again to hold fast. And ever since, it's something we've used in our letters. I even gave her a medallion with it engraved upon it."

To his disappointment, the moment Maleen's name was mentioned, his father's curious expression became sympathetic. Rob wanted to scream. He'd known this would happen.

"Roburts," his father said gently. "I know...I know this is hard. Losing Maleen and then having to promise your heart to another. But..." He held his arms up helplessly. "I'm not sure what to tell you. It's been seven years."

"You haven't heard it all!" Rob cried. "And before assuming this is all in my head, did you hear Mother?"

"I heard her." His father pinched the bridge of his nose and sighed. "All right. Tell me what else you have to say."

"When we returned home, I went and found Luc–Father Luca. He reacted just as you are now until I mentioned that Priscilla is from Vaksam. Then he told me that an evil magician's book of magic had been stolen there, and not long after the disappearance of the book, mysterious evils began taking place around the Vaksam palace. People driven mad and being murdered!"

"We never heard any such reports." The king frowned. "And I sent my best men to do a thorough search. I believe we even had one of our ladies stay within their court for several weeks, listening to gossip and reporting it to us."

"If...if you'll pardon me, Your Majesty."

They all turned to see Luca rising from the corner in which he'd been hiding. "It's true. From what we were told, the crown did all they could to hide the source of the rumors. I only knew because one of my old mentors had interviewed a servant who escaped and wrote to tell me about it. The girl died just after he spoke with her." With a shaking hand, he withdrew the green candle from his robes. "There was also this."

"What is that?" Rob's mother leaned forward.

"It was a gift from one of my teachers," Luca said, his voice still shaking slightly. "It's not useful for finding sophisticated power, but to a point, it can detect dark magic when the object is held to the flame." He put his hand in front of the candle, as though it were lit. "The flame turns green whenever it comes into contact with dark powers. The weaker ones, at least."

"And did you find anything?" Rob's mother asked, sounding somewhat breathless.

Luca nodded. "We, um...we did. In the princess's chambers."

"I've sent a letter to Destin," Rob said, speaking hurriedly once again before his father could talk. "And Father Luca has also penned a letter to the priests in Vaksam, though we're not sure if the crown will allow them to leave the country." Rob paused as his father walked to the sitting chair at the foot of his bed and sat slowly, his left hand at his temple. His mother met Rob's eye and shook her head slightly as Rob began to open his mouth again. *Let him think*, she mouthed. So Rob waited as patiently as he could while his father stared miserably at the far wall. Finally, he spoke.

"I know you miss her." His voice was quiet, gentler than before. "We all do. But," he sighed, "we cannot afford another seven years of war. We just can't. And we've already signed the betrothal papers. You're as good as married in their eyes!"

"Can we afford a queen who might be steeped in darkness?" Rob's mother asked, delicately arching her eyebrows.

"No, I don't mean...What I mean is that lots of people go walking through a princess's room. Her guards, her servants, her lady's maid. One bit of evidence can't tie your charges directly to her." He looked up. "I can't call off the unification of two kingdoms on mere conjecture."

"Well, no," Rob said, feeling exasperated. "But oughtn't we at least investigate?"

The king let out a gusty sigh and rubbed his hands over his eyes. "Very well. I'll order a more thorough inspection of her room. I'll even give you a fortnight to get a reply from the Fortiers. We'll...say you were afflicted by a war injury or something." The king's gaze then bored into Rob's. "But if nothing comes up, you can't back out of this. That's an order." He stormed to the door to one of the inner chambers, and for a second, Rob was sure he would slam it shut behind him. But then he paused, and after a moment, turned. "I'm sorry, son," he said in a tired voice. "I really am." Then he closed the door behind him.

CHAPTER 22
FATES

Maleen was sitting on the window seat, staring out at the garden below. She recognized a few of the kitchen staff that were out weeding and once again desperately wished she could be outside, too. She also wished she could wave at them and make signs for help. But the guards were watching her, and Priscilla was determined to keep them locked up in the room when they weren't officially required elsewhere in the castle.

Notice had been sent that morning, not long after her return, that the princess's presence was requested by the queen in her study. Priscilla had read it aloud and then set it down on the table with a thoughtful expression. Whether or not it was her own suspicion or she recognized the hope in Maleen's eyes, she had announced that she would be going instead of Maleen.

"So you don't need me after all!" Maleen had cried indignantly.

"I never said I was going as myself," Priscilla had replied gently, as though shushing an overtired child. "I'll be going as the princess's old governess. It appears that the queen has some unfortunate business she wishes to discuss with me." She pursed her lips for a moment then smiled. "Yes, I think you'll have the morning to do as you like. Within the rooms, of course. And I'll inform Her Majesty that the princess has a headache, and she can tell me whatever she wishes to be passed along."

"They haven't seen you around," Maleen pouted. "They won't know who you are." She wasn't at all disappointed not to be wearing Priscilla's face, but she had been working on some more secret hints to drop at the afternoon tea she'd been invited to with the prince. It seemed, however, that Priscilla had suspected what she was up to.

"No, dear, this is something I need to take care of, I'm afraid. You can sit here and rest. Isn't that what you wanted after all?" And so Priscilla had donned her own disguise and shuffled out of the room while Maleen had retreated, grumbling to herself, to the window seat.

And now, hours later, Maleen couldn't help scowling to herself as she reflected that the whole situation was rather ridiculous. She'd been stuck in a tower for seven years, and yet she couldn't remember ever being quite this bored. For the last hour, she'd been staring down at the corner of the garden that seemed to be set aside for herbs, and she was trying to distinguish one bush from the next, though that was difficult to do from such a distance.

The door opened, and an old woman hobbled in. The guards shut the door behind her and locked it again as the old woman removed her wraps and slowly, slowly straightened and began to grow.

"Well," Priscilla said as she returned to her usual self, her skin stretching to become more taut, losing most of its assumed age spots and lines to become what it usually was these days. She shook her hair out in front of the mirror and smiled. "That was enlightening."

Maleen glared at her.

Finally, Priscilla stopped primping and finally looked back

at Maleen, and Maleen prepared herself for the worst. She'd defied Priscilla in the most obvious way possible in the carriage, then again at the well, and as she hadn't been punished yet, she was fully expecting to suffer Priscilla's wrath now.

But the look on Rob's stern face that morning had been worth it.

"I've been informed," Priscilla said lightly, "that my wedding will be postponed for two weeks." She walked toward Maleen, and Maleen did her best to turn back to the window as if she didn't care.

She tried to sound incredibly bored. "Oh, has it?"

"Yes. Apparently, the prince is suffering from some war injuries and is in too much pain to carry through with the ceremony and ensuing celebrations." She sniffed. "It's interesting, though, that he mentioned no such discomfort this morning."

Maleen ignored her.

"You know," Priscilla continued, "after your little outburst at the well, I had planned all sorts of punishments for you. I've studied them in great detail, you see. Not in the hopes of using them, however. I would much rather coax obedience than coerce it. But as you're determined to ruin everything, I can't let such conduct slide."

"I'm not afraid of you," Maleen whispered. It was a lie. She was afraid. The pain Priscilla had inflicted on her the night before made her muscles throb every time she closed her eyes.

"No, I'm afraid you're not. At least not enough. But then I realized that this extension in my betrothal is actually a good thing." She went back to a bag she'd placed by the door and pulled something from it. Out of the corner of her eye, Maleen could see Priscilla unfolding a piece of parchment. "I did some exploring of the city this morning. I have a few friends here, you see. And I've discovered a number of your friends as well."

Maleen stiffened.

"Let's see. I believe you were quite fond of an old man

named...ah yes. Here it is. James Wickson? He was your old steward, was he not?"

Maleen reminded herself to keep breathing.

"And who else? There's a family here. Jim and his family. I believe his mother works here at the castle. And it seems they have extended family here as well. How cozy. And then there are several more servants I've discovered who once worked for your family, but I think you'll be most pleased to learn the where-abouts of a Miss Emille Morales."

Maleen had done her best to don a mask of indifference. To let Priscilla know how much these names meant to her would be like handing over the key to what had been a carefully guarded treasure. But at the sound of her old governess's name, Maleen flinched, and Priscilla smiled.

"I thought that would get your attention." She went into her private chambers, and after a moment, returned with a small leather drawstring pouch. She came and sat on the floor beside Maleen's window seat as though they were the best of friends, and she dumped the contents of the bag onto the floor. A pile of thin metal rectangles spilled out, each about the size of Maleen's thumb. Priscilla counted out two dozen of them and then, pulling her list toward her, picked one up and started carving letters into it with a pen knife she produced from her reticule.

Maleen leaned closer. As soon as she realized what Priscilla was doing, she snatched the little rectangle out of her hand and ran to the doors that led out to the balcony. As she struggled to throw the sash open, however, she was grabbed by one of the guards as the other wrenched the rectangle from her hand.

"I wouldn't do that," Priscilla said pleasantly. "If you throw that, dear Phoebe is going to fall and hit the ground as though she were the one tossed. It wouldn't be a pretty ending."

The guard handed the rectangle back as the other one held Maleen.

"Do you wish me to lock her in her room?" he asked.

"No, leave her here. Now that she knows what will happen to her friends should she try to destroy these, I doubt she'll try again."

The guards returned to their corners, and Maleen could only watch as Priscilla continued to scratch names into the little metal tokens. Finally, she finished and beamed up at Maleen.

"There, dear. When we do get another invitation to dine or dance or whatever with the prince, I expect you'll be on your best behavior. Because you know what I can do." She picked up the rectangles and gently put them back in the bag. "And what I can do to your friends should you try sending the prince another message."

Then she stood and dusted off her hands. "I'm hungry. Aren't you? Let's tell the kitchen to send something up to the room. I'm thinking more of that bisque." She waved her hand toward the door. "Maleen, be a dear, won't you?"

Woodenly, Maleen stood and went to the door to call for a servant. As she did, Priscilla stood as well and returned to her room, where Maleen heard the sounds of her friends' fates being locked in the princess's large wooden chest.

CHAPTER 23
THE WOMAN AND THE WOLF

Rob looked down at Priscilla and her ridiculous pout. If Maleen was anywhere near, she was doing a good job of hiding because she would have died before using such tactics.

"It's been five days since you began feeling poorly," Priscilla was saying. "You're sure you can't continue with the wedding? We could scale back the ball after if you wish. I wouldn't even make you dance." Her pout turned into a sly grin. "You could make a statement, thanking everyone for visiting, then you and I could make our way up to our rooms to...relax." She traced the arm he was using to escort her with the tip of her finger.

Rob recoiled. He hadn't meant to. It had been reflexive. But she was asking him to go somewhere with her that he had only ever imagined venturing into with Maleen. And to his disgust, if he was honest with himself, his body wanted to follow. He was a man, and this woman knew how to get his blood rushing. His head, however, knew better, and his heart wanted to retch with disgust. How, he wondered, had he ever been able to think even for a moment that he could possibly be happy with this woman? As wise as his father was, this union had been a terrible idea.

Unfortunately, his father had been right in that they couldn't afford another war. And by the calculating look on Priscilla's face, she was thinking the same thing. Withdrawing her hand from his arm, she sniffed and stiffly smoothed her skirts.

"Just so you know," she said, her voice suddenly cold, "we won't be able to pause our marriage when you're struck with these maladies in the future." Then she sighed and looked back up at him. This time, her voice was softer, and so were her eyes. "Why won't you let me help you?" she asked in a quiet voice. "Isn't that what wedlock entails? Leaning on one another when we're weak?"

How talented she was. In less than two minutes, she'd worn four completely different countenances, and each had been just as convincing as the last. She'd even managed, in spite of his best efforts to remain impervious, to get his blood racing with just the slightest touch. No, this marriage could not take place.

But as little as Rob wished to wed her, he had to tread with care.

"I am asking you to help me now," he said, taking one of her hands in his. Her expression softened further as he kissed it gently. Two could play that game. Also, it didn't hurt if he pretended it was Maleen's hand instead of Priscilla's.

Don't get your hopes up, a voice that sounded a lot like wisdom whispered in his ear. But it was too late. He was hoping with everything he had. And if he was wrong?

He wouldn't even think about that right now.

"Very well," she said with an indulgent smile. "If that's what you need, then I shall give it." She thought for a moment. "I actually had some friends living in the city that I wished to seek out. So perhaps this is for the better."

Rob encouraged her to find everyone she needed. He even offered her a royal escort whenever she desired. Anything to push off the wedding. He had nine days left.

Two days passed, and with only one week left until the wedding, Rob was sure his father might try to force the issue. But continued warnings from the queen, assurances that Rob wasn't making these claims from a broken heart, won him the second week's reprieve. Which, he found out five days later, was exactly what he needed.

"Your Highness."

Rob turned from where he had been staring out the window in his study to see Gregory, who was looking quite put out.

"There is a young couple here from Vaksam demanding to see you." He scowled. "Commoners from the look of it."

"Demanding?"

"Yes, demanding. Quite rudely, I might add. The only reason I even dared to bother you is that they came bearing a letter with the Fortier crest." He held out a sealed parchment.

Rob's heart thundered so fast his next words sounded breathless.

"Bring them here!"

His servant blinked at him a few times before bowing and nodding back at the servant standing in the door. "Bring them in."

A few minutes later, a man, woman, and a little girl were ushered into the study. The man looked to be about Rob's height and age, and he had carefully trimmed scruff on his chin. The way he walked, however, was the most noticeable thing about him. His gait, while upright, was nearly feral, and his eyes roamed the room warily.

The woman had hair so blond it was nearly white, and she wore a startlingly red cloak. She was lovely, but the handsome angles of her face were now pulled taut by worry.

The only one in the group who didn't look stressed or suspicious was the little girl, who appeared to be about six or seven. She grinned up at him, quite unabashed, the freckles sprinkled across her nose and cheeks making her expression even more ornery. Her honey-brown eyes sparkled with a light that reminded him painfully of another little girl who had grinned up at him years ago. He knelt and took one of her hands in his.

"And who might you be?" he asked softly.

"I'm Ilse." She beamed. "What happened to your arm?"

"Ilse!" Her mother looked horrified.

Rob just laughed. "I was fighting a troll, and he thought I looked delicious."

Her eyes sparkled even more. "Were you?"

"No, that's why he spit me out."

Ilse's laugh echoed through the room, and the sound of it seemed to put everyone more at ease.

"How can I be of service?" Rob asked, standing.

The couple exchanged a glance, and worry was etched on their faces once more.

"I am Kurt," the man said, "and this is my wife, Liesel. And we are from Vaksam."

"We were contacted by Prince Henri of Destin," the woman said, holding out the parchment Rob's servant had held before. "He said you were looking for information concerning our princess."

"Our *imposter* princess," Kurt spat.

"Please," Rob said, gesturing to the armchairs by the fire. "Let us sit. And if it would please you, I could have your daughter escorted to the menagerie. My old nurse maid has been wishing we had more children about the castle." Something she had mentioned to him often since he'd come of marriageable age.

"I want to see the wolves!" Ilse chimed, at which her father winced.

"Or we have other places..." Rob began, but Liesel shook her head.

"The menagerie will be fine. We thank you, Your Highness." She looked severely at the little girl. "You obey and do as you're told. And I'm not to hear of you touching anything you're not supposed to. Understood?"

The severity on the woman's face seemed unjustified until the little girl beamed up at her mother again. "Of course, Mother." And in spite of his other concerns, Rob nearly laughed. She seemed far more like Maleen than Rob could have ever guessed possible. If his guess was correct, her mother had reason to be concerned.

When Ilse had been escorted away, Rob faced her parents. For a long moment, no one spoke. Rob wasn't sure what they were here for, but whatever it was was clearly making them uncomfortable. But if they were from Henri, he would give them all the time in the world. Finally, Liesel broke the silence.

"I suppose before we begin, you need to understand why Prince Henri encouraged us to come." She took a deep breath then paused as a servant bustled in to serve tea. Only when the servant was gone did she speak again.

"I was born and raised in the vineyard region of Vaksam. I lived with my grandparents there after my mother fell sick, and they took us in so they could care for her. My father, however, was so heartbroken by her illness that when he was offered the promise of a special healer deep in a wood far from my mother's old home, he accepted. And he took my mother and me with him."

She drew in a slow breath and rubbed one hand across the back of the other. When she spoke, her voice trembled slightly. "On my first night there, I realized we had been brought under false pretenses, and it was on that night that my mother died." She swallowed. "I was so frightened that I tried to run away, back to my grandparents. But as I ran, a wolf bit the back of my hand."

"Only your hand?" Rob asked. "He didn't attack you further?"

"He wasn't trying to attack her," Kurt said in a low voice. "He was marking her."

Rob stared, transfixed. He hadn't the slightest idea of what this story had to do with Maleen and Priscilla, but it was getting more interesting by the word.

Liesel nodded. "Little did I know, I was marked to be a future wife of the village head. But not the village I had been moved to. It was a village of...of others." She glanced at Kurt, and he nodded. "I was found by a kind woodcutter and returned to my father. Kurt helped me escape when we were a little older. Unfortunately, it was only for a time, though, for when summoned years later, I was unable to stay away."

Rob must have looked confused because Kurt broke in. "She was forced to return, thanks to the mark."

"You said it wasn't the forest village you were summoned to," Rob said. "What do you mean?"

"She was summoned to my village." Kurt frowned more deeply. "We weren't far from the other village, but we preferred to stay hidden for obvious reasons."

Whatever the reasons were, they weren't obvious to Rob. "What did they summon you for?" he asked, though he had a bad feeling about it.

"My turn had come to marry the village chief," Liesel said, her chin raised. "So that he could siphon my humanity and share it with his people to prevent them from losing their own humanity completely."

"And who was the chief?" Rob asked in a low voice, prepared to hear the worst. What awful things had this poor woman lived through?

"I was."

Rob turned and looked at Kurt, whose face had darkened like a cloud of smoke over a forest fire.

"My uncle was the one who had marked her, but as my

father knew I loved her, he allowed me to summon her for my own."

"But why would you do that?" Rob whispered. He tried to imagine calling Maleen to...what was it? Drain her of her humanity? Whatever that meant, it sounded sinister.

"Because if I hadn't, my father would have."

"Before you judge him," Liesel said, "you must understand. His village was originally made up of the children of one man. A magician of the darkest sort, who in an attempt to gain glory, used dark powers to change his own children's very natures."

Rob blinked. "Their natures?"

Kurt frowned, and Rob could tell the conversation was bringing up memories he'd rather forget. He immediately felt ashamed of his horror and determined to try and make them as comfortable as possible.

"I...I don't mean to be rude at all," he hastened to explain. "I only–we don't hear this kind of story much in Metakinos. I'm sorry, I'm simply trying to understand."

"It's the kind of story we hope to prevent in the future," Liesel said with a sad smile. "Ergo, our shocking appearance here." She looked at Kurt. "Go on."

He nodded, but instead of talking, stared into the fire for a long time. When he did speak, his voice was nearly inaudible. "The curse...we're still not sure how to explain it. We think he meant it to be a protection for himself and his children. But instead of allowing change only when desired, his sons and daughters began changing shape whenever they lost control. Got angry. Scared. Any feeling of extreme passion could induce it. Strangers were brought in for marriage without knowing who and what kind of family they were marrying into until it was too late." He shook his head. "But what they suffered was nothing compared to what the chief's wife...wives would suffer."

"The magician," Liesel took up, "realized quickly that they

were losing their humanity too fast. So he rearranged his original spell to allow for a way of keeping some humanity among his children."

"You were that loophole," Rob said softly. "Weren't you?"

She gave him a sad smile. "The chief, according to the magic, had to marry a Pure Blood, or a woman completely uncontaminated by the curse, meaning she had to come from the outside world. So the human village nearby—the one my father had been lured to—would purposefully invite families with young daughters into the village in order to protect their own girls."

"You said wives," Rob said. "Were there more than one at a time?"

Liesel shook her head. "No. It wasn't that. It was more—"

"The magic drained them of life," Kurt said in a hard voice. "As soon as one died, another had to be found."

"Or what?" Rob asked, glancing between the two.

Kurt shrugged. "We would lose our humanity completely. An entire village of wolves would be set upon the surrounding areas. They might even leave the forest. Countless lives would have been lost. And every single soul in that village would have lost his humanity for the rest of his life."

Wolves. They would turn into wolves. That must have been why Kurt had grimaced when Ilse had wanted to see the wolves.

"So...what happened?" Rob asked, clearing his throat. "It seems you don't have that trouble anymore."

Liesel's smile was more genuine this time as she looked at Kurt with adoration. "We broke it." Then she looked back at him. "The price was heavy, but by the Maker's grace, we found a way." Her smile widened. "And we weren't the only ones. Others found a way to break it, too."

"Ours, however," Kurt said, "was more impactful. I was the chief, so what happened to me affected everyone else there."

Rob studied them each in turn. So they were from Vaksam. And they had escaped dark magic. Henri's choice to send them was making more sense. "It would seem, then," he said slowly, "that you might be able to help me. Or at least, Henri seemed to think so."

"Unfortunately," Liesel said, "our story isn't quite finished. After my husband's people were freed from the curse, we left the forest entirely and began to travel. Our daughter was born soon after, and we lived our lives quite happily for several years, roaming back and forth between my grandparents' vineyard and our own adventures until we received some startling news from Kurt's brother."

"My brother," Kurt said, "had stayed behind with those of our village who wanted to remain in the forest. And with him, he had kept the magician's book, where the magician had transcribed his experiments and other magical ventures. We'd thought that if someone from the village had a reversal of some sort, it would be good to have the original book, should we need to find a cure. But two years ago, my brother wrote to inform me that there had been a raid on the village, and someone had stolen it."

"Not long after," Leisel continued, "we were contacted by holy men from the Vaksam palace. They believed there were dark powers at work there, but they didn't know of anyone else in the region who would recognize them. Word had spread of our history by then, and we were the only ones familiar, it seemed, with such power."

"What did you find?" Rob asked, his heart tripping over itself.

Kurt frowned. "It was...difficult to say. We didn't have much time to look, as the holy men snuck us into the palace without the king's permission. Some of the magic did feel familiar, though. I'm not sure how to describe it other than that. But there were other powers at work as well."

"We took our findings to the king," Liesel said, "but he didn't want to listen. In fact, he had us thrown out. If it hadn't been for the Fortiers, who were traveling through at that time, we might have given up completely. But the priests contacted them on our behalf, and they found us a home near the palace and have sent money to sustain us. In return, they've asked us to remain there on watch. So I set up an apothecary shop, and Kurt has found work at a nearby mill, where we've been waiting until the Fortiers gave us a sign." She tilted her head slightly. "And here we are."

Rob ran his hand through his hair and found speech difficult for a few very long minutes. He turned instead to look down upon the menagerie, where he could just see the top of Ilse's blond head bouncing up and down beside the bear's cage.

"I cannot express to you what your visit has meant to me," he finally said, turning back to her parents. "Not only have you possibly saved me from an unhappy marriage, but my kingdom from ruin as well."

"She's here, isn't she?" Kurt asked.

"Who?" Rob asked.

"Our *princess*." Kurt sneered as he said the word. "I can smell her."

Rob, who had assumed they'd simply heard the news of the betrothal, froze. After a moment, he shook his head. "Well, I can't say you're wrong. She's housed several floors above this one." Then he gave a start and strode over to his writing table, where he'd left the sealed message. "The letter!" He paused, his knife on the wax. "Did Henri say I was supposed to open it now?"

"He sent word that we should present this note in order to gain access to you," Liesel said. "But he instructed that the letter you now hold in your hand was to be given only to you."

Rob thought about that for a moment before nodding and breaking the seal.

Roburts,

I am sorry I can't come to you in person at the moment. As it is, I'm quite vexed at being unable. You were right to question Lady Priscilla. (I refuse to call her by such a high title as princess when all evidence suggests that title was maliciously earned.) My family has been following her for several years. Unfortunately, we haven't found anything that will tie her to the use of dark power directly, but all signs point to it.

From what my family can tell, Priscilla has taken not one but several kinds of dark power and has tried through some sort of amalgamation to force them together. We've guessed that she's used not only magic found in that cursed book, but she's also stolen Fae strength from what we can tell as well, though we're not sure where she could have found it. And I'm convinced there are other forms of dark powers there as well, but unless I see them for myself, I'm not able to say for sure. Unfortunately, the girl's uncle has not been cooperative in the least, so our efforts have been hampered. But we are making headway.

Take care, Rob. I'll come as soon as I'm able. But under no circumstances should you marry that girl. My parents are in the utmost agreement on this, so if you can't take my word for it, take theirs.

Until next we meet,
Henri Fortier

Kurt and Liesel were not in the least bit surprised that Henri had warned Rob against marriage of any sort with their princess. They were, however, hesitant to stay in the palace when Rob pressed them to take up their own rooms. What they could do, aside from tell his father what they had told him, he wasn't sure, particularly as the letter from Henri Fortier, crown prince of the strongest kingdom in the western realm and possessor of his own incredible power, would carry the most weight.

But having them near made him feel less as if insanity were knocking at his door. And he was eager to discuss a new plan with them as well, something which would allow him to catch Priscilla in the act.

Also, watching Ilse was much like seeing Maleen once again. And he so desperately wanted to see her again.

.

CHAPTER 24
EMILLE

Thirteen days after the wedding had been postponed, Priscilla joyfully announced during breakfast that everything would proceed as planned. Rob was feeling better, and a new date for the wedding would be set within the next week.

"I had hoped it would take place the very next day, but a few days can be spared," she said as she smiled down at her eggs. "Everything must be perfect, after all. This is my wedding." She giggled. Then she put her spoon down and smiled affectionately at Maleen. "And you, my love, have nearly played your part. In just a few days, this will all be over."

If the price for disobedience hadn't been someone else's head, Maleen would have retorted that she was sure Priscilla would make sure Maleen never had any part ever again. But thoughts of the metal rectangles kept her mouth shut.

She wasn't allowed to linger at breakfast. As soon as Priscilla was finished, the table was cleared away by Priscilla's silent maidservants, and Maleen found herself stripped and then dressed once again. This time, she was wearing a wedding dress.

"The prince will be calling you soon to discuss wedding

details," Priscilla said as her maidservants measured and pinned the gown Maleen was wearing. "But before you go, I have someone I'd like you to see." She nodded at one of her guards standing at the door of her bedchambers. The guard disappeared inside for a moment before returning, dragging something along behind him.

Or someone, rather. The body was that of a woman, but her head was covered with a cloth bag, and her wrists were bound. She seemed to be conscious, but resisted little as the guard roughly pulled her toward a chair set against the wall. He shoved her into a sitting position and yanked off the bag on the woman's head.

"Emille!" Maleen shrieked, running to her old governess's side, ignoring the maidservants' protestations.

Emille it was indeed. But this Emille was far different from the tall, proud woman Maleen remembered. Her shoulders were hunched, and her hair, far from the neat curls she had pinned up every day, was in a messy knot at the back of her head, pieces of her hair escaping in every direction. A gag was tied around her mouth, but when she saw Maleen, she began to struggle against her bindings and gag, her desperate words coming out as incoherent mumblings.

"I thought this would be a lovely little reunion," Priscilla said, bouncing on her toes and clapping. "I remember how close you two were."

"What have you done to her?" Maleen did her best to find the knot at the back of the gag, but even as she did, she received a zinging shock. Looking up from the floor, where she'd fallen painfully on her elbow, she gaped. "You enchanted the bindings, didn't you?"

Priscilla smiled genially. "I can't have you trying to help her escape." She laughed. "She's here to ensure *you* don't escape. Isn't irony wonderful?"

Maleen glowered at Priscilla. "I take it you have a new plan."

"Oh, not a new plan. Just one to make sure you behave this time." She removed the bag of metal rectangles from her vanity and began searching through it. Finally, she found the one with Emille's name on it.

"No." Maleen took a step forward, but before she could finish, Priscilla grinned and whispered something to the little piece of metal. Emille began choking from behind her gag. This time, when Maleen ran to her side and removed the gag, she wasn't shocked, nor did Priscilla stop her. When it was off, though, she felt just as helpless. Emille was turning blue, the sounds of her choked gasps filling the room.

"I'll do what you want!" Maleen screamed, tears streaming down her face. "Just stop!"

Then it was over as soon as it had begun. Priscilla smiled sweetly and dropped the rectangle back in the bag as Maleen helped Emille back up onto the chair, from which she'd fallen.

"I'm sorry," Maleen whispered tearfully, tracing her old governess's face with her fingers. "I didn't know she would–"

"August," Priscilla said sweetly, "please affix Lady Emille's gag back on. I have the room muffled now, but it won't be so when I'm working. And Arabella, I need you to help Maleen finish getting ready." She beamed at Maleen. "You're attending a garden tea."

Maleen waited for Rob to come so he could escort her to the tea, and only the puppet smile Priscilla forced onto her face kept her from dissolving into tears.

She had been so close. Rob had taken the hint. She knew he

had because he had immediately delayed the wedding. Priscilla's rooms had been searched twice. The palace had tried to hide their intentions both times, but no one was fooled. Priscilla had even found it slightly amusing. Especially when the holy man appeared both times to conduct the searches himself.

As if anyone in his right mind would send a holy man to examine the room's structure or to clear the rooms of invisible mites.

To make it all worse, help had been so close. Not only had the holy man come, but Rob had been there as well. Maleen had been unable to send the searchers even a small message, though. As soon as they'd appeared, Priscilla had whisked her away to a different room each time they searched.

But close wasn't enough, and Priscilla knew she had broken her. Maleen couldn't watch her mother's best friend die. Because that's what she knew Priscilla would make her do. She would probably laugh and clap in delight as Maleen was forced to see Emille struggle for every last breath.

"Princess?"

Maleen looked up to realize that she had been joined by the prince's entourage. His hand was outstretched, and he was looking at her with appropriate concern. "Are you well?"

For the first time since she had returned, Maleen saw that some of the ice in his eyes had thawed, and suddenly, she could see the Rob she knew in their depths. Only...Rob had been found just in time for Maleen to disappear.

"Yes," Maleen flashed him a practiced smile. "I was only hoping you were feeling better today."

The light in his eyes flickered slightly, but he answered just as smoothly as she had. "Much, thank you. My physician has discovered a new herbal remedy that seems to help." He held his arm out again. "Shall we?"

He led her to a part of the palace she'd never seen before, through a large stone hall with an outer wall made entirely of windows. The back of the palace had more pillars like those at the front of the palace, and more steps. But these steps led down into a winding garden filled with green bushes, vines, and trees, sprinkled with flowers of every color, and dotted by circular pavilions.

"Oh!" Maleen breathed, and this time, she wasn't sure if it was her or Priscilla who was more enchanted. "This is magical!" Then she turned to him. "Could we have our wedding out here?"

Definitely Priscilla.

He laughed a little. "I'm afraid the wedding will take place at a church across the city. It's tradition. We'll have a large procession that spans the city. You and I will walk together as the people surround us and wish blessings upon us. Then after the ceremony, we'll begin our celebration here." He tilted his head slightly as he studied her. "I wrote telling you of our traditions before you accepted the suit. Do you remember?"

"Oh, yes." Priscilla put an absurd pout on Maleen's face. "I'd forgotten."

"My parents will be down in a few minutes," he said, leading them past the chairs and tables which had been set for the tea and into one of the winding stone walkways. "Why don't we take a turn about the garden and get to know each other a little better?"

Maleen's heart leaped at this opportunity. Then it sank down into the ground. If only he'd done this sooner!

Unaware of her situation, however, he continued. "When I was little, I had a favorite part of the palace." His gaze narrowed slightly. "Which part do you think it was?"

She could do it. She could say, "Menagerie." The answer was just on the tip of her tongue. Because whether or not she could disobey Priscilla wasn't the question. She knew she could. But with Emille in Priscilla's gasp, Maleen couldn't bring herself to do it. So instead, she submitted to Priscilla's stupid tittering.

"The throne room? I can only imagine you made such trouble when you were little." Priscilla forced Maleen's hand up to his short curls, where she attempted to muss them.

His face immediately hardened, and Maleen wanted to cry. *I'm here! I'm here and I can't get out!* But her mouth simply continued to utter whatever Priscilla's did.

The day continued as such, only it grew worse with each passing hour. Question after question he tossed her, questions she knew the answers to as well as she knew herself.

"What's your favorite dessert?"

It was miniature white cakes with raspberry and mint.

"Lemon tarts," Priscilla answered instead.

"What animal did I fear the most as a child?"

Coyotes. He'd been bitten by one the first time he'd accompanied his father on a hunt.

"Bears?" Priscilla guessed.

And so they went on, the look of disgust growing with each answer she gave. She could have stopped it at any time. But the memory of Emille's choking still filled her ears, and she knew without a doubt, as Priscilla had wanted her to, that Priscilla would do all of that and more to each person whose name resided in that hateful little bag.

Help me, Maleen cried out silently to the Maker. But the Maker didn't seem to hear her. Or if he did, he had other plans.

The tea itself was torture. Rob was clearly upset, and Maleen had absolutely no appetite for the morsels Priscilla forced into her mouth. Even worse were the fake smiles and girlish giggles she was forced to produce over and over again.

When she was nearly too exhausted to say or do one more thing, Rob stood and stiffly held out his arm. "You look tired," he said. "Perhaps you would like to return to your chambers and rest." His voice was pleasant, but his eyes were hard. And as Maleen allowed him to silently escort her to her rooms, she thought it just might kill her.

CHAPTER 25
NO ONE

Rob didn't return to speak to his parents after the tea. He knew they would be waiting for him. After his disastrous experiment, though, one performed in front of his father, no less, he simply couldn't do it. He couldn't admit defeat. So once Priscilla had been returned to her quarters, he stormed down to the stable and barked for one of his servants to ready his horse.

He had been so close to hearing her say the words. All he had needed was a little more evidence to convince his father, who he knew had been listening in. He had given her every opportunity to betray herself that morning. If Maleen could only have given him a few, or even one starkly inappropriate answer, his father would have relented.

He had been sure at first that the witness of Liesel and Kurt would have moved his father. It hadn't. Father Luca's insistence that there was a particular darkness about the palace had done even less. Only the letter from the Fortiers had served to give him pause, but when his father realized the letter was from the prince of Destin, rather than the king, he'd become hardened once again. Two more unsuccessful searches of the princess's quarters had only served to strengthen the king's conviction that Rob was desperate and had concocted the whole scheme in order to save himself from what he feared.

Today had been his father's final test. And they'd failed.

Once he was on his horse, he made his way to the edge of town and allowed the massive beast to break into a gallop as soon as they were free from the crowded streets. Storm clouds hovered on the horizon, drawing closer and darker with each second, but Rob was too angry to turn back. The clouds reflected how he felt, and he welcomed them all the more for it.

The rain hit him like a wall of rock, huge drops stinging his skin where they pelted him, but he only turned his face up to the sky. He let them wash away every foolish hope he'd entertained over the past few weeks. Whatever Priscilla was doing... whomever she was manipulating wasn't Maleen. And if it was Maleen, she had chosen to stop fighting. Well, he was done fighting, too. And he was done feeling broken. Whatever woman his father chose for him to marry, he would marry.

But they couldn't make him like it.

He would have stayed out in the storm until it drowned him, but at the sound of his animal's protests, he finally turned back. If no one else had, his horse had earned his affection.

Dripping, he made his way back through the halls. Servants skittered to clean his sopping mess behind him, and courtiers took one look at his face and fled, but he didn't stop or slow until he reached his father's study. He hesitated only a moment outside of it.

This conversation would happen eventually. He might as well get it over with now.

"Come in," his father called at the sound of his knock.

Rob walked in. His father had been speaking with his steward in the far corner by the window. They were holding several long lists in their hands, but they both stopped speaking when he walked in.

"Roburts!" his father exclaimed. "Whatever–"

"Our list of acquisitions from Vaksam, if I'm not mistaken." Rob nodded at the lists in their hands. "So it seems you've made your decision."

The king reddened slightly, but he didn't deny it.

"I believe Marianne needed my help in the kitchens," his father's steward said quietly. "I'll return later to finish this, Your Majesty."

Rob's father nodded and took the list from his steward's hands. They waited to speak until the steward had shut the door.

"Roburts." His father let out a deep sigh. "I know this is difficult for you."

Rob just glared, and his father shook his head.

"I...I understand what Maleen meant to you, Roburts."

"And how would you know that?"

His father met his glare, warning in his eyes. "Because your mother is that to me."

Rob folded his arms. "You're not listening to Mother in this."

"Your mother didn't see the death and suffering that I did!" his father shouted, throwing the lists down on the table. "She didn't spend seven years watching the sons of other men and women die because her own son was a fool!"

Rob hadn't thought he could hurt more than he already did. But, apparently, he had been wrong. His eyes stung, and he clenched his jaw to keep his emotions at bay.

His father groaned and ran his hands through his hair before leaning heavily against his writing table.

"I'm sorry, son. That was inappropriate."

"Not undeserved, though," Rob said coldly.

"No, it was undeserved." His father looked up at him again, this time looking very tired himself. "What her uncle did was an act of war. And while I wouldn't have chosen the...path you did, he was even more to blame than you." He straightened and looked out the window, though the rain was falling so hard there was little to be seen.

"Your mother and I always believed you and Maleen could be the start of a new era," he said softly. He turned to Rob, suddenly seeming much older. "We loved her like a daughter. It killed your mother to watch that little girl grow up motherless. And after losing your sister at birth..." He was lost in thought for a moment before shaking his head. "But sometimes, the Maker has other plans. And Rob?"

"Yes?"

"Just because you lost Maleen doesn't mean you have to lose everything else."

"Would you say that if it had been Mother?" Rob growled. He was being obstinate, but the pain in his chest was too great to be anything else.

His father's lips thinned. "If your mother had died, I would have done everything in my power to raise you as best as I could. I would have led my kingdom. I would have embraced fatherhood and the crown to the best of my limited abilities."

"I never had the privilege of fatherhood," Rob spat.

"No. But you could!" His father leaned toward him over the writing table. "Rob, she wouldn't have wanted you to waste away! Maleen had more life in her than anyone else I've ever known. Do you think she would have wanted you to throw away your life just because she lost hers?"

"So you suggest I take a wife I don't love to sire a child so I might find it?"

His father laughed ruefully. "You think your mother and I were in love when we married? Good gracious, son. We'd never seen each other before meeting at the altar. But we learned to love." He straightened. "And you will, too. If you only give yourself the chance."

Rob rubbed his hands over his eyes. "Father, Priscilla...she's not who you think she is—"

"Yes." His father's voice had hardened once again. "As you've told me many times." He shook his head. "Son, I have tried my best to help you. To encourage you and walk beside you in this. But you are pushing me to a place neither of us want to be."

"But—"

"You have a duty to this kingdom!" his father thundered. "And if you won't let me help you as a father, then you'll listen to me as your king!"

Rob stared at his father.

"Roburts, as your king, I *command* you to marry that girl! And if you don't, I will disinherit you from your position as future king!"

His father breathed hard as Rob stared at him. For several eternal moments, no one spoke. Rob wanted to vomit. He and his father had never spoken to one another this way. Not even during the length of the war. And it threatened to undo him.

"Very well," he finally managed to force out in a hoarse whisper. "If you're determined to have her on the throne, then I will do as you command." He finally dared to flash his father a look, where he saw the regret already flooding his father's face.

"Rob—" he began weakly, but Rob held up a hand.

"I'll do it to protect our people from her. Because I love them." He clenched his jaw and swallowed. "But I will never love *her*."

And with those words, he turned and stalked out of the room.

As he did, though, a new idea came to him. A form of rebellion, one last stab in the dark at the hope Priscilla's strange persona had awakened in him. If he was right, it would mean everything. If he wasn't, then no one would ever know.

No one but him.

CHAPTER 26
THANK YOU

Y ou know," Priscilla said as she straightened the train of Maleen's wedding dress, "I really thought I would be jealous of you when the time came for the wedding. But I'm really not. As tight as we've got you squeezed into that thing, I'm really enjoying the freedom to breathe." Then she playfully swatted Maleen's arm. "Don't look so dour, love. Today's the fitting. Tomorrow's the wedding. Then I'll make sure you never have to set eyes on this place again."

Maleen stifled a growl as Priscilla's servant poked her in the ribs with yet another stay. Corsets had gone out of mode in recent years, after Queen Isabelle had refused to wear them. But Priscilla had insisted on having the tiniest waist ever seen at a wedding.

Which meant Maleen would have the tiniest waist ever seen at a wedding.

It also meant she could barely breathe.

The wedding was tomorrow, and Priscilla was just glowing. Meanwhile, poor Emille was still in the chair in the corner. Maleen could tell that it hurt her to sit upright in the wooden seat, hour after hour. She hadn't been able to convince them to let her move the poor woman to the cushioned window seat, which had become Maleen's, but she had, at least, been allowed to place a pillow as a cushion beneath Emille. At night, Maleen slept beside her, so that Emille might lean against her for support. She was only allowed to remove the gag for eating and drinking, and then it had to go right back on again.

If anyone had ever been asked to create a torturous situation designed to breed misery specific to Maleen, this would be it. And Priscilla knew this. She hadn't wiped that smug smile off her face since she'd been informed the wedding was back on. It was the same smile she'd flashed at Maleen back when Maleen was fifteen, and Rob had asked Priscilla to dance because she was of age and Maleen wasn't.

"Think of the opportunity I'm giving you," Priscilla said as she took the tiara off of Maleen's head and put it on her own. "You're getting to live out your fantasy. Maybe your life didn't take the path you'd hoped, but you're getting what no jilted lover has before. You're wedding the man you loved! You've got the wedding gown, the tiara, the parade...you'll even get the kiss."

Maleen scoffed. "And you'll be enjoying it as well."

"Naturally. I *am* going to be his wife."

Maleen tasted bile at the back of her throat.

Perhaps that was the worst part of all of this. Priscilla was right. She was getting everything she'd dreamed of. Rob would lead her at his side through the streets, surrounded by all the people who loved him. She would be dripping with the world's most expensive silks and gauzes and jewels, and then...

Then he would swear to love Priscilla, kiss Maleen, and then she would never see him again. Priscilla would have him in her clutches, and most likely, Maleen and anyone that could be used as a witness against her, would die.

"You enjoy that tiny waist," Priscilla said, picking up her

fifth truffle in five minutes. "I'll be pregnant in no time, so it's not as if it really matters to me."

Maleen froze.

A memory, much like a little mouse, niggled at her mind. She had to search for a few moments in order to find what had triggered it.

What are you thinking?

They had been standing under the moonlight, and Rob had been playing with a lock of her hair. How did she remember all that?

She had given him an ornery grin.

Only that I'm going to have your babies.

His eyes had gleamed as they'd moved from her eyes to her mouth. *Mmm*, he'd said, kissing her softly. *Yes, you will.*

And now, Priscilla would be the one to have his babies. Except, they wouldn't be his babies alone. They would be hers, too. And without a doubt, they would be subject to all of the vile compliments, lies, and manipulation that Maleen was being subjected to now. Except, their fate would be far worse. Because she would either force them into submission through means Maleen didn't even want to think about...or she would make them as twisted and vile as she was. Even worse, Rob's people–and Maleen's–would suffer the same fate.

Rob would suffer as well.

A spark hissed to life inside of her, and Maleen ground her teeth. There had to be a way.

Maleen spent the rest of the day in thoughtful silence. Priscilla didn't seem to notice this, but that was actually good. She was so wrapped up in wedding plans, all issued from the safety of her chambers, that she didn't think twice when Maleen requested to have a special tea prepared for Emille.

"For some reason, she's been having a difficult time sleeping," she said, glaring at Priscilla.

Priscilla laughed at her scowl. "Of course, love. She's dying tomorrow. We might as well make her comfortable today."

She was in such good graces that she even allowed Maleen to write her own list of teas and herbs to send down to the kitchen with the castle servant who appeared when summoned.

Soon after, Maleen's requested selection of herbs and teas was delivered. Instead of having the tea prepared for her by the kitchen staff, however, Maleen had requested the tea leaves be served dry. "For better mixing," she told Priscilla when Priscilla sent her a curious glance. For a moment, Maleen wondered if Priscilla would object, but she sent her thanks up to the Maker when Priscilla finally shrugged and went back to what she was doing.

Left alone, Maleen mixed a little of it for Emille and let the older woman drink, which she did desperately. But what Priscilla didn't see, however, was that Maleen had removed most of the chamomile from the bowl and crushed it in with the two other herbs.

If nothing else, during her seven years in the tower, Maleen had read. She had read book upon book full of knowledge she would probably never need, and she doubted many other people would ever be interested in such things as the various breeds of milk cows or the mating habits of the common ground squirrel. But there had been several very useful books, a few that she had read more than once, on the many uses of common herbs. And through these books, she'd learned that the sleeping powers of chamomile could be multiplied when combined with mashed capper thorns and oil of lemon.

Maleen even pretended to drink some of Emille's tea before

going to bed. Then she made sure that Priscilla saw her lie down and pretend to breathe deeply. Her heart, however, far from resting, was racing in her chest as Priscilla ordered the lights out and the servants to their own beds.

The guards would be the most difficult. But as they couldn't injure her, being as she was Priscilla's puppet, she held the upper hand. Standing silently, she grabbed a handful of the mixture she'd mashed into a powder earlier, and waited.

Sure enough, the first guard came at her within seconds. Maleen held her breath and smashed the mixture against his face as he grabbed her left arm. Within seconds, he was snoring on the floor.

Because it was dark, the other guards didn't see what had made their comrade fall, so it was easier to knock them unconscious in turn until they were all snoring on the floor.

Emille, who had been watching, whimpered, but Maleen didn't have time to untie her just yet. The guards would only be unconscious for an hour at best, which left her very little time. So she went to Priscilla's room and tossed the rest of the powder at Priscilla and her guards as well.

She didn't bother trying to escape through the door or the windows. Priscilla put an enchantment on each every night, preventing anyone but herself or her guards from opening them. Nor did Maleen try to strike anyone with a knife. The only weapon at her disposal was the pen knife. She could try to take the guards' weapons, but their sleep was so light she was afraid a single touch might jostle them awake.

She did, however, go over to the vanity and pull out the little bag of metal rectangles. Her hands trembled as she removed her pen knife. If she made a mistake, she could end up killing the very people she was trying to protect. But if she succeeded...

Priscilla would get everything she deserved, and Maleen's loved ones would be safe.

Maleen held the knife above Jim's rectangle, but her hand was shaking so hard at first that she didn't dare touch the knife to it.

"Do mine first."

Maleen jerked her head up to see that Emille had loosened her gag enough to whisper over the top. Had she been able to do that the whole time? Not that it would have mattered. If they'd seen her, Priscilla or her guards would have simply pulled it up again.

"What?" Maleen's whisper broke.

"I know what you're trying to do." Emille gave her a sad smile. "I would try to talk you out of it, but I know you won't listen." She took a deep breath. "So do mine first. Then you'll know if it can be done."

Maleen stared at her friend for a long moment before nodding slowly. The thought of testing her theory on Emille threatened to put her into a panic attack, but Emille was right. It would be better to know if she was unsuccessful on the first person rather than the fourth or tenth or fifteenth. So she pushed Jim's little rectangle away and searched by the light of the moon until she found Emille's.

Please don't let me kill her, she prayed.

With tremulous breaths, she took the knife's point and tried to run it through Emille's name. But no, it wouldn't let her do that. Apparently, she needed to put down another victim first.

Very well, then. On the other side of the rectangle, Maleen did her best to write Priscilla's name. She pressed hard, but try as she might, her hand wouldn't write.

Her breaths began to come in and out too fast. The magic would not let her write Priscilla's name. She had intended to visit the witch's evil back upon her, but it seemed Priscilla's intent to punish others had been well-crafted. Maleen stared blankly down at the little piece of metal for a long time, unsure of what to do. Everything had depended upon her scratching out the names of her loved ones and substituting the princess's name instead, allowing the princess to defeat herself.

Unless...

Her stomach nearly convulsed as she tried once again to put the pen knife to the metal. If it wouldn't allow her to turn the magic upon the dark princess, perhaps it would allow...

Yes. She'd done it. She let out a shaky sigh as she turned the little metal rectangle toward the moonlight leaking in. There in rough lines was her own name instead. This time, she tried once again to scratch out Emille's name, the knife slid easily through the letters.

When she was finished, she hardly dared to raise her eyes to where her mentor sat, terrified by the silence. Was Emille dead? Had Maleen just killed the closest person she'd ever had to a mother?

But there was no blood. Instead, Emille was smiling gently down at her.

"I always knew you would be brilliant," the older woman said, tears running down her eyes. "I just didn't want it to be like this." Her shoulders shook as she sobbed silently. "I didn't want to leave you, love. I tried so hard to stay, but I was injured, and they made me—"

Maleen jumped to her feet and ran to her and held her face. "Never once did I doubt your love," she whispered.

"Tomorrow," Emille said, her gaze going to the guards as she spoke, "I want you to do everything in your power to expose her. Don't think about me. I'll do my best to escape. But whether or not I'm successful, you must free your people. And yourself."

Maleen's throat felt so tight she couldn't answer. Her instinct was to protest and insist that she needed to get Emille to safety. But her friend was right. Even if she got away, thousands more would suffer. This, Maleen realized, would be their final adventure together. Still unable to speak, Maleen kissed her beloved mentor on the cheek and went back to the rectangles and stared at them.

She had wondered at one point if crossing the names out on the rectangles might suffice to cancel Priscilla's darkness. But based on her admittedly limited readings of Sortheleige, she got the feeling this kind of darkness couldn't simply be canceled. It had to be destroyed. And there were very few who knew how. The Fortier family from Destin knew how. So did Queen Arianna of the Merpeople, and a few holy men scattered about the western realm, but Maleen wasn't confident enough in her knowledge to risk leaving Priscilla any avenue to her friends. So with a steadier hand this time, Maleen crossed the other names off one by one and wrote her name on the back of each little piece of metal, confidence and peace slowly pooling in her mind with each one.

A soft knock sounded at the door just as she finished the final tile. Maleen darted to it. "Hello?" she softly called out, hoping Priscilla's muffling spell had died.

"Maleen?" came a strangely familiar voice.

"Jalyna?" she whispered back.

"Mother got your note."

Maleen nearly fainted from relief.

"She's trying to spread the word," Jalyna continued. "We'll be gone by morning, but she wanted me to tell you first. So you wouldn't worry."

"Oh. Thank you," Maleen called back, unsure of what else to say.

"Maleen?"

"Yes?"

There was a pause. "Thank you. For saving my family." And with that, she was gone.

CHAPTER 27
HOLD FAST

"Happy wedding day, Maleen!"

Maleen twisted and groaned at the sound of Priscilla's voice, but that only made Priscilla laugh.

"Congratulations to both of us! Look how far we've come!" And with that, Maleen was forced out of bed. Priscilla nearly forced her to eat breakfast, too, until Maleen told her that if she did, she would promptly be sick.

Skipping breakfast was the only liberty allowed her that morning, however. Maleen was directed to stand so the maids could begin their preparations. And stand. And stand. As they worked, Maleen could only imagine what the rest of the palace might think, having a princess who refused to allow them to help with her wedding preparations, rarely leaving her room except to be attended by the prince.

She wouldn't be allowed to find out, though, because Priscilla had timed her arrival to the parade so she would arrive just in time to begin.

"Remember," Priscilla said, holding up the bag of rectangles and shaking it, "you would be wise not to try anything. Not only do I have these, but I know where every single one of your friends lives and works. One mistake from you, and they'll all be punished."

Maleen had to work hard not to smile. No, only one would face that danger. And she was ready.

Still, Maleen couldn't help wondering what her parents had felt as they died. Had they been afraid? Or worried? Had they suffered? To her surprise, Maleen wasn't afraid. She was sure that Priscilla would punish her. Probably punish her to death once she realized what Maleen had done. But the body could only hang on so long, and if Maleen was to go, she could be glad her death would be a noble one. She would leave this world for the next without fear.

Thank you, she prayed silently as Priscilla placed the tiara on her head. *You've allowed me to be queen even here.*

In a way, it was what Maleen had always wanted. Not the pain and suffering. That had never been her desire. But a meaningful life. Maleen had always desired to protect her people from evil, to stop any harm that might come to them. And while this death certainly wouldn't be attended by mass mourning or white flowers in the streets, as was Ertrique's custom, she was confident that the Maker had given her a way to be the queen that her people, even if they would remain ignorant of it, needed her to be.

The queen that Rob had, at one time, believed she could be. But before Rob or anyone else could be completely free, she had yet one task to finish.

Wearing Priscilla's face for the last time, she stepped out the door and was immediately offered escort by Metakinos's royal guards. They surrounded her as she walked down to the entry hall and out the doors to the drive where Rob was waiting.

Maleen's heart stopped when she saw him. Even with only one arm, he was the handsomest man in the world. Or perhaps that made him more handsome. His dark curls had been cut short again, which was a pity. She would have liked to reach up and tousle them once more. The cut of his jaw was well defined by the set of his military collar, and arm or no arm, his shoulders sent shivers down her spine.

The light was gone from his eyes, but Maleen understood why this time. She had failed his last test, and he felt abandoned, just as she had begun to make him hope. Now that her friends were shielded from Priscilla's wrath, though...now he could know the truth. He must know the truth.

"Are you ready?" he asked in a clipped tone.

"More than ready." Priscilla smiled bashfully.

He nodded once then gave the signal for the parade to begin. Maleen heard the sounds of music and singing coming from the front of the procession. Rob guided her to the center of the road, two servant girls following them as they held up her wedding train. As they made their way into the city, people crowded one another on each side of the street, throwing flowers, waving, and calling out blessings. All over, smaller groups broke into song. Maleen nearly allowed herself to smile when she heard several lines being sung from Ertrique's customary wedding songs.

But she couldn't go on as if this would last forever. It was now or never.

She tightened her grip on his arm just enough to make him turn and look at her. Closing her eyes, she focused on breaking the magic long enough to utter a few words.

"Hold fast," she whispered.

Her punishment was immediate. Maleen's back felt as if someone had stuck a knife into it, and she stumbled. Rob caught her. When she was recovered enough from the pain to open her eyes, his face was near hers.

"What was that?" he whispered.

"Oh, nothing." Priscilla made her breathlessly laugh. "I think I stepped on a dry nettle twig." She took a deep breath. "Shall we go on?"

The line of people around them had come to a halt, and Rob frowned as he searched her face. "You're sure you feel well enough?"

She nodded, though really, she felt like curling up and dying. Priscilla's attack, quick as it had been, had felt the way Maleen had always imagined a lightning bolt to feel. But after Priscilla's repeated insistence that she was well, slowly they began to walk again, and Maleen began to prepare herself for her second attack. She would have to take care. Priscilla was punishing her for sure. Her nerves still throbbed, and there was a lingering pain that ran along her spine. But Priscilla couldn't punish her too much. Not yet, at least. She needed Maleen to finish this. And finish this Maleen would.

As they neared a footbridge that ran over a brook, Maleen would have liked to take another deep breath. But that would warn Priscilla of what she was about to do, so as they stepped onto the bridge, she tried again. But this time, she was prepared for the pain. And she made her voice louder for it.

"Hold fast."

She wasn't prepared after all. A flash of white, hot pain hit her head, and she swayed. Rob caught her, but instead of setting her on her feet, he kept her close.

"Maleen?" he whispered. "If you're in there, please tell me!"

But Priscilla just shoved him off lightly. "I'm only a little woozy from skipping breakfast. You'll have to forgive me, Your Highness."

He stared at her.

"Roburts?" the king called to them from his place in the carriage behind them, "is everything well?"

Rob was slow to take his gaze from her face, but eventually, he nodded and they continued walking again.

Word was beginning to spread about the faltering princess. Twice now, the parade had been held up. And as the church was coming into view, Maleen knew she had to do it once more. Her head hurt so badly she could barely stand up straight, but she could survive one more time. And if she didn't? Well, perhaps Priscilla wouldn't get the wedding she had planned on after all.

Rob couldn't marry a princess who was dead.

They reached the steps of the church. But instead of entering, as Priscilla's magic was urging her to do, Maleen knelt and placed her hand on the door. This time, as she uttered the words, they were stilted and weak, her focus unraveling due to the continuous pounding in her head.

"Hold...fast."

Then she stood, so tired from fighting that she was unable to even look at Rob, and had to let him lead her through the doors.

She had little knowledge of what went on around her after she reached the altar, as remaining upright took all of her strength. She would have gladly fainted if Priscilla had let her. But she was aware the whole time of Rob's hand in hers. So instead of fighting the pain, she chose to focus on the pressure of his fingers and the low rumble of his voice, reverberating in her chest.

"Your Highness?"

Maleen opened her eyes to see the priest looking at her with wide eyes.

"Yes?" she asked.

"Um...do you vow to respect and honor your husband, to cherish him faithfully all your days, and do you, before the Maker and all these witnesses, covenant to sacrifice of yourself for his good?"

Maleen smiled, and she knew it wasn't from Priscilla.

"I do."

"Then," the priest said, with a small sigh of relief, "I present His Royal Highness and his bride!"

Rob stepped closer, and to her great confusion, Maleen realized that the light was in his eyes once again. But this was a new light. Determination, she realized. And ferocity. A look like he might wear on the battlefield. Was it there because of her? Had he heard her desperate warning? Did he understand that her words were a cry for help?

"I have something I want to give you," he said, a soft smile on his lips as he placed a golden chain in her hands. Hanging from it was a pink jewel the size of an olive.

"This," he said, touching the gem, "is a special jewel. It's tradition for the king to give his bride a jewel with their names engraved on it together." He looked her in the eyes. "An unbreakable stone for an unbreakable love." And without giving her a chance to respond, he pulled her close with his good arm. Then his mouth was on hers, and Maleen was seventeen again as he'd kissed her under the stars, surrounded by flowers dripping with silver raindrops that glistened under the light of the moon like diamonds.

But no, this was far beyond anything she had felt that night. The way he pressed his hand against the small of her back, his lips moving on hers. Slow. Strong. Sure. He tasted of mint and sunshine, and Maleen found herself clutching at his coat, as if holding on might let her remain here in this moment forever. He let go and looked at her as a starving man might look at a feast, his hand lifting up to trace the side of her face.

"I know your kiss," he murmured, running the backs of his knuckles down her cheek.

Maleen smiled in spite of the searing pain Priscilla sent down her legs.

"This isn't going to be easy," he whispered. "I'll need you to do something for me."

"Anything," Maleen whispered, unsure of whether or not she or Priscilla was speaking.

"Hold fast," he said, his fingers tightening slightly on her shoulder. Then he turned her to face the crowd, which had filled the church, and held up their clasped hands, the jewel dangling between them, and the people let out a cheer.

They were shuffled out to an open carriage after that, from which Maleen and Rob waved to the people outside the church, pausing every so often to toss coins from a basket sitting between them.

In some twisted way, Maleen thought as she watched him, Priscilla had been right. If she couldn't have her own happily ever after with the man of her dreams, at least she had today. And Priscilla would never be able to take that away.

The carriage ride couldn't last forever, though, and soon they were back at the palace. Maleen had resisted Priscilla every chance she'd gotten. But no matter how hard she tried to shake it, she knew Priscilla's invisible chains were still around her, and the effort it took to resist was making her tired. She wasn't free yet. Even worse, she would have to see what Priscilla had done to Emille in her absence. Or, more likely, what she would do when Maleen finally returned.

"I know you asked to prepare in your own chambers," Rob said before leaving the carriage. "But when you're ready, I'll be in the honeymoon suite." His cheeks reddened slightly. Maleen's cheeks heated as well. An odd thing to say, considering he seemed to know what kind of game Priscilla was at. But she had no choice in the matter. Because against her will, she was already speaking again.

"I'll be there soon," Priscilla giggled, and with one last desperate look behind her, Maleen was escorted back to her chambers.

As soon as the door was shut and locked, Maleen faced her manipulator. But she had little time to look as a handful of small, metal rectangles was thrown at her face.

"So you've chosen to take their places," Priscilla hissed, no longer from Maleen's mouth. "Very well, then. Their fates shall be yours as well." Then she paused, and a smile crept over her face. A smile that made her look every bit like the witch she had become. Maleen tried to look around her to see if Emille was still alive, but Priscilla blocked her view as she drew closer.

"No. Do you know what? Since you've made it your business to alert him to your presence here, then you'll both suffer for it. He's going to lose you the way he should have lost you years ago." She looked at the guard, and as she did, Maleen could feel Priscilla's features leave her face.

"Take her to the stream in the garden. Drown her as well as you can, and I'll do the same." She looked at Maleen, her smile vanishing like smoke. "And this time, he won't be able to save you."

CHAPTER 28
THE TRUTH

Rob's head swirled as he watched his bride make her way back to her chambers. Maleen was in there. He was sure of it. Whatever had silenced her into submission in the garden seemed to be gone now. Three times, she'd given him the warning. And when she'd kissed him...

He'd only ever shared her kiss one night of their lives. But he'd never forgotten.

Should he let her go to her chambers? He'd nearly followed her to make sure she was safe. But the appearance of a familiar face around the corner stopped him. He knew his parents, who had followed his carriage in their own, were waiting to congratulate him, or at least, his father was. His mother was about as unhappy regarding the marriage as he had been. He didn't stop to wait for them, though. Instead, he followed the familiar face to where it had disappeared down a smaller hall to the right.

"Henri!" he called quietly. Sure enough, there was a hulking figure in a dark blue cloak, standing in a corner. The figure turned to reveal the face of Destin's crown prince.

"You're here!" he cried. Then, unable to stop himself, he

went on. "Did you sense it?" he asked breathlessly. Henri was older than he was by several years, and they had never been intimate friends, but if there was anyone in the world he could trust to be honest, it would be him.

Henri nodded grimly. "There's definitely Fae power here." His frown deepened. "And several others as well. But they're in raw form and poorly cobbled together."

"Liesel and Kurt said you had investigated Priscilla before?"

"We tried, but her uncle, the one who adopted her, was most unhelpful. Which we can only guess means he was complicit." He looked down the hall in the direction the princess had gone. "Unfortunately, her sloppy combination of dark powers means it will be even more dangerous to confront her."

Rob paused. "Shouldn't we confront her?"

"Absolutely. I just mean it will be more difficult to do so without someone getting hurt. Do you have your sword?"

Rob drew it in response, though not without a fleeting sense of shame. After losing his arm, he'd had to change his weapon to a short sword, something light enough that he could use it single-handedly. But Henri didn't give his sword a second glance. Instead, he looked at the guards standing near the entrance. "Bring them with us."

Rob paused. "Should we warn my parents?"

Henri considered then shook his head. "No. The fewer people who know what we're doing, the less likely she is to be prepared. Let's go."

Before they could go very far, they were greeted with a chorus of shocked cries and hit by a barrage of questions as they passed the wedding party.

"Rob!" the king called. "What is the meaning of this?" Then he seemed to see Henri and blanched. "Prince Henri!"

Henri nodded respectfully. "I'm sorry, Your Highness, but you have a dangerous witch in your home. I'll explain later."

THE TRUTH • 295

Rob's father continued to call after them, but Rob followed Henri, praying the whole way that they weren't too late. Only as they approached Priscilla's door did Rob realize he hadn't even told Henri where Priscilla was staying. But somehow the prince had known.

"Your Highnesses?"

They turned just before reaching her door to see Kurt behind them.

"Might I join you?"

Rob opened his mouth to say no, he should be with his family, but Henri spoke first.

"Of course. We could use someone of your talent."

Unable to argue with Henri, Rob simply shrugged and they started walking again. When they reached Priscilla's door, the two sentries who were usually standing guard outside were gone. Henri nodded at Rob, who went up to the door and banged on it.

"Priscilla, come out, please. We need to talk."

"Ask away!" she called without opening the door. Henri nodded again, so Rob tried once more.

"What was it you said to me when we were walking? Something about behind held or holding?"

"I think you were hearing things, love," she laughed. "I was commenting on the weather."

Something in Rob broke, and with a shout of anger, he kicked down the door. A burly guard who must have been inside the room stepped between him and the princess. Before he could engage them, though, Henri had used a crossbow on one, and Kurt had leaped at the other, his leap more like an animal than a man. Rob darted through as soon as they were out of the way.

Priscilla was sitting on the floor, a pile of rough metal rectangles in a heap before her. She was dropping them, one by one, into a basin of water. Her eyes were closed as she muttered inaudible whispers over the basin. A sweet, sickly scent filled Rob's nose, and he had the sudden urge to vomit.

"Figured it out, did you?" Priscilla finally opened her eyes and looked up at him. And for a second, Rob froze.

It was Priscilla who was looking at him. But it wasn't. Instead of the youthful, blooming girl he'd been courting, this woman's face was at least thirty years older than it had been the last time he'd seen her. Dark bags and wrinkles surrounded her eyes, and her face was covered in unnatural lines. She leered at him now.

"You might be looking for Maleen, but you married me, my love," she chirped. "Which means I now have rights over your house and kingdoms."

Henri strode forward and grabbed her by the front of her dress, lifting her up off the ground. "Where's the girl, witch?" he growled.

"Only meeting the fate she should have met years ago," she spat back.

Henri opened his mouth, but before he could speak, a scream pierced the air. It came from the open window. Rob's heart stopped.

It was the same scream that had haunted him since boyhood.

A rope was tied to the balcony and was hanging out over the banister. Rob ran to it and looked out over the edge.

Maleen was there, and she was being pressed down into the water by one of Priscilla's guards, who was forcing her face beneath its surface.

"Sire, no!" one of his own guards shouted after him, but he was too late. Rob had grabbed the rope with his good arm and was over the ledge in a moment. Unfortunately, he'd forgotten briefly that he only had one arm, and the rope burned his hand so badly he hit the ground at an odd angle.

Ignoring that pain in his knee, however, he sprinted toward

Priscilla's man and shoved his sword deep into the man's heart. Blood pooled out around them as his heavy body hit the ground. It splashed onto Rob's clothes as he knelt down and pulled Maleen up out of the water. Dragging her onto the bank, he helped her into a sitting position so she could cough up the water.

But the cough never came. Instead, she continued struggling for breath, her hands at her throat. Panic churned in his stomach as he stared, not sure what to do. He began beating her on the back, hoping to dislodge the water.

"She won't stop choking!" he cried as Henri and the others came up beside him. "I don't know what to do!"

Henri put his hand to her neck and closed his eyes for a long second.

"Blast. I wish my mother was here!" Henri closed his eyes. Then he opened them and leaned toward Rob. "What she's suffering from is Fae magic. That means she isn't really choking. But the magic tricks her into feeling like she is." He looked down at Maleen. "You have to breathe deeply!" he told her. "You're not actually choking!"

Instead of breathing deeply, Maleen began to turn blue.

"You." Henri turned to Rob. "You have to convince her. If she doesn't breathe, she'll die."

Rob pulled her into his lap and cradled her there. Brushing her hair with his hand, he leaned close and pressed his face against hers, his mouth beside her ear.

"I know it's been a long seven years. But I need you to trust me."

He pulled back enough to see her eyes on him. They were half closed.

"What she did to you is a lie," he whispered. "I know I've asked it of you so many times before. But I need you to hold fast for me one more time."

She twitched in his arms.

"You know the truth!" he said, his voice rising as her eyes fluttered shut. "Cling to it! Hold fast, Maleen! Hold fast!"

CHAPTER 29
MINE

Spots swam in Maleen's vision. She couldn't dislodge the water from her throat. Every time she tried, it caught, and she fell a little further into the dark. Henri called it a lie. But what could he know? He wasn't the one who couldn't breathe.

Maybe it would be easier to give in. Just let the water take her. No more fighting. No more pain.

"You know the truth!" Rob screamed in her ear. "Cling to it! Hold fast, Maleen! Hold fast!" His voice shook, and she could feel his tears on her face.

His tears were real. A stark contrast to what was caught in her throat. Just as the truth she'd been killing herself to tell him was in complete contrast to every lie Priscilla had ever told and forced her to tell. Priscilla had used her heinously in every way possible, but Rob would never lie to her.

"Breathe!" he roared in her ear.

Help me find the truth, she prayed silently. *Because I'm not sure I can find it on my own.*

And then, with what she knew would be her last attempt, she pulled in a deep lungful of air.

The air gave her the ability to open her eyes again. And

though her vision was still fuzzy, she could see Rob's face, inches from hers as he pressed his forehead against hers, his tears washing over her face.

"I did," she managed to croak.

He pulled back and stared at her, his green eyes red.

"Hold fast," she croaked, though her voice was slightly stronger this time. "I did."

This time, she felt him slide his hand beneath her head. Then he lifted it and pressed his lips against hers, and she closed her eyes again. But this time, it was to feel nothing but him.

When he finally released her, it seemed the entire palace was in the garden surrounding them. The sound of the queen's cry when she saw Maleen and Rob covered in blood was only silenced by Prince Henri's interference. There were voices everywhere, and eventually, Rob finally allowed her to stand, but he kept his arm around her waist, pressing her tightly against his side.

Eventually, Henri convinced Rob's parents and all the concerned onlookers to allow Maleen and Rob to go to their chambers to be seen by physicians. During their confrontation in her chambers, he had been forced to kill Priscilla. Now that she was safe, Henri told everyone, what Maleen needed more than anything was rest.

Maleen couldn't have agreed more. This time, it was she who was waited on, hand and foot. And while she would certainly never bring up any of the servants' past actions, she couldn't help but notice that those she recognized blushed every time their eyes met hers.

Of course, before she had allowed herself to rest, she pleaded with Prince Henri to find Emille. And it wasn't long before he sent word back that Emille hadn't been tortured and killed. Rather, one of the Vaksam guards admitted to having taken pity on her, thinking she reminded him of his own mother, and had secreted her away when Priscilla had ordered her dead. Once Emille was discovered, Maleen was more than happy to allow herself to be attended to.

Several hours later, she was invited to supper with Rob, his parents, Emille, and Prince Henri. Maleen had been given another room far from Priscilla's to get ready in, but she felt a distinctly familiar thrill run through her when a knock sounded, and it was opened to reveal Rob. Unlike the times before, however, he was smiling at her.

Shyly, Maleen accepted his proffered arm, and they walked for a moment in silence before Maleen could wait no longer. Looking around, she pulled them outside and into a corner of the garden, which had already been cleared of any sign of the violence that had been done there earlier in the day. Coming to a stop in one of the pavilions, which was so surrounded by trees that the pavilion itself was nearly invisible, she took his hand in hers and studied it, suddenly unsure how to utter the words that were about to burst from her chest.

"What is it?" His voice was gentle.

She smiled and shook her head but realized that tears were closer to the surface than she had believed them to be. "I..." She swallowed and tried again. "I just need to know." Finally, she was able to look him in the eye. "Why didn't you come for me? Back in the tower, I mean?" Her voice hitched. "I waited for you. I knew that if I just–"

"Maleen." His eyes widened. "Don't you know how the war started?"

She shook her head.

"As soon as you were locked in that tower, I went home and rallied my best soldiers. Against my father's wishes, I led them back to your palace. Unfortunately, your uncle discovered us before we could make it." He tucked a lock of hair behind her ear. "The war started because I came for you." He gave her a sheepish smile. "In a stupid way, mind you. I didn't stop to think that maybe I could free you another way. But don't ever for a moment think I meant to abandon you."

Maleen stood silently for a long time as this sank in. He hadn't abandoned her. He'd started a war for her. She felt tears beginning to fall again, but for more reasons than she could express. Relief. Sorrow. Heartache. They had hoped their love would bring two worlds together. Instead, they had torn their countries apart.

"Hey, hey," he whispered, lifting her face to look into his. "Don't you dare think this is your fault. I made my decisions. Your uncle made his. But if it makes you feel better, we learned recently that your uncle had planned to make war on us anyway." He gave her a sad smile. "I suppose I simply gave him an excuse for an early start." He took her hand and brought it to his lips. Frowning, he brushed his lips over her fingers.

"You...you don't know what it was like. The torture of knowing you were waiting for me and not being able to cross such a short distance to get you. And then, when we finally won, I went out to your tower to find that your own soldiers had destroyed it and set it on fire." His voice shook slightly. "So when I saw you in that market on the way back, I thought it was my mind playing tricks on me. I'd just had confirmation that you were dead." He paused, and when he spoke, his voice was a whole octave deeper. "Words can't express how very much I wanted to die."

Maleen traced his face with her fingertips, moving them down his temple, along his jaw, along his neck, and over to his shoulder. He closed his eyes and leaned his head back at her touch.

"What happened?" she asked softly, fingering the empty sleeve.

He shrugged and opened his eyes. "Your beloved hero wasn't as invincible as he believed himself to be." Then he shook his head. "When I think about what a young, stupid puppy I was—"

She put her fingers on his lips and smiled. "I loved that boy." She stood on the tips of her toes and gently pressed a kiss against his lips. "And I love this man," she breathed, her lips still on his.

"You know," he breathed back, "we're supposed to be in the dining hall by now. But I know for a fact that our honeymoon suite is ready and waiting."

Her heart nearly jumped out of her chest, but then she sighed. "You might have kissed me today, but you married Priscilla."

"Did I?" Rob smiled and arched a dark brow as he reached up and gently traced the thin golden chain that hung from her neck. Picking up the pink gem pendant, he pinched it between his fingers and held it up for her to see with the light of the moon's illumination.

"Do you see that etching in the light?" he asked.

"No. But...oh, wait!" She leaned in closer and just made out the names. Then she gasped. Not only was her name beside his, but below each name was the year of their respective births.

"But...you gave me this just this morning! How did you know?"

He smiled, and it was more genuine this time. "It's tradition in Metakinos for the groom to offer his new bride a gift with their names inscribed upon it." He turned the gem in his hand. "Priscilla's face might have been visible, but I knew you were somewhere in there. And I wasn't about to marry the wrong girl." His smile turned impish. "I don't know if you recall, but I *might* also have asked the holy man to omit Priscilla's name from the vows." His face sobered, but his eyes sparkled. "Titles only and all that."

This time, it was Maleen who pulled him into a kiss. A kiss

that was far more passionate than the one they had shared that morning in the church.

"You are so beautiful," he murmured. Maleen let out a strangled cry and kissed him harder. He buried his good hand in her hair and sighed against her lips.

Before they could enjoy the moment too much, however, someone cleared her throat.

They both looked down to see the queen looking at them with arched brows and folded arms. Maleen's face heated as if it was on fire.

"Sorry, Mother," Rob said, looking not the least bit sorry. "Maleen had something she wanted to ask me."

"Oh, we all have questions." This time, the queen's mouth quirked up at the corner, and Maleen could see that her eyes were twinkling. "I thought that was the point of this dinner."

Rob laughed, and Maleen found herself laughing as well. And as she walked down the pavilion steps back to the main path, the queen put her arms around Maleen's shoulders and squeezed.

"I know it's selfish of me," she whispered in Maleen's ear, "but I lost a daughter once. And from the first time I saw you standing there alone and motherless, I wished you could be mine."

Something, some hole in Maleen's heart that she had nearly forgotten was there, healed in that moment. And Maleen stopped walking and threw herself into the queen's arms. And the queen held her back. It wasn't the stiff, formal embrace of familiar monarchs, but the tight, warm embrace of a mother and child. Then Rob took her arm again and tucked it beneath his, and at that moment, as they headed toward the castle, Maleen knew everything would be all right.

EPILOGUE

Priscilla's experimental jabs into the darkness had affected, upon further investigation, many more injured parties than were first thought. As soon as the truth about what she'd done was made known, stories of exaggerated trade agreements, castle staff deaths, and the disappearance of citizens who had displeased the Vaksam crown began to flood in. Henri stayed with Rob's family for another month to help them sort out all the damage that had been done. Henri's father, High King Everard Fortier, made it known that he was on the way to Vaksam himself.

"He's not in the mood to fool around after what happened here," Henri told Maleen after receiving a letter from his father. "It seems he truly does have gout, but that's not going to spare him from the crimes he committed in lying and scheming while using his niece's dark magic to get what he wanted."

"So..." Maleen had frowned. "He's not going to start a war?"

Henri snorted. "The western realm has a binding agreement that no crown shall knowingly enter into use of dark magic, and Vaksam was part of that agreement. Starting a war would be incredibly stupid, and somehow, I doubt the old man has the desire for war when his heir was just killed and his gout keeps him in his bedchambers."

It was decided quickly that the best way to move forward would be to unite the remnants of Ertrique with Metakinos under one crown. When the plan was first proposed, Maleen feared the outcry of her people and accusations of betrayal. But to her surprise, her survival and ascension to the throne were met with wild approval by the people of both kingdoms.

"I'm not sure why you're so surprised," Rob said one day after they had spoken with several local governors in the region. "Uniting the two kingdoms means a permanent end to the war that tore their lives apart for seven years."

Unfortunately, the countryside itself wouldn't be healed so easily. Entire villages had been decimated, and many families were struggling to recover, as Maleen's uncle had drained their resources to feed his army. Rebel militias had to be stamped out, and royal property had to be repossessed from the outlaws who had claimed it.

And yet even their recovery began to take shape. It was discovered soon upon return to Maleen's palace that her grandparents had at one time seen fit to purchase samples of the seeds from various farms all over the country. Hundreds of barrels of the many seed types were discovered in a cool cellar that had been dug beneath the Ertriquen palace. These were immediately tracked to their original regions and were distributed quickly in preparation for the next year.

Maleen also found that her place as rightful queen hadn't been forgotten by their allies. Food and other resources began to arrive not long after the wedding, just as autumn began to set in. Maleen cried as she read each letter from her old friends and relatives, overwhelmed by their generosity.

She was particularly struck by the letter from Princess Olivia of Ombrin. It arrived not long after her liberation, but she read it often. For some reason, Princess Olivia's words had an unusual healing quality to them, like aloe to a burn. The night of her coronation was one such night, and after all of her preparations had been made, she stole away to her personal chambers to read it once more.

My Dearest Maleen,

In truth, there's no way to make up for the loss of seven years. I weep as I pen this, thinking of all you have suffered. You must have felt so completely alone. I cannot go back and explain it to the dear child who was shut up in that tower, waiting for a faithful friend to rescue her. Hopefully, however, I can help you understand why there wasn't more interference from outside kingdoms. I will also labor to offer hope for your future.

As soon as you were locked in the tower, Launce and I set off immediately for Destin. We wasted no time in meeting with Everard and Isa concerning your situation. (In case you've forgotten, Launce is Queen Isa's brother, which means we get to enjoy a faster audience with our sister and brother-in-law than the average monarch.)

Everard was immediately ready to set off with an envoy to force your uncle into diplomacy when your uncle sent word of his own. It seems he had anticipated our interference, and he threatened to set fire to his own people's cities and villages if we so much as crossed into your country. He would, he claimed, tell everyone in his country that he was right, and the other kingdoms were making war upon you. He then went into other threats that he would release upon his own people as well, blaming us in the process.

Everard could have easily disposed of him alone given the threat, but your uncle also claimed to have dozens of secret agents ready to deploy the same punishment. Because of your uncle's violent history, we feared for your people. Cobren and Destin did all we could to discourage war. Everard had long suspected your uncle was preparing to make war on Metakinos, and it seems that his fears were justified.

As soon as the war broke out, we refused to sell your uncle weapons, and most of the other kingdoms followed suit. Unfortunately, illegal trade is lucrative, and your uncle found sellers more than willing to bring him weapons that way. He drained your kingdom's coffers in his attempt to take Metakinos, and his people suffered for it. We did what we could, leaving supplies at the border towns under the cover of night, but I fear it wasn't nearly enough.

I hated that war. It stole so much from your people and the people around them. And from you, my darling girl. We had always believed that you and Rob would be the answer to the struggles between your kingdoms.

I have asked Everard if he knows what happened to your parents, and though he has no sure answer, he's fairly sure that they were killed by an anonymous political rival who was opposed to the work they were doing in order to find peace with Metakinos. You, it seemed, were destined by the Maker to finish their work.

I'm afraid my children are vying for my attention, so we will have to finish this conversation at some later date, but before I go, I wish to offer a gentle caution.

Don't allow what has happened to make you bitter. As terrible as this war was, the Maker seems to have prepared a way of peace for you and your people. Even though a fire destroys a forest, the ashes of that fire make the soil fertile and ready for planting. Your people at one time weren't all ready for such a union between Ertrique and Metakinos, as evidenced by your parents' murders. But they are now.

The Maker has made you and Rob beacons of hope and endurance. You both have scars. So do your people. And you are now stronger for them. Use those scars to show your people how to be resilient. Have joy in the path you are now set to run,

trusting in the truth that the Maker's plans are good. Despair is
common. You are uncommon, set aside for something good.
Now run your race knowing that yours will be a happy end.

    Yours Always,
    Olivia

"Who's that from?"

Maleen turned to see Rob walking in.

"Olivia." She smiled and put the letter away as he came to stand behind her chair. He gathered her hair in his hand and pulled it to the side.

"Are you almost ready?"

"I am. But are your parents sure about this?"

"Mmm." He bent, and his lips slid gently along the nape of her neck. She shivered with delight. "They've been ready to retire since the moment they realized I had married you instead of Priscilla."

"We should probably go," she said, getting to her feet, but he only turned her and pulled her against his chest, his hand tight on her hip. His lips met hers, and she was only too happy to acquiesce.

She would have happily continued, but a knock on the door interrupted them, and then it was really time to go.

A raging sense of déjà vu hit her as he led her into the ballroom. This was her home. There was Emille, smiling brilliantly from the side of the dais where Maleen and Rob were to ascend. Two thrones...her parents' thrones as she'd always known them, stood in the center. Hundreds of people packed the ballroom, glittering with silver, gold, and diamonds that reflected in the light of the hundreds of candles surrounding them.

"Your Highnesses." James, the palace steward, more lined and thinner than he had been eight years ago, bowed and gestured to the thrones, where Rob's parents stood. Maleen flashed him a familiar smile, and he sent her a grin of his own. The silence was pregnant as Maleen and Rob came to stand in front of the thrones, Rob on the left and Maleen on the right. Their hands were clasped as Rob's father moved to stand before them.

"Kneel," he said, his eyes crinkling kindly as he smiled down at them. They obeyed, and he turned to address the crowd.

"Eight years ago today, it was announced in this very room that this man and woman had betrothed themselves to one another. In a heinous act of insanity, Duke Perseus sought to separate them from one another. A long and terrible war ensued, and many lives were lost. And so we were led to believe that Princess Maleen's was among them."

He paused, and when he spoke again, Maleen could hear the smile in his voice. "But the Maker preserved her, as he preserved my son. And now they kneel before you, ready to serve you, their people and neighbors, as no monarchs of these two kingdoms have before. Today, in them, centuries of anger and distrust are laid to rest, and a new era is born." He turned back to Maleen and Rob. "Are you ready?"

"I am," they said in unison.

"Good then." He nodded to his wife, who was standing beside him. The queen held Maleen's crown, which had been her mother's, and Rob's father removed his own.

"Before the Maker and this cloud of witnesses, do you swear to lead your people, united in good faith, with honor and integrity until the Maker brings you into Eternal Bliss?"

"I do."

"Will you seek the preservation of peace in every way possible and to protect your people by any means necessary when it's not?"

"I do."

He smiled. "Do you swear to love one another, your people,

your neighbors, and your God for as long as you each shall live?"

"I do."

"Then," he said, "I now pronounce you King Roburts and Queen Maleen of the united kingdom of Entrikamos." The weight of the thin gold crown came to rest on Maleen's brow. And with it, the reality of what was really taking place.

"Now," the king said, his eyes shining with tears, "I bid you rise and greet the world."

A roar went up from the people around them, and Maleen felt her own eyes pricking as she looked over at her husband. They had done it. Their people were one. And so were they.

After the coronation took place, the floor was cleared for the new king and queen's first dance, and once again, Maleen was hit with the sensation that she had been in that very moment before.

Unlike the last time, though, Rob's hand was steady on her waist as he drew her near, and when the music began, she knew this dance was just the beginning.

"Thank you for wearing pink," he murmured as they spun.

She laughed. "The seamstresses were rather scandalized." She paused so he could spin her out and then spoke again when they were closer. "Out of curiosity, why did you wish for me to wear pink?"

He raised his brows. "Haven't you guessed?"

She shook her head.

"Because we were very rudely interrupted eight years ago when you looked ravishing in such a gown. And I felt we needed to start where we had left off."

The people around them laughed as Maleen stopped dancing and pulled his face down for a kiss.

A while later, they stole away from the dance floor to take a stroll through the newly revitalized garden. The plants weren't old enough yet to have wound around the trellises, but their new pink buds were beginning to peek up from the little green shrubs that ran in lines and circles all along the grounds.

"I have something I've been meaning to ask," Rob said as they walked hand in hand along the newly cobbled winding path.

"What's that?"

He stopped walking and drew her close again. "You had given up during that walk in the garden when I kept asking you questions to get you to betray Priscilla. I know you told me she had threatened everyone you knew, but..." His mouth turned up at the corner as he caught her hand and kissed it. "What changed your mind? What made you fight?"

Maleen thought back for a moment. She'd explained, of course, how she had come up with a way to defeat Priscilla, which had allowed her to take matters into her own hands. But upon reflection, she remembered that there *had* been a moment in which she'd chosen to fight. Then, as it hit her, she laughed.

"What?" he asked with a grin.

Maleen, still laughing, shook her head. "Priscilla announced to me that in less than a year, she would be having your babies."

Rob's eyebrows shot up high, which only made Maleen laugh harder. "Really? That was it?"

Maleen traced the white military sash that lay across his chest. "But you had already promised," she said, giving him an ornery grin, "that that was my job."

Rob threw his head back and laughed, and Maleen lay her head on his chest, thanking the Maker for all that life had come to be.

He took her chin in his fingers and brought her face up to his. "If the world ever tries to convince you otherwise, just remember. You always have been and forever will be the love of my life." He kissed her temple, and she felt him smile against her skin. "My wife and the mother of my children." He slid his mouth over to her forehead and pressed his lips against it. "And always my queen." This time, his mouth found hers. Maleen was only too happy to comply.

The White Slipper
A Clean Fantasy Fairy Tale Retelling of The White Slipper
(The Nevertold Fairy Tale Novellas, Book #1)

An Excerpt

You look tired," a deep voice said.

River gave a little jump.

"I'm sorry," Avery whispered, pressing a cup of tea into her hand. "I didn't mean to startle you."

River shook her head and bent her head appreciatively over the tea, inhaling deeply. It smelled of lemon, thyme, and one other flavor she couldn't make out. She took a sip and sighed. "Thank you. I didn't realize I needed that."

Avery frowned slightly. "It's been three weeks since the accident, and you've hardly slept more than four hours at a time."

River raised one brow. "And how do you know that?"

He gave her an equally wry smile. "Servants talk." Then he leaned forward. "I do wish you would stay in your own rooms, at least for a few nights. There are more than enough servants to look after him."

River looked back down at her father again and frowned. He was dozing at the moment, but he could wake up at any time. He always did around this time in the afternoon. "I can't," she whispered. "He needs me here."

"Your father's advisers need you, too," the prince said, taking a sip of his own tea.

River sighed. "I met with them yesterday."

"That's the funny thing about a kingdom," Avery said with a shrug. "No matter how many times you tend to it, it seems to need tending again the next day."

River traced the rim of her cup with her finger. Her aunt decried the habit, saying it dirtied the cup. But today, she was too tired to care. "You know," she said slowly, "if you stayed with him, I would feel more comfortable meeting the advisers more often."

Avery's brow creased. "You know it doesn't really matter whether it's me or his valet or the physician's assistant. He can't tell who's there while he sleeps."

River looked down at her father's pale face and gently touched his hand. "I think he can."

Before Avery could argue, low voices sounded at the door, and after a moment, it was opened to reveal a young man. As soon as she saw him, River's heart plummeted.

It was the runner.

"What news do you carry?" Avery asked the runner as he bowed low. The young man, who could hardly be called more than a boy, looked briefly at Avery before returning his gaze to River.

"Your Highness," he said, bowing again. "You sent me out three weeks ago to find the doctor who made the shoe."

River nodded.

"He's dead, isn't he?" asked a rough voice.

Everyone turned to see the king's red eyes open and fixed upon the runner. The young man scrambled to bow low yet again, keeping his eyes on the ground as he rose and spoke. "He is, Sire."

The king let out a gusty sigh and nodded. "It was only to be expected. Couldn't get him to make second when he was here. And now the fool is gone, and I suppose I'm supposed to follow."

The room was silent as River, Avery, and the doctors and other attendants watched the king. At first, River wondered if he might rant as he sometimes did when he was feverish. Then she wondered if he might curl up and become unresponsive the way he often did when his pain was at its worst. Instead, however, she found his sharp gaze fixed on her and Avery.

"I'd like everyone to leave me," her father said, pushing himself up into a sitting position in the bed. "River, you stay."

River blinked at him as everyone did as the king wished. Avery offered a small smile and a nod as he, too, left the room. A moment later, she and her father were alone.

"Rest," he said softly, patting the edge of the bed. River, who had been sitting on a small stool beside the bed, was careful not to jostle the mattress when she leaned over. When she was finally settled, her head resting on the soft blanket, she heard herself release a sigh. He began to rub her hair the way he had when she was little, and she closed her eyes.

"You've been sleeping in here," he finally said.

River kept her eyes shut, but she nodded. He was silent for a while longer, then he spoke again.

"No one has come to help you?" His voice was so scratchy his words were difficult to understand, but River didn't care. For a moment, at least, he was thinking clearly. The king had returned. For the moment, she felt safe.

"Aunt has been helping the treasurer," River said slowly. "And Vonaparte has been very gracious in helping the cook organize and prepare the meals. Mistress Lonnie has been expertly organizing the servants, and General Thaden has been running the troops through their usual exercises."

The king watched her carefully for another moment before nodding again. "And Prince Avery," he said slowly. "How is he at quests?"

"I...I suppose he's quite good," River stuttered. "I've never seen him try." What was her father getting at?

To her surprise, the king simply nodded and patted her hand. "I'm sure he is. His father was quite ambitious in his own day..." He paused for a moment to adjust his position. But as he moved, he froze and then winced before panting slightly. "Call one of my lawyers. Make it...Jefferies. I have a declaration to make before their blasted soothing tea puts me to sleep again."

Nodding, River got up and did as he bid. What was he up to?

River and the rest of the palace had been terrified that this second bout with his injury would make him as weak and helpless as it had the first time. To their relief, however, it hadn't. For while the physicians' healing tea did often put him to sleep, and he often woke in the night, moaning and pale, he had seemed less shocked by his pain this time, more resigned to what was and what needed to be.

After calling for Jeffries, River returned to his bedside, and studied her father. There was no feverish light in his eyes, no confused fog that sometimes filled them when he was in the most pain. Instead, there was a grim determination.

That determination was somewhat frightening.

"Father," River said slowly, "won't you tell me what you're doing?"

He turned and watched her for a long moment, his gaze haggard but sharp. "Do you really wish to know?"

"Of course."

He studied her a moment longer before giving her a sad smile. "You'll learn soon enough."

Usually, River knew what her father was planning. He'd taken special pains to include her in his rulings and deliberations over the past two years, making sure she understood why he was making this decision or that. They'd discussed judicial hearings and court debates, and River had been required to share her opinion with him so they might discuss it as he made his own judgments. He'd consulted her about taxes and aid rendered to the poor. They'd spent many a late night talking about their plans for the kingdom's future. This tight-lipped silence was new to her, and River decided as they waited that she didn't like it.

When Jefferies finally arrived, the king sat as tall as he could, though River could see just how much it pained him by the beads of sweat rolling down his temples. A few of the other lawyers bustled in as well, all holding quills, ink, parchments, and wax, and several of the courtiers followed as well. Avery loitered in the doorway, sending River an encouraging smile. River expected her father to chase the extra people out, as he'd summoned only Jefferies, but instead, he merely nodded to the others.

"I only called for one, but very well. You'll all hear what I say eventually. And word will get out faster this way."

"About what?" Avery mouthed to River.

She shrugged as her father turned to her.

"Daughter," he said with another sad smile. "Before we begin, I'm afraid that you're going to be very angry with me." He glanced at Avery, then back at her. "I never thought I would need to take these steps. But we are where we are." He paused, the soft light leaving his eyes and the grim determination returning. "You are my daughter," he said, his voice hardening slightly, "and I must also remind you that you're a princess first and foremost, and your duty is to your people."

"Of course, Father," she said, bowing her head. Really, such a reminder was almost insulting. Had he forgotten how she'd sat faithfully beside him every day for the last two years?

The king cleared his throat. "Let it be declared," he said, his voice regaining something of its former strength, "that whatever man finds a method by which to replicate the lost balsam slipper or its effects shall have my kingdom as his own inheritance." He paused and glanced at River. "And my daughter's hand in marriage."

River stood and gaped at her father. Had he really just

promised to give the kingdom...to give *her* to a complete stranger?

"Furthermore," the king continued, as though he hadn't just shattered River's world, "my successor, should someone complete the quest, will be the man who successfully performs the feat. Not his master or employer. Only the man himself."

A strange sound came from her right, and River turned to see Avery pale. Part of River's mind told her that this response in itself was troubling, but her head was still spinning too much to comprehend it.

For her entire life, River had been promised that she would marry only when she was ready, and only to the man they both deemed worthy. Once she'd come of marriageable age, she'd been the envy of her friends and the point of desire for many of the men. Heiress to the throne with the power to choose one's king made River arguably the most privileged woman in the realm.

Until now. Now, River was destined to marry whoever met the king's demands. Be he ancient, filthy, conniving, dumb, or cruel, he would be River's destiny.

Only a lifetime of training kept River from publicly demanding that the king explain himself. Whatever kind of father he was, as he had just reminded River, he was still king. Power might have been promised her, but that power was not yet hers.

It might never be now.

"Daughter?"

River realized everyone was looking at her.

"I'm sorry, Father," she said stiffly. "I didn't hear you."

"I asked if I have your agreement," her father said, gazing steadily at her.

River straightened. "As you wish, Father." And before her mouth could utter something truly disastrous or her stinging eyes betray her, River stormed out of the room.

Will Princess River find happiness in spite of her father's royal edict? Find out *The White Slipper: A Clean Fantasy Fairy Tale Retelling of The White Slipper*. *The White Slipper* is the first of the Nevertold Fairy Tale Novellas, and you can get it for *free* on all major ebook retailers.

Dear Reader,

Thank you so much for coming along with Maleen and Rob in their fight for freedom and a happily-ever-after. I hope you had fun! If you'd like more stories about them and other fairy tale characters, you can get them by becoming one of Brit's Bookish Mages by joining my newsletter team. You'll get free bonus content, sneak peaks, book coupons, and more!

Also, if you enjoyed The Sentinel's Song, it would be a huge help if you could leave a rating or review on your favorite ebook retailer or Goodreads to help other readers discover new books.
As always, thanks!

About the Author

Brittany lives with her Prince Charming, their little fairy, and their little prince in a ~~sparkling~~ (decently clean) castle in whatever kingdom the Air Force has most recently placed them. When she's not writing, Brittany can be found chasing her kids around with her DSLR and belting it in the church worship team.

Facebook: Facebook.com/BFichterFiction
Subscribe: BrittanyFichterFiction.com
Email: BrittanyFichterFiction@gmail.com
Instagram: @BrittanyFichterFiction

THE SEVEN YEARS PRINCESS: A RETELLING OF MAID MALEEN

Copyright © 2022 Brittany Fichter

The Seven Years Princess / Brittany Fichter. -- 1st ed.

Edited by Theresa Emms